OVERLAY

OVERLAY

Blaine C. Readler

Full Arc
Press

OVERLAY

Published by Full Arc Press

This is a work of fiction. Names, characters, places, and incidents, other than obvious historical figures and events, are either the product of the author's wild imagination or are used fictitiously. Any resemblance to actual events, locales, organizations, or persons, living, dead, or one foot in the grave, although inevitable and in a weird way complimentary to the author, since it shows he is not so insulated from reality that the products of his imagination are totally alien to the average mind, is nevertheless entirely coincidental and beyond the intent of either the author or the publisher.

Visit us at: http://www.readler.com

E-mail: blaine@readler.com

ISBN: 978-0-9834973-4-9

Printed in the United States of America

First Edition: 2013

To all those who believe that truth is an infinitely layered onion.

ACKNOWLEDGEMENTS

Thanks to Tim O'lena for a first read-through, sweeping up typos along the way.

As always, enthusiastic cheers of gratitude to MTB for tackling the near-hopeless task of wrestling the words into a semblance of prose.

And a big thank you to Chris Wilson for lending her graphic wisdom (both interpretations) and aid for the cover.

There are only two forces in the world, the sword and the spirit. In the long run the sword will always be conquered by the spirit.
—Napoleon Bonaparte

It is the nature of man to rise to greatness if greatness is expected of him.
—John Steinbeck

PART I

ENTRY

Chapter 1

I felt my heart pounding in my throat during the whole frantic dash to the hospital after the call from Clintock, Kirsten's professor. The nurse at the entrance desk was obviously used to babbling wild-eyed madmen, for she ignored my sputtering and spittle as she calmly directed me to the third floor of Scripps Hospital in La Jolla after searching out Kirsten's name on her monitor. I explained in a rush that she was my fiancée, and the nurse told me that that was nice. One of the elevators stood open, waiting, and I jabbed the third-floor button, then jabbed it a few more times for good measure. The door lumbered closed, objecting to my pushiness by taking its sweet old time. I felt the subtle surge of ascent, and then the elevator seemed to float, weightless in suspended eternity.

Instinctively, I checked my level of anxiety. This was a habit developed over the years, ever since the first massive attack when I was eighteen. Although that first debilitating onset was situational, the culmination of conflicting pulls between my parents' expectations and a teen need for peer acceptance, I had slowly come to realize that the angst I had been wrestling with over the years was something else. I had developed what is called anticipatory anxiety. I can be frightened into anxiety by the fear of lapsing into anxiety.

Now I had a truly legitimate reason to be floored with a full-blown panic onslaught. I should have seen the whole thing coming. Kirsten had been dropping hints for weeks, but I chose to ignore them, hoping this new obsession would fade like all the others. I had every reason to be paralyzed with anxiety now, but my years of self-training were paying off: I was terrified for her, and angry with myself, but that was normal.

Satisfied that my mind didn't require any of the damping exercises I had mastered, I turned my thoughts to the professor's call. This was the first time I had a moment to think, the first opportunity to replay his words. "Jordan," he'd said in his ever-earnest voice, "this is Burney Clintock. There's been an ... accident. Kirsten is all right, but she's in a coma."

The tsunami of my life crushing in on itself had slammed home at that second, but I remember thinking, *how can she be all right if she's in a coma?* What I said, though, was, "*What!*"

"She's stable. Don't worry. But I need to talk to you. Can you come to the hospital soon?"

What kind of question was that? *Um, let me check my schedule—my fiancée might be dying? Sure, I think I can fit you in.*

Clintock hadn't waited for a reply. "She overdosed," he had explained in that earnest tone, as though she had made a splendid choice for self extinction.

"On what?" I squeaked. Kirsten didn't have any drugs. She wouldn't even take aspirin for a headache.

"Ativan."

"An anti-anxiety drug?"

I had researched the whole spectrum of chemical solutions years ago, but had decided in the end against them.

"It's sometimes used for insomnia."

"A sleeping pill? But that's crazy—is it dangerous? Is she going to be okay?" He'd already said that she was. My brain was spinning in the mud, throwing up a spray of confused panic.

"She's in no danger from the drug."

"But what do the doctors say—"

"Jordan, we can talk about it when you get here. We shouldn't discuss this on the phone."

Floating now in suffocating elevator limbo, I wondered at how the phone call had ended. Professor Clintock had said that Kirsten was in no danger from the drug. Then why was she in a coma? The implication was that there was some other danger. Maybe indirect brain damage? I had an aunt who had narcolepsy and died of a brain aneurism after hitting her head during a cataplexy attack. Maybe Kirsten hit her head when she passed out.

Clintock might not want to talk about something so horrible on the phone.

The elevator door grudgingly slid open, and I burst through and sprinted past startled visitors waiting to go down. Inside the room, I found Clintock sitting in a chair reading a book next to an iconic image of Sleeping Beauty. Her lustrous auburn hair had been brushed and lay coyly, sweetly spread across the pillow. Beautiful, loving Kirsten seemed to be dozing peacefully, the professor waiting patiently for her to awaken for coffee and toast. The effect was made all the more fairy tale by my own very different experience of Kirsten in the morning—hair matted and pajamas all twisted from aerobic tossing and turning, and cracker crumbs mashed against her forehead and cheek, remnants of a midnight snack.

Clintock looked up expectantly as I went to the bedside. Now that I was finally here, I was at a loss about what to do. My level of adrenaline had prepared me to fight off a gang of hoodlums, or maybe lift a two-ton car off of her. But here she lay, seemingly safe and sound. Except for the monitor clipped to her finger, she could just have well have settled onto her parent's living room sofa for a nap.

I looked to Clintock who had laid the book upside-down on his knee. "Where's the doctor?" I asked.

The lean, grizzled man shrugged. "He stopped by a while ago. He's around somewhere."

I looked at my slumbering soulmate and back to the earnest face that said so little. "How about a nurse or two? Shouldn't they be running tests or something? An I-V maybe? She's just . . . lying there."

He shrugged again, as though this was one of those questions whose answer had been long proven unattainable. "They did a lot of tests in the emergency room. I guess they've concluded that she's in no immediate danger."

"She came through the emergency room?"

Again the shrug. "Of course."

"How long was she there?"

He considered a moment. "About an hour."

"An hour! You were there?"

He nodded earnestly. "I brought her."

The adrenaline was finding an outlet. "You brought my fiancée to the hospital emergency room, and then waited for an hour to call me? What the hell!"

"It's actually been more than that. She's been here for about a half hour."

My face must have broadcast my storm of emotions, for he finally seemed to take the situation seriously. "I would have called you immediately if she had really been in any danger. Obviously."

"Obviously," I repeated, the sarcasm thick enough to precipitate a mist of vitriol. "Because, of course, you are a doctor." I realized that technically he was. "I mean, a medical doctor," I added.

He studied me a moment, then stood up, laying the book on the chair. I saw that the title was *Satanism and Witchcraft: The Classic Study of Medieval Superstition.* Kirsten was taking one of his comparative literature classes on adult fantasy. Our tiny apartment had been slowly filling up with piles of books just like this. "We need to talk," he said.

"We sure do," I concurred.

Just then a middle-aged nurse bustled in, glanced at us, and went to the monitor and wrote something on her pad.

"Let's go where we can talk," he suggested, heading for the door.

"You're afraid Kirsten will hear?"

"Not Kirsten," he replied, pausing at the entrance. "Others."

The nurse threw a quick look our way, but ignored the comment.

I followed the professor down a hall, then another, then up a flight of stairs, and outside onto an open deck, what once might have been a smoking lounge. Clintock held the door for me, and pushed it quickly shut as soon as I was through.

I glanced through the window set into the door, but there was nobody behind us. "Are you afraid of being followed?" I asked.

The earnest stare he returned seemed to indicate that my comment was not as sarcastic as I intended.

The fourth-floor smoking balcony opened to a dramatic vista of the wave-tossed cliffs of La Jolla, and in the misty sunshine beyond, the Pacific Beach pier, and blue with distance, Point Loma beyond that, guarding the entrance to the great San Diego Harbor.

Clintock stepped towards the balcony rail and turned to study the fifteen feet of wall above us leading to the roof, as though actually suspicious of spies leaning microphones over the edge on booms.

I had chatted with Clintock at a couple of parties, and despite his seemingly intense and serious manner, had found him easy to talk to. I had decided that it was because, contrary to his demeanor and in contrast to Kirsten's other professors, he didn't take himself too seriously.

I remembered vividly the first time I'd met him. One of the seniors had just been accepted to Stanford for graduate study, and was throwing a celebration party at her home in Carmel Mountain. Kirsten and I were sprawled on a sofa watching the cult film Koyaanisqatsi, while clouds of resin-rich pot hovered about us. I hadn't smoked the stuff since my breakdown, but just the secondhand intake of the potent strain was probably as effective as the joints I'd shared in my teens. Whether from the newly legalized drug, or the spellbinding flow of disparate images from the eccentric film coupled with Philip Glass's masterful score, I had zoned out, and was transfixed by a goateed commentator who was addressing the camera, seeming, in fact, to be talking directly to me. And so I didn't notice that the professor was squatting next to me until he lay a hand on my knee and spoke my name. I snapped to, and found him looking at me in that ever-earnest stare. He introduced himself and then, as though not sure what to do next, reached out and shook my hand. Only then did he greet Kirsten, which seemed a bit odd to me. The whole time, he never took his eyes off me. If politeness requires committing your complete attention, then Clintock was the most polite person I'd ever met at a party.

"I didn't call you right away," he finally explained, "because I knew that Kirsten was in no danger—no medical danger, that is."

"You said that she overdosed on Ativan!"

The professor gazed at me a moment, then glanced quickly around to make sure nobody was crawling over the balcony rail. He stepped forward so that he could talk into my ear. "She took only three pills," he said quietly.

I stepped back and looked him in the eye. "How do you know?"

"Kirsten stole the pills from a friend, and that's all that was in the bottle. Her blood level was hardly above what would be expected for someone on prescribed treatment."

"Then why would the doctors call it an overdose?"

"I think only because they couldn't find anything else wrong with her. And they won't."

He watched me closely. "Also, she left a note," he added.

"A suicide note?"

He paused and then nodded. "Close enough."

"What did it say?"

In answer, he reached into his pocket and handed me a folded piece of paper. I recognized the stationary Kirsten's mother had given her. The note read:

> *To all those that I love, and who love me, please know that I am not really gone, but have only stepped sideways to a place better suited to my soul. Even though you can't see me, be comforted that I am safe and happy.*
>
> *Jordan, our separation is just temporary. I am confident that you will eventually find the way, and when you do, we will be wed in a place where we don't have to say the words, "until death do us part."*

The note blurred as my eyes filled with tears, and I caught a sob and stifled it. Seeing her handwriting hit me harder than watching her lying in a hospital bed, where she just seemed to be sleeping. The written words—her own words—spoke irrefutable proof of her intentions. Remorse dragged at me and my knees felt weak.

"I should have seen it coming," I murmured, struggling to keep my voice from wavering. "No, I *did* see it coming, but I ignored it."

Clintock watched me curiously. "What did you see coming? Suicide?"

"No! No, not suicide."

"Then what?"

"She wasn't depressed. It wasn't that. It was more . . . an obsession."

"An obsession?"

"Yeah." I looked at the literature scholar and grinned for the first time since receiving his call. "Your class."

Her professor showed no appreciation for my lighthearted turn. He just stared at me, as though I had maybe insulted him.

"She immersed herself in all that . . . fantasy and magic," I went on. "You should see our apartment. It looks like a bookstore for the black arts. The last few weeks her approach morphed somehow. Instead of an entertained interest, I could see that she was taking it way too seriously. I should have gotten some help, but she's been through these obsessive fads before. A year ago it was the Second Great Awakening and The Book of Mormon; six months later it was Rastafarian meditation. I thought it would just pass."

The wiry older man turned his stare from me to the waves booming against the rock bluffs of La Jolla. He seemed to be contemplating the eternal push and pull of the ocean.

"But it looks like we got lucky this time," I offered, trying to break the impasse. "If there's nothing wrong with Kirsten, she should pull out of this . . . sleep."

Clintock finally turned his gaze back to me, and its hard resolve suggested that my words were foolish. The dread returned and my chest tightened with premonition. "You said that the doctors wouldn't find anything else wrong with her," I reminded him, "that she wasn't in any *medical* danger; what did you mean?"

He still didn't say anything, but after a few seconds he sighed and nodded. He glanced again to the roof and both sides of the deck, and then took my elbow and led me back to the door. "We need to talk, but not here."

We took the elevator back down, and he led me outside, to the parking lot. He took off at a brisk stride and motioned for me to come up next to him. "Will you do exactly what I tell you?" he asked.

I looked at him in wonder at the request, but shrugged and nodded.

"Okay, stay as close behind me as you can," he directed, and instantly took off at a jog.

After a moment's surprise, I ran after him. He ran quickly for a man past retirement age, but I caught him, and stayed on his heels. We ran along past car after car until he held up his remote and pinched it, and a Ford Explorer just ahead blinked its lights in acknowledgement. He threw open the rear door, grabbed me by the shoulder, and shoved me inside, calling out for me to move over. A moment later he slammed the door shut behind him and sat panting.

I peered cautiously past him, expecting to see men in black suits running up to the car, but there was no one in the parking lot except for one couple two rows away staring at us, astonished.

"What was that all about?" I asked. "I don't see anybody."

"You can't," he replied breathing hard. "That's the whole point."

"The point of what?"

"Where Kirsten has gone."

I stared at him. Was he mad? "We saw her lying in a bed not ten minutes ago," I explained cautiously.

He looked at me, and the distant hardness melted. His gaze reached out to me, inviting me to join him in his secret. "Indeed, Jordan. You saw her body lying there, but her mind is gone."

I suddenly felt cold despite the flush of the mad dash across the parking lot. Were we looking at the worst scenario for a coma? "What are you saying? There's some traumatic brain damage? That the coma is irreversible?"

"This has nothing to do with her brain. There's nothing wrong with the workings inside her head. The problem is that she's just no longer there."

My own brain was spinning with exasperation. "Professor Clintock, enough with the riddles. What the hell are you trying to say?"

He put his hand on my shoulder, as though consoling me. "Jordan, Kirsten's mind—her soul—is no longer part of her body. She has transferred."

"Where? *Where!*"

He sighed. "This is not easy to explain. The best I can describe in a simple way is that she is now in purgatory."

Chapter 2

I blinked. Clintock sat watching me. "What in God's name are you talking about?" I exclaimed. "Kirsten isn't even Catholic."

"It was a simplistic analogy. She's not really in purgatory—there is no such thing. Besides, she would have to die first, even if there were."

"But you just said that she was 'gone.' How is that different from being dead?"

"The difference is that she might—just might—be able to come back."

I studied the old man for some clue to his sincerity. "From purgatory."

He shook his head, rejecting the word in frustration. "It's not purgatory. Forget purgatory. Just accept that her soul has gone to a different place."

I wondered what the hell I was doing, talking about Kirsten's 'soul' leaving her body. "What place? Another planet? A different star? Kansas?"

He sighed, blowing air through puffed cheeks, struggling to communicate. "It's not so much a place as a . . . dimension."

I snorted. This was getting out of hand. "What, are we now in the Twilight Zone?"

He smiled sardonically. "You're getting warmer."

But I was getting frustrated. "Look, can we cut the crap? How do you know all this?" I remembered the class he taught, the book he was reading in the hospital room. "Are you saying that this is some sort of witchcraft or something?"

He sighed again and thought a moment. "It's not witchcraft. There's no such thing as witchcraft any more than a purgatory. Both myths, however, derive from this same source, the place where Kirsten has gone."

"How do you *know* this?"

"It's been my life study. There are hints and vague references throughout history in the superstitions and fables of western culture. I've developed software that scans through centuries of written myths—thousands upon thousands of documents—searching for common threads."

"A text-based correlation function," I noted automatically.

He paused. "Kirsten mentioned that you are an engineer. I could have used your help."

"You still can if it helps to get her back."

Ho-boy, I thought. *I sound like I'm buying into the whole nonsense.*

"We'll need your help, all right," he assured, "but not to develop correlation software."

"Wait a second," I protested. "Correlation operations aren't absolute. They can only search for what you tell them to look for."

Clintock nodded. "They're biased. So much so with cultural subjects that given enough material, you can find whatever you please. If you were so inclined, you could demonstrate that humans can breathe fire and dogs can talk."

I snorted. This was exasperating beyond endurance. "So, you're contradicting yourself. You admit that you spent your life searching and then finding something that you fabricated completely for yourself."

The professor's eyes seemed to glint with appreciation. "You don't understand the whole picture. My years of searching through the tales of our past hinted at the truth, but there was not nearly enough detail, enough accuracy, to reveal a clear view. Not nearly enough. But what the common threads did glean were markers—pointers—to the final source."

I held up my hands in supplication. "And what is that?"

He smiled, reached behind the seat to the cargo area where the top of a shiny copper ball peeked over the seat back, and handed me a manila envelope. I looked at him, and he nodded for me to open it. Inside I found a sheaf of perhaps thirty pages. At first I thought that they were ancient parchment, but when I slipped the bundle from the envelope, I recognized that they were scanned reproductions. I glanced at the beautifully formed cursive words, and saw that they were not English.

"Latin?" I asked, looking up to find the professor watching me closely.

He nodded, apparently pleased that I had gotten it right.

"What is it?" I asked.

"The story of a sixth century monk who made the transfer, but managed to get back."

I glanced again at the copies, feeling a surge of intrigue, but still deeply suspicious. "Dante?" I asked, without giving the notion much thought.

Clintock smiled. "No, this is not *The Divine Comedy*. For one, it would weigh about five pounds, and for another, Dante was not a monk. The great Italian poet probably took inspiration from the story, however. Only scholars know of it now, but during the early Middle Ages, it was well known. The original version was written by Justinian Exiguus, who was subsequently excommunicated when he refused to recant what was considered to be blasphemy by Pope Adrian. The tale remained popular, though, and the Vatican recognized, perhaps better than today, that banning a story outright just serves to enhance its appeal, so the Pope commissioned a sanitized version that was presented as an allegory of heaven and hell."

I hefted the slim manuscript. "I take it that this is a copy of Exiguus's original version?"

"Indeed. That is a photocopy of his manuscript—his hand-written pages."

I looked at the first sheet again. The florid, evenly flowing lettering from the quill pen seemed to lean forward against a bracing wind, as though pushing its message determinedly through restraining prejudices. "How did you get it?" I asked.

"That is a long and mostly boring story, for which we don't have time. Let's just say that I have gambled almost everything I have acquiring it. If the world understood its true value—and danger—you would not be holding a copy now."

"What's the story about, the grand secrets revealed?"

Clintock raised one eyebrow, suggesting I rethink my sarcasm. "His journey, what he saw. But more importantly for us, directions."

"Directions? Is that possible without GPS?"

He ignored my quip. "Instructions on how to transfer—how to get to the overlay."

"And how to get back," I added helpfully.

The professor looked at me a moment, then said, "Time is of the essence. The longer Kirsten's there, the more difficult it will be for her to return."

I suddenly felt like a shit. Kirsten, beautiful loving Kirsten, lay senseless in a coma, and here I was making jokes. "How do we get her back?"

"You need to go and get her."

"*Me?* How can I? I don't even know what's going on—I mean, I'll do whatever it takes to help her but ... I mean, you're the expert. Can't we both go?"

He shook his head resolutely. "That's the problem. I know too much."

"How can you know too much? This isn't a CIA operation."

He looked at me, searching. I wanted to reach up to feel whether there was something sitting on my nose.

"You'll just have to trust me on this," he finally replied. "Besides, Kirsten wouldn't follow me back. It has to be you, someone she loves."

This gave me pause. Not that it was me that she would follow, but that she was in a position to follow. "I had the idea that she—her mind—was tucked away somewhere, hibernating."

"Oh, no," the scholar corrected adamantly. "She's fully conscious. This is exactly why it's you that must go. You must convince her."

"She did go there of her own accord," I agreed. There was that damnable note.

Clintock was looking at me with that earnest examination. "Yes and no."

"What do you mean? Did someone force her?"

"No. You can't be forced into the overlay. But you can be enticed—there's really no time for all of this."

"Fine, fine. Just tell me what I need to know. This is the second time that you called it the overlay. Should I know what that's about?"

He sighed and gazed out the window a moment. "According to Exiguus, this other dimension is similar to Earth. He uses an odd conjunction of two words: 'cubor,' which means 'to lie, or lay down,' and 'tegere,' which means to cover, as in clothing, but also in the sense of protection. From his cultural references and analogies of his period, I interpreted this to mean an overlay, like the plastic sheets that mapmakers and geologists once used to show layers of features, one on top the other."

"How similar to Earth? Will I recognize anything?"

He shrugged. "Exiguus seemed to think that everything was very familiar. But he also talked about another part that was special, that he hinted at being heaven. This is what got him excommunicated. Nobody was supposed to have access to heaven without a ticket from the Pope."

"So . . . do you think that this place is actually, you know, like heaven and hell? Where God and angels live?"

I sounded goofy. But the whole thing *was* goofy.

Clintock smiled, what I took maybe to be a bit condescendingly. "Exiguus described what he saw in the context of his times, when heaven and hell were taken for granted as something real. Caribbean natives assumed Columbus's ships to be giant birds— their brains mapped what their eyes saw onto the existing reality in their heads. I suppose that this was the same for Exiguus."

I suddenly felt dizzy, and realized it was because I was buying the story. It was like pulling up in front of your house to find flames shooting skyward through the roof, astounding beyond any expectation, but impossible to disbelieve.

But if it was real, there had to be some rational explanation. No matter how outlandish the concept, I couldn't climb on board with just some metaphysical hand-waving. "Where did this other dimension—this overlay—come from? I mean, like, is it as big as our whole universe?"

For once, Clintock lost his intense eagerness, and retreated to uncertainty. "I don't know. All I have is Exiguus's manuscript. If there is some legitimate scientific explanation, there was no science in his day to guide him. All I have is my own theory."

"Well, let's hear it."

The professor looked at me from under a doubtful brow. "It sounds crazy."

"Ha! How can it possibly get any crazier?"

He sighed. "Okay. I think that aliens visited Earth four to five thousand years ago and set it all up."

The interior of the car fell dead silent as I stared at him. "It just got crazier. What on Earth leads you to think this?"

He closed his eyes a moment in exasperation. "We're getting side-tracked, and we're wasting time. I'll just say that the evidence surfaced unexpectedly from cultures all over the world. I'll show you someday . . ."

"If I get back."

"Of course you'll get back. But you have to go *now*. Every minute counts."

"Fine! Fine. Let's go."

I reached for the door handle to move around to the front seat, assuming that Clintock would be driving us somewhere, but he grabbed my wrist in an iron clench. "Don't open the door!" he cried.

"Why!" I responded with equal alarm.

The professor looked pained, as though wanting to explain, but unable to.

"Is it for the same reason that we ran to the car like we were fleeing from a poison gas attack?" I asked.

He seemed stuck, stubbornly resisting. "We don't want anybody listening to us," he finally conceded.

I waved my arm around at the empty parking lot. "Who? The seagulls?"

"You have to *go!*" he yelled. "Now!"

He was getting angry, and I knew that this equated with the escalating danger to Kirsten. "Go," I muttered determinedly as I tried to crawl forward between the front seats, "I have to go."

"What the hell are you *doing?*" he asked, clearly frustrated.

"Are you going to drive the car from back here?" I asked, matching his frustration and then some.

"No, no," he exclaimed, finally understanding. "You're leaving from right here."

I glanced around. "I'm transferring to a different dimension from the backseat of an SUV?"

"Yes," he replied. His tone indicated that this should be obvious.

I shrugged. "Fine," I said, sitting back down. I looked at him. "I'm ready."

I wasn't sure what to expect. Maybe he would snap his fingers, or wiggle the tip of his nose back and forth. Instead, he pulled a plastic medicine bottle from his pocket, opened it, and handed me two small, white pills.

"What's this?" I asked.

"Rohypnol. Chew them before swallowing."

I looked at the shiny round tablets lying in my palm. "Isn't this the date-rape drug?"

"Its use in sexual assault has been highly overrated by the media," he replied as he rifled through the pile of photocopies. He looked up at me. "What are you waiting for? It's just a fast-acting sedative."

I wanted to ask for some Ativan instead, but popped the pills into my mouth and chewed as instructed. The resulting sludge was bitter, the taste of pharmaceutical domination.

"Ah, here it is," Clintock announced, taking one sheet from the pile. He studied it a moment, then asked, "How are you feeling?"

"Confused and disoriented."

My extra-dimensional coach glanced at me in alarm.

"Not from the drug," I reassured. "Just the concept of warping the only reality I've ever known. I don't feel anything from the date-rape drug."

"You will soon," he assured, returning to his study. "And you shouldn't call it that," he added.

I waited, looking across the parking lot where a few people wandered here and there, trying to remember where they parked. I wondered if this would be my last view of my own world. I suddenly realized that the professor was talking to me. I turned to him, and blinked. The movement seemed to proceed in slow motion.

Clintock smiled. "I think you're about ready."

"I think I'm ready for beddy-bye."

"No!" he commanded. "Don't go to sleep. Hang in there just a couple of more minutes. "Now, when I tell you, I want you to close your eyes—but don't fall asleep—and picture yourself floating up and up. Imagine that you are rising right through the roof of the car. While you do that, listen closely to the words that I speak. You won't understand them, but listen closely anyway."

"What words?" I asked. I sounded dopy, even to myself.

"It's an incantation," he explained, pointing to the sheet that he held out for me to see. I had difficulty focusing, but I saw what looked like a square filled with letters.

"It's an ancient two-dimensional palindrome," he explained, "quite amazing, actually."

I forced myself to see the words. This is what I saw:

S A T O R
A R E P O
T E N E T
O P E R A
R O T A S

I stared at this grid of unintelligible letters, vaguely understanding what he meant. I could see that the letters read the same both forward and backwards, as well as up and down. The professor was explaining that it was Latin, and that the enigmatic matrix had been found scratched into walls uncovered in Pompeii, and as far north as ancient Roman settlements unearthed in Britain. I was having trouble following his flood of information, but I tried. He was describing something about how the direct translation was approximately, *Sower Arepo holds the wheels of work*, and that although some scholars have interpreted deeper meaning from the direct translation—for example, because the Latin word *sator* can mean both sower, but also a divine progenitor—a common legend holds that it also served as a secret sign that nascent persecuted Christians used to flag their identity covertly to each other. The letters can be arranged to form a cross consisting of a vertical and a horizontal Pater Noster, which means "Our Father" —the first two words of the Lord's Prayer—surrounded by four protective points of Alpha and Omega, God's reference to himself in Revelations.

As Clintock spoke, he watched me closely, almost as though his lecture was something rote, something that he had delivered many times, requiring little attention from his conscious mind. He was now explaining something about how palindromes held special meaning to ancient mystics, since they believed that the symmetry of the letters confused the Devil, hiding the meaning from him.

As though waking from a dream, I suddenly realized that he had stopped, and was gazing expectantly at me. "Okay," he said quietly, "it's time."

I saw that this flood of information was simply meant to distract me from the blanket that the pills were lowering over my brain, like counting backwards after being administered anesthesia.

I felt a wave of despair. I was about to be launched on a mission of which I knew only the goal, absolutely nothing of the means. I started to question him, but he seemed to anticipate this. "The only advice I can give you is that you must find Kirsten. Convince her to come back."

"That's it? That's all you can tell me?"

He lifted his shoulders. "I'm sorry. You'll have to figure it out as you go."

"But, how do I get back?"

"I'm going to explain that in due time. Right now, you just have to relax."

I stared past him, curious about a bird that had landed precariously on the whip antenna of a nearby truck. I didn't care anymore that I had no clue what I needed to do. That I was about to embark on a journey bizarre beyond imagining, I was aware; I just didn't care. A tiny kernel of hard logic deep within my cerebral cortex knew that the Rohypnol was casting its spell, but it was far outnumbered by all the rest of me's that didn't give a hoot about this or anything else.

I felt his hand on my shoulder gently pushing me back into the seat. "Close your eyes," he said, "but don't sleep. The only things you can think of are the words that I am speaking. Just my words. Listen carefully. In one hour, you will hear sirens, maybe close, or maybe in the distance. When you hear the sirens, it will be time to come home. No matter where you are, or what you are doing, it will be time to come home, and you will come home. You may meet others while you are there. One of them may be a powerful force, a domineering tyrant. He has been called the Devil, but he was once just a man, like you or me. Avoid him if you can, run from him if not. Do not trust him, and do not believe what he tells you."

The kernel of hard logic in my brain shouted a warning to back out while I had the chance, but it was too tiny to be of any consequence. I was ready to go.

"You will now begin to rise," Clintock continued. "Up, up, you are rising right through the roof of the car."

He began a slow chant that I knew was the ancient, mystical, sacred palindrome. "*Sator—arepo—*"

I was indeed rising. I could feel it. My arms had become weightless, mere tufts of feathers. My torso and legs followed.

"*—tenet—opera—*"

My eyes were closed, but I could see—or perhaps I was just imagining. I felt and saw my head rise, right through the roof of the car.

Clintock's voice was omnipotent. It was the entire universe, and as he intoned the final word of the incantation, I sensed the whole Earth burst about me like a massive, fragile bubble that had been poised to dissolve all my life.

"*ROTAS!*"

I opened my eyes. The familiar world of the hospital parking lot still surrounded me. Nothing had changed.

Except that I was now standing on top of the car.

Chapter 3

The effect of the sedative had completely worn off. I could think clearly again, acutely aware of details—the sheen of the sun reflecting off the smooth-worn pavement; the intricate metal latticework of the telecommunications towers on top of Black Mountain in the distance; the critical screech of the seagulls holding court on top of the hospital; and the surge and gurgle of the ocean below the bluff. It was like stepping outside on a brisk March morning after gazing at the world through dirty windows all winter, or perhaps waking from a confusing dream.

Considering that the Rohypnol had worn off, I concluded that some time had passed—hours, probably. I had no clue, though, how I happened to be standing on top of the professor's car. I guessed that Clintock must have hypnotized me. Why he would have instructed me to forget how I had gotten there was a mystery. Indeed, the thought that he might have been commanding my actions for who-knew-how-long was deeply disturbing.

In any case, I figured I had better get down before I dented the metal surface. I hopped off, and only as I stepped into the air did I realize that a six-foot jump onto hard pavement was pushing the limits of a safe fall. The leap didn't carry the sense of danger, though, and this was confirmed by my pillow-gentle landing.

That was very strange.

I told myself that I might still be dreaming, but I was overcome by an inescapable dread, which urged me not to look inside the car. But I had to. I turned and saw two people in the backseat. One was obviously Clintock, his thin, curly gray hair immediately recognizable. The other was not so easily distinguished, as he was slouched down in the seat, as though asleep. The professor was reaching over to tilt the seat back, trying to better position this unconscious person.

Uh, oh.

It can't be, I pleaded with myself. But I knew that it had to be. Who else *could* it be? I had never viewed myself from this angle, but I had seen myself in enough pictures to recognize that this was indeed my body.

My body. Holy hell. What was the "me" standing here outside the car, then? A ghost? I slapped my chest, dreading that my hands would pass through, into insubstantial innards. But they stopped short against a solid surface, albeit one that didn't exactly thump.

I felt panicky; not the doomed dread of my well-worn anticipatory anxiety, but full-blown legitimate fear of a situation far, far beyond my wildest ken, and possibly without escape.

Despite a welling terror of coming face-to-face with myself, I had to find out from the professor—the only person who could help me—what the hell was going on. I reached out and grabbed the door handle, but it didn't budge. Assuming that it was locked, I tried the front door. Also locked. I ran around to the other side, but both door handles were as immovable as if they were welded in place.

Allowing myself one quick glance at myself lying back in the car seat, my head lolling to the side, seeming lifeless, I pounded on the window to get Clintock's attention. It felt like I was pounding the back of a firm sofa with fists made of styrofoam. Even if he couldn't hear my blows, I didn't understand why he didn't notice me standing not three feet from him. At that moment he glanced up, and appeared to look right through me. It was as if I were invisible.

The realization stopped me cold. I would have crapped in my pants, except that it was slowly dawning on me that there was no crap to excrete.

As the British might say, I was buggered.

My one overriding desire, a desperation of overarching urgency, was to get myself back into my body. How I would do this, I had no clue. Maybe if I just lay on top of me, I would sink back in. Whatever the means, I had to get *to* me first. Was this why the professor had been so insistent that we be sequestered away in the car? Was he specifically preventing me from reuniting with myself?

Then it hit home that this nightmare nether existence in which I found myself might just be exactly the plan. In the short few minutes I'd had to contemplate my imminent "transfer," I had imagined slipping off to sleep and waking in some dream world where people fly about speaking in rhymed metaphors. But Exiguus had written that the other dimension was similar to Earth, and more to the point, the professor had called it the "overlay." The other dimension wasn't just similar to Earth; it *was* Earth, and I was the overlay.

I was breathing hard, my old friend the fight-or-flight reaction to panic. It had the feel of habit, though. A morbid curiosity suggested that I stop breathing. I did. I waited. Nothing changed. I just stood there waiting. *Shit!* Bad idea. I was only freaking myself out. I started breathing in earnest, but now the whole process felt disingenuous.

Don't think about the weirdness, I warned myself. Focus on a specific task. This was an exercise I had developed early in my struggle to cope with my anxiety. It was probably one reason that I had gone into engineering, a field that allowed me to completely immerse myself in real-world puzzles, logical mental games that not only occupied me exclusively for hours and days, but for which I was paid. And I did indeed have a task, the entire reason for my situation in the first place: Kirsten!

My heart leapt at the thought, or rather, the memory of a heart leaping when I'd had the actual organ. I realized that there was probably a Kirsten overlay version around somewhere. I had a mission: find her and convince her to come back.

But, how to *get* back? Was it really just a matter of merging into my comatose body? Would I indeed just lie on top of me and slip inside, like I was settling into a hot tub? I had a dreaded suspicion that were I to even get to my body, I would find it as impermeable as the window of Clintock's car. My memory of the minutes before the transfer were foggy, just like my brain had been at the time, but I remembered that the professor had given me instructions. I replayed as best I could the sequence of those moments. He'd said that in about an hour I'd hear a siren, and then it would be time to come home . . . and I would come home. That was it? No incantations to utter? No secret button somewhere to push?

I was buggered for sure.

The task. Get to the task. "Kirsten!" I called. To my virtual ears, it sounded like I had yelled into a pillow. I called again, louder. The figurative pillow just got bigger in turn.

Think! She would have emerged from her body up there on the third floor of the hospital. She might still be hanging around there. In any case, it was a good starting point.

I took off at a trot across the parking lot. Jogging along, I felt weightless, as I assumed I probably was, being of insubstantial other-dimensional stuff. My feet barely touched the pavement before pushing off again. If I indeed carried no mass, then according to Newton's second law of motion, I should be able to accelerate with no expenditure of energy. I should be able to outrun trains, like Superman. I pumped my legs faster. Or rather, I tried. Even though each step still felt as though it was pushing nothing, I couldn't get my legs alternating any faster than a good sprint in my molecule-based body. It was eerily like the dreams I occasionally had where I tried to run, but my feet seemed mired in molasses. Maybe the air was holding me back. I didn't know, but so far, being a liberated spirit didn't seem to offer any benefits.

Suddenly, a woman stepped out directly in front of me from behind a van. I had a split second to react, and all I could manage was a shout before I crashed into her. I stumbled to the side and turned back to help her, but my apologies were cut short when I saw that she was walking away as though nothing had happened. To her, nothing had. I had urged myself not to think about the weirdness, but I couldn't help myself. I ran to catch up with her, calling. I unconsciously interpreted her complete obliviousness as rude. It was instinct. I ran past her, turned and stood directly in her path, arms outstretched in defiant challenge. Her gaze was that of someone blind, seeing nothing. She saw plenty, just not me.

Incredulous, I stood my ground as she reached me without a hint of hesitation. A second later I was bumped aside as a balloon might be before a car.

I regained my footing and trotted off again towards the hospital. As I again passed the woman, I tapped her on her head, just for spite. Her fine, lustrous hair felt stiff to my hand, like a mass of spun glass. I glanced back, and was surprised to see her brush her hand against her ear, as though shooing away a fly. This was intriguing, but I had to keep my focus on Kirsten, so I left the unsuspecting Earthling to her peace and continued on.

After a few more steps, however, I stopped short. Ahead, at the patient pickup area in front of the double-wide hospital doors, a taxi stood with the back door open. A pudgy, middle-age woman with short, gray hair stood holding the door handle, glancing around as though expecting someone. I caught a glimpse of the rear end of a woman entering. A man wearing a beret was right behind her, practically pushing her forward as he climbed in as well. All the while, the elderly woman gazed about, seemingly unaware of the two passengers who had climbed in right before her nose.

I recognized that rear end. I would know it anywhere. It was Kirsten's.

I ran forward, shouting. I was not surprised when the elderly woman ignored me and, with one last glance around, shrugged, climbed in and slammed the door shut. I was closer now, not fifty feet away when the taxi pulled away. Kirsten's face appeared in the rear window. She was leaning across the elderly woman who looked straight ahead, right through her. Kirsten looked puzzled, then astonished, and I saw her mouth open and I heard her yell something from inside. But by now the taxi was picking up speed, carrying the love of my life away.

I stood there, supremely frustrated that I had missed her by mere seconds, and I uttered a curse. People continued to enter and leave through the double doors, unaware of me, but their inattention seemed a snub. I took the opportunity to vent, bellowing my anger at each of them, knowing they couldn't hear me. One young man hustled out on the heels of a rotund woman, and when I yelled at him in turn, he seemed to look right into my eyes as he raised one hand in defense. "Hey, man," he cautioned, looking directly at me. "Take it easy. You're going to blow a carotid."

I froze and blinked. The young man continued to look me in the eye, clearly seeing me. He looked to be late twenties, dressed in clean jeans and T-shirt that was about three sizes too big. The white shirt was dappled with multi-colored tie-die patterns. His hairline had receded early for his age, but the rest of his hair was thick and curly.

"You Jordan?" he asked pleasantly.

I just stared at him. "You can see me," I finally said.

The young man smiled. "I can feel you, as well," he added, holding out his hand. "I'm Zorba."

I looked at it dumbly, and then managed to recover enough to put my own hand out to shake his. The man's hand was soft and alive. Actually, it felt inert, like holding a stuffed sausage, but in a world now consisting of impenetrable hardness, this was as alive as I was going to find.

"Welcome to Neverland," Zorba said, breaking the handshake and throwing his arms wide to encompass the mundane view of a bustling hospital. A young boy ran by and knocked Zorba's feet out from under him, but as he he tumbled sideways, he deftly pushed off the sidewalk with his hands and spun back onto his feet.

I shook my head, trying to absorb it all. "Neverland? Like in Peter Pan?"

Zorba looked at me doubtfully. "It's a joke. Do you *know* where you are?"

"Not really, but I know that I'm happy to be talking to somebody."

He nodded knowingly. "It's disconcerting at first. You'll get used to it."

"I hope not."

He eyed me with that doubtful skepticism. "I was warned that you might be an odd duck."

I leaned in. "Warned by whom?"

He shrugged. "Boney. Well, not by Boney himself. He doesn't talk to the likes of me. The word came down from the Soldat."

"But who's Boney?"

He didn't answer. He just stood there studying me, effortlessly stepping aside when a man came hurrying through. "When did you arrive?" he finally asked.

"You mean here, in Neverland? A few minutes ago."

Zorba furrowed his brow at this. "Are you serious? You've just arrived?"

I shrugged.

"No party?" he asked.

I shook my head, clueless.

"I mean, nobody waiting to orient you when you came through?"

"No. Is there usually?"

"Of course. I've never heard of somebody coming through out of nowhere. Where's your corpus?"

"My who-wah?"

"Your body, your flesh and blood that you left behind."

I indicated away across the parking lot. "In a car."

Suddenly, I was sent flying. I had a quick glimpse of another child running away along the sidewalk. Firm fingers caught my shoulders, and set me back on the ground. "Let's get out of the line of fire," Zorba suggested, and I followed him into the landscaping along the building. "How in God's name did you get here?" he asked.

"I was sedated, and then I guess sort of hypnotized while an incantation was read—"

"You had help? From a corpus?"

"If you mean somebody made of molecules, then yes."

"This is very strange," he mused, more doubtful than ever. "Very strange indeed."

"Why?"

I agreed whole heartedly that the whole damn thing was way more than strange, but I understood that he meant just my transfer.

He looked at me as though he'd forgotten I was there. "First of all, an arrival is rare enough that word would have spread long ahead of time, but I've never heard of an unassisted ascend."

He pronounced it with the accent on the first syllable, so that it sounded more like, "ass-end."

"I did have assistance."

"I mean from this end. Nobody comes through without that."

"How about Exiguus?" I offered, glad to proffer even a little insight into the madness.

"Who?" he asked.

"Exiguus—the Middle Ages monk who made the transfer and came back to tell about it."

Now Zorba gave me a look daring me to continue with this outrageous fib. "That's not possible," he stated flatly.

Whispers of terror again tingled my spine, which had no real nerves to tingle. "Er, do you mean that it's not possible for a Middle Ages monk to make the transfer, or . . ."

"The 'or' part," he finished.

"Oh shit."

Zorba's look of disbelief morphed to concern. "Jordan, did you ascend knowing what you were doing?"

How to answer such a question? "How can I know what I don't know? All I do know is that I've come to get Kirsten back."

Now Zorba's eyes went round, surprises heaping on top of surprises. "How do you know Kirsten?"

"She's my fiancée—how do *you* know her?"

"Everybody knows about Kirsten."

I raised an eyebrow.

"Everybody in Halfway," he qualified.

"Halfway?"

He spread his arms. "Where you are now."

"Why is it called Halfway?"

Zorba lifted his shoulders to the obvious. "You're halfway between Earth and heaven."

I was speechless. My brain, or mind, or soul, or whatever was executing the I-Think-Therefore-I-Am was overloading.

Zorba looked worried. "Jordan, where did you think you were going?"

"I told you," I muttered, my words seeming to come of their own volition. "To get Kirsten."

My spiritual guide heaved a big sigh of resignation. Breathing serves purposes other than gathering oxygen. "We obviously both have a lot to catch up on," he finally said, "but we should probably get to a safe house."

"A safe house," I repeated woodenly.

"Just what it sounds like: a place that's safe."

"Safe from what?" I asked, barely caring, hardly even wanting to know the answer.

"The Soldats told me that JJ is nearby."

I just looked at him. My input processing buffer was full.

"A Rogue," he explained anyway.

"Right," I replied, agreeing. I would have agreed if he'd told me that JJ was a termite.

I realized that Zorba was staring at me. "You're burnished," he declared.

"Right."

He smiled. "It happens to new arrivals who try to take things too quickly. You just need rest once we make the safe house."

"Right," I murmured. Rest sounded great, irresistible, in fact.

Just then, a car alarm went off. It was only for a couple of seconds, but it seemed to echo in my mind. One of the last things the professor had told me was that sirens would mark the time for my return. It had been mere minutes since I had arrived, but the car alarm reminded me why I was there in the first place. "No!" I said, rubbing my eyes with my knuckles to clear the fog. "I've got to get to Kirsten!"

Zorba shook his head. "Sorry. She's off to Rancho Sante Fe. The Soldats told me to take you to a safe house in Pacific Beach."

"Where in Rancho Sante Fe?" I demanded. I had only ever driven through the wealthy enclave. From the road, the society of mansion homes looked like an expansive garden, but a garden locked securely away behind ornate wooden gates.

My new spectral friend's mouth was set firm. "It doesn't matter. We were told to go to Pacific Beach."

"By the Soldats. Screw the Soldats, whoever they are."

"You shouldn't talk like that," Zorba admonished. "You don't understand."

I was already walking away, though. I had no idea how I was going to get to Rancho Santa Fe, nor how I would find Kirsten once I did, but I was damned if I was going to be led around like a child. It occurred to me that I might be damned in more than a figurative sense, but I had come to save my fiancée, and that's what I was going to do.

"Wait!" Zorba called, running to catch up with me. "You can't walk. It's ten miles."

I stopped, turned to him, jumped out of the way of a passerby, and said, "What do you suggest?"

He chewed his lip. "I'll tell you what: come with me to Pacific Beach, and I promise I'll try to get you to see Kirsten."

"You'll 'try'? America 'tried' to stay out of WWII, Lyndon Johnson 'tried' to end poverty. No deal," I declared, starting off again.

Zorba grabbed my arm. "Wait. You're right, I can't promise that I'll succeed, but I can promise that I'll do my best, and you can bet that whatever I come up with will be ten times better than if you go it alone."

I looked at him. To the random visitors bustling past, this man was invisible, but to me, a fellow limbo soul, his youthful face seemed real and substantial, and it spoke of honorable intent. "Okay," I conceded. "It's your game, for now."

My Halfway host led me through the dynamic obstacle course of arriving and exiting hospital visitors to the curb directly in front of the double doors, where cars were pulling up to take in hobbling or wheel-chair-bound discharged patients. He instructed me to listen to people's conversations, either to companions, or talking on cell phones. The idea was to find somebody heading in our general direction—in our case south—and to catch a surreptitious ride. He explained that the overlay citizens of Halfway referred to this as a hitch. I also noticed that he referred to himself as a Wop, and as we walked about, leaning in to one conversation after another, he told me that he wasn't sure where the name came from. He guessed that it was just borrowed from the pejorative used for the flood of Italian immigrants of the early twentieth century. He remembered that when he'd first arrived, the old timers viewed newbies like himself as wet behind the ears, easy targets to be taken advantage of.

"When did you arrive?" I asked, ducking away as an elderly woman suddenly swung her arm wide as a gesture to emphasize a point to her daughter.

"At seven-ten PM, on March sixteenth, nineteen sixty-nine. It was an unusually warm evening."

"I guess you wouldn't forget the details of an event like—wait! Did you say nineteen sixty-nine?"

He nodded. "The Boston Bruins scored eight goals in one period—an NHL record."

"Er, I take it that's hockey?" *That would make him, like, seventy years old!* I thought. "So, I guess people don't age in Halfway."

"What's there to age with?" he answered without looking at me. He had his ear pressed against another man's head where he held a cell phone.

I stopped, frozen. I realized that his body—his Earthly body—would now be long dead. Whatever the veracity of the professor's claim that I could return, there was no going back for Zorba. Or most other Wops, for that matter. I glanced at him, leaning against the man talking on the cell phone. This at least explained his clothes.

A thought occurred to me. "How old is the oldest Halfwayer?"

" 'Halfwayer?' You're not going to be taken seriously if you keep talking like that."

"Okay, the oldest Wop."

He stepped back from the man, unsatisfied. "I don't really know. I've met Soldats who were born in the nineteenth century. But I only know the Wops in the San Diego and Los Angeles area. I've heard rumors of guys—and women—a lot older."

"Hmm, then I guess that would mean that Halfway has been in existence only—"

"There's Boney, of course."

"How old is Boney?"

He shrugged. "A couple hundred years—more like two-hundred and fifty, I guess. And he's not even the oldest."

"Who is Boney?"

He threw me a quizzical glance. "You really don't know?"

"How the hell can I know? You haven't—what?"

Zorba was staring past me in alarm.

I wasn't sure what he was looking at, but then I saw a man striding purposefully towards us down the sidewalk fifty yards away. As he hurried along, he passed one person after another who never gave him a glance, even though he was practically stepping on their feet. He wore a tan short-sleeve shirt with multiple flap-covered pockets, the kind of shirt I associated with guys that went fishing, or on safari hunts. He was handsome, in a sixties James Bond sort of way, with dark hair, full sideburns, and a soft, confident grin.

"Who is it?" I asked.

Zorba uttered a curse. "That's JJ—we have to get out of here."

I stared at the approaching man. There was something familiar about him. "I think I've seen him before."

"Probably in the papers—no, you're too young; maybe in documentaries. We can talk about it later. We have to go."

Zorba was pulling me by the elbow. "I'm sure I've seen pictures of him," I insisted.

"That's JJ, and we can't let him catch us. Get in," he urged.

My new friend was practically pushing me into the back of a van that was open, waiting for an infirmed patient.

The approaching man's gaze settled on me, and his eyes lit up in victory. He sprinted forward. "Uh, oh," I said.

I turned back to find that the driver of the van, a young man, had already helped the elderly discharged patient into the seat and was about to slide the side door closed. Zorba was inside, on the other side of the white-haired lady, calling frantically for me to climb in. "She's in my way!" I cried, catching the infectious panic from my friend. Our pursuer had covered half the distance to us. I had no idea why he was dangerous, but the sense of urgent doom caused the virtual flesh on my scalp to tingle.

"Climb over her!" Zorba called.

The woman looked to be about ninety years old. Her bones would break like pretzels.

Then I remembered.

I grabbed her head and hauled myself inside. Her soft cotton dress felt like formed iron as I pulled myself past, her eyes looking through me, unconcerned. Suddenly I was catapulted forward by the door closing behind me, and I landed headfirst on Zorba, who, unlike living people, provided a soft landing. He helped me turn around into an upright position again. JJ had now reached the van, and ran around to where the young driver was climbing into the front seat. Not in time, however. The driver slammed the door closed, nearly catching JJ's wrist.

Safe.

I felt the flush of what an hour ago would have been a wash of adrenaline in a flesh-and-blood body, but JJ gazed at me through the window calmly, almost serenely. Another man, middle-aged with a neatly trimmed Van Dyke, and watchful, intelligent eyes, ran up behind our assailant and looked at me intently. JJ glanced briefly at the newcomer, and then extended his hand forward and carefully pushed it through the glass. I stared transfixed as his fingers appeared on my side, followed by the rest of his hand. The utter shock of the arm unexpectedly sliding through solid glass immobilized my will, and I just watched as JJ grabbed me by the throat. I could have reminded myself that since I wasn't actually breathing, he couldn't actually choke me, but my lifelong absolute dependency on air caused me to reflexively struggle with frantic desperation against a grip that seemed stronger than should be possible. The handsome man at the other end of the arm watched me carefully, almost tenderly. He spoke. "She'll be mine."

At that moment, the van started to pull away. My assailant walked along beside us, but soon had to trot to keep up. Meanwhile, Zorba was beating against the gripping wrist with fists balled together like a sledgehammer. JJ finally let go, and his hand slid silently back through the window and we pulled away. Behind us, the safari-shirt man watched calmly, seeming confident that this was just the preamble.

"Jesus! Who the hell *is* that guy!" I yelled, rubbing my neck. It hurt!

"Jim Jones," Zorba replied.

It took a moment for this to sink in; the juxtaposition of two of the most common names in the English world carried an infamous legacy. "You mean the Jim Jones that orchestrated the mass suicide of a thousand people in Guyana?"

"Nine hundred, fourteen. Over two-hundred children."

I sat squeezed in next to Zorba, silently absorbing this.

Our companion in the van, the elderly passenger, gazed out her window, oblivious to our encounter with the perpetrator of the greatest American man-made disaster prior to the fall of the World Trade Center.

Chapter 4

"Jim Jones—*the* Jim Jones—is alive here?" I asked, incredulous at the injustice that a man so heinous would be allowed to survive. This monster of a man must surely be the powerful force, the domineering tyrant that Professor Clintock had warned about, the man some called the Devil.

"He's not alive," Zorba reminded, although my new friend seemed preoccupied, only half listening to me. We had climbed over the back of the seat into the rear cargo area where we had more room, and he sat with his arms wrapped around his knees.

"But he's still *here!* After killing all those poor, deluded people—even kids!"

Zorba glanced distractedly at me. "More than half came along with him. There's probably a hundred or more still left, the core of his flock."

That answer launched a dozen more questions in my mind, but I chose the one most pressing. "What was he after?" I asked.

This pulled him back completely. "Kirsten," he replied confidently. "And we have to warn Boney."

"Boney—who in God's name is Boney?"

Zorba looked at me a moment and then grinned, nodding. "I forget sometimes just how insulated the living are. 'Boney' is the nickname that the English gave him. They were afraid of him, afraid that he would set his sights on their island."

I remembered that he had placed Boney's age at two hundred and fifty years, which would put him just around the end of the eighteenth century. "Oh no!" I exclaimed.

Zorba shrugged. "Why not?"

I shook my head in consternation. Things couldn't be *this* bizarre. "Napoleon? Napoleon *Bonaparte*?"

Zorba just smiled.

Why not, indeed? Zorba was born sometime in the forties; Jim Jones, in the twenties or thirties. Maybe there was no limit. Maybe, two hundred and fifty was considered a spring chicken.

"He stuck his hand right through the glass," I said.

"He did," Zorba agreed, peering around, keeping track of where our oblivious ride was taking us. We were heading north on the coast Highway 101.

I slowly pushed the tips of my fingers against the window. It felt like a stone wall.

"You can't do it," he warned. "I can't either."

"What's so special about Jim Jones? Other than the obvious."

"He's been to heaven. You learn these sorts of things there. Boney kicked him out. That's the definition of a Rogue: someone who's been kicked out."

"A fallen angel," I mused, struggling to join the idea of an angel with somebody like Jim Jones.

Zorba glanced at me. "Heaven is just a name. Don't take it too literally. Boney doesn't even want us to call it that."

"What does he call it?"

"Home."

"Huh," I uttered perceptively. "I guess it's better than Elba."

My friend looked at me, perplexed.

"The first island where the English banished him after his defeat, before Saint Helena," I explained.

His quizzical expression turned dark. "Boney doesn't talk about his time before ascension."

"And I take it that we don't either."

Zorba nodded.

"How do you get into heaven?" I asked. It was strange hearing me say those words. I hadn't asked that question since Sunday school.

He bounced his shoulders in a little shrug. "Boney decides that it's time."

"*Boney* decides . . . so, he really is, like—"

"Don't go there. He can't bring you in—you have to figure that out yourself—but he can block you. Boney isn't God. He's just sort of the leader, or—"

"General?"

He shrugged again.

"How about Emperor?"

Zorba threw me scrunched eyebrows.

"I take it we don't make fun of the Little General."

He looked at me, exasperated.

"Well, Bonaparte *liked* that title. His men meant it in an endearing way."

"Whatever. Like I said, he doesn't like references to the time before his ascension."

"What about the name you use—Boney?" I asked.

I could see that my host was getting annoyed with my persistence. "I don't know. Maybe he just likes that it was used by people who feared him."

I wondered about that, but I bit my tongue, deciding not to annoy my only Halfway contact any further. There were way too many questions, though, to give him his peace. "Does everybody come through Halfway?"

"What do you mean? You can't get to heaven without first learning the ropes in Halfway, if that's what you mean."

"No. I mean, does everybody come to Halfway when they, you know—"

"When they die? No, of course not."

I realized that this was a dumb question. If it were so, then the world would be jammed with dead people walking around hitching free rides. "How do they get here?"

"How did you get here?"

"I, um . . ." I had to think about this. "Professor Clintock helped me—executed it, actually."

"He didn't send you here. You brought yourself."

"No. He really did do it. He gave me a sedative, and then he spoke this incantation—"

"Yeah, yeah, all that maybe helps, but nobody can just send you here. You have to *want* to come. You have to *believe*."

"Believe *what*? I didn't know what the hell I was getting into!"

Zorba studied me, squinting, as though trying to figure out my game. "You *are* an odd duck." He shook his head, finding me hard to swallow. "Ending up here without a clear path and desire is like closing your eyes, walking randomly for months, and ending up in Hawaii."

"Er, there's an ocean between here and Hawaii."

"Exactamundo, Cunningham."

"Hey! I thought you said that you died in nineteen sixty-nine."

"I did. I watch tons of TV. Not a lot else to do. It's not like I can open a book and read it."

I hadn't thought about that. It sent virtual shivers down my virtual spine. "In any case, there wasn't anything to believe. I didn't know what I was getting into."

He studied me. "What about Kirsten?"

"What about her?"

"You said that you followed her here."

"Yeah. I'm taking her back."

He looked skeptical, but seemed to let that thought go. "I think that she was your path."

"She's my fiancée. She's *supposed* to be my path for the rest of our lives."

"You know what I mean." He tapped his finger against his chin. "Boney obviously had an idea that you might be coming, but your ascension must have caught him by surprise. Otherwise, the Soldats would have been waiting for you."

"Why did they send you?"

"I was the only Wop in the immediate area. Trust me, I wouldn't have been their first pick otherwise."

All of this brought home my mission. "But where were they taking her? I assume that the guy in the beret that hustled her into the taxi was one of the Soldats. In fact, at the time, I thought they'd called the taxi."

"They did," Zorba confirmed out of hand. I could see that he was pulling something together in his mind.

"How?" I recalled the scene in my head. "The pudgy gray-haired woman! She was holding the door!" I remembered, though, that she seemed not to see Kirsten and Mr. Beret.

"She's a candidate, a pliable candidate, almost ready for first ascension. She thinks that she's psychic, but it's Boney whispering to her—that's just an expression; he's able to influence her. He probably convinced her with a premonition or intuition that she had to take a taxi from the hospital to Kirsten's destination."

"He can do that?"

"Most everybody in heaven can influence to a greater or lesser degree, but only the living that are listening—candidates—can be influenced to the degree of that woman."

"Meaning that they believe."

"You're catching on."

"I don't want to seem obstinate, but you haven't told me why they've taken Kirsten to Rancho Sante Fe."

He watched me for many fake heartbeats. "I don't know for sure—they don't tell me things like that—but I can guess. They're probably prepping her for an expedited second ascension."

"A second ascension, let me guess: that's rising up to heaven?"

"Heaven isn't 'up,' but essentially, yes. It normally takes months to get ready, but every now and then Boney takes an interest and helps a Wop prepare."

I could feel my ire building, whatever that was. "Let me guess again: these 'special interests' of Boney just happen to be beautiful young women."

Zorba chuckled. "Jordan, we all wish—Wops and Soldats alike—that sex was an option for us. No, I'll bet Boney wants Kirsten as a shepherd."

I sighed with breath only useful for such purposes. "Napoleon keeps flocks of sheep in heaven? Reminds him of his youth in France?"

"There's no animals in heaven. How do you think people like the candidate that arranged the taxi became connected in the first place? Using the previous analogy, if you didn't know about Hawaii, why would you ever think of setting off in the first place?"

"What about Kirsten? She figured out how to get here on her own."

" 'fraid not, Jordan. Candidates are generally paired with Soldats, but I heard that Boney took Kirsten under his wing personally."

"Because . . . he wants to use her as a shepherd."

"Yep. The word on the street is that he thinks she has special talents."

It hit me like a window shade snapping open on a dark room. Kirsten had always been enamored with all things mystical. Her interests were so broad, though, that I had assumed that the pentagrams drawn on her wall, the dragon sculptures, even Professor Clintock's class, were but a part of the wide-ranging, eclectic mix. But I recalled now how she had been particularly engrossed in paranormal extremes the last few weeks. Just a couple of days before, she had told me that she thought she could sense people's auras. Belief was necessary to make first ascension, according to Zorba. One plus one equals two.

She had been duped.

At least from my perspective.

"She believed that orbs were following her around," I said. "I didn't take it seriously. She'd had other crazy ideas that passed with time."

Zorba nodded.

"Is this the talent Boney thinks she has?"

"The orbs she saw were probably just Boney's influence," Zorba explained. "They're a side-effect, sort of like the ghostly glint you get in a picture when the sun is shining on the lens. No, the talent that Boney is after is her ability to get people to trust her."

"She doesn't *get* people to trust her. They just do. It's because she's trust-*worthy*!"

"Hey! Take it easy. The point is that people do trust her."

"How is that a talent? At least, one that's useful to Boney?"

He smiled at me, at my naiveté. "She'll be great at drawing recruits."

"Recruits?"

"Candidates. Ascensions to Halfway. Boot camp troops."

I wagged my head, trying desperately to shake off this lie. "She wouldn't do that! She would never entice people into giving up their lives."

"She wouldn't? What if she thought she was giving them the greatest favor she could offer? Inviting them into the grandest club there ever was?"

I looked at him. "Do you believe that?"

He held out his hands. "I'm here. I wouldn't be if I hadn't believed that."

Something in his tone wasn't completely convincing. "You use the past tense. What do you believe now?"

He didn't reply for a few moments, and then just said, "I have no complaints." Then he said, "Science and modern medicine has really cramped Boney's style."

I knew he was trying to change the subject, but I was struggling to grasp the idea of Kirsten—beautiful, kind Kirsten—seducing innocent, gullible people. The trouble was, I could imagine her in the role if she truly thought she was helping. "How so?" I asked, relieved to have the subject changed.

"Science teaches belief in the wrong things."

"Science has it all wrong?"

"No, it has it mostly right; that's the problem. For centuries, maybe thousands of years, heaven has used superstition, the occult, magic—anything mystical that fosters the idea of accessible supernatural powers. Believing in magical powers beyond what you're born with is effective training for a first ascension—"

"Hold it. Are you saying that Napoleon is responsible for all this? He came up with it all?"

"No, of course not. It's been the standard toolbox of heaven from the beginning. Science has been ruining it, and it's gotten to the point where Boney has to scrabble to find candidates."

"Uh, oh. I see. That's where Kirsten comes in."

"Boney sees her as his answer for the war preparations. She's not only going to recruit candidates directly, but she's going to select ones that she can train to become recruiters themselves—"

"Whoa, I'm still back at the war preparations. What war?"

He looked at me with concern. "I think I'm blabbing too much. This is stuff you don't learn until later." He seemed to muse to himself. "This is such an aberration. You're supposed to have a whole program waiting for you when you arrive at Halfway."

"Fine," I stated impatiently. "I'm an aberration. Let's go with that. No program, no need to follow any schedule. What about this war?"

He chewed his lip a moment, then seemed to decide. "Boney's planning a preemptive strike against the other heavens."

I closed my eyes and took a meditative breath. If I had possessed a real brain, I thought it might have exploded by now. "Other heavens?" I repeated.

"Er, yeah. See? This is why there's supposed to be a program. How do I explain? The Creators set up multiple heavens—one for each major cultural region on Earth—"

"Clintock thought that it was aliens who created Heaven and Hell, or should I say, Heaven and Halfway?"

Zorba lifted his shoulders. "I've heard that theory. Nobody really knows; it was so long ago."

"You're saying that there's a heaven for America, and other ones for France, and Spain, and Lithuania?"

He shook his head. "No, those are countries with different languages, but they all share a common cultural history: ancient Greece. Remember, the heavens were probably created thousands of years ago, before there *was* an ancient Greece. But ancient Greece expanded on the earlier Mycenaean and Phoenician civilizations. Heaven—*our* heaven—includes all of North and South America, Europe, and I think a lot of the Middle East. I know that there's a different Chinese heaven and an Indian heaven—that's the south Asian India. There may be others, I don't know."

"You know your history and geography."

"History Channel."

"Huh," I said. "So, if I hitched a ride on a boat or airplane, I would pass into those other Halfways, assuming they have Halfways."

"No, not at all . . . it's really not easy to explain. You see, our heaven spans the whole Earth—so do the others. If you got on a plane, you could fly completely around the whole planet and never leave our Halfway."

I tried to capture this concept. "In the same sense, a Chinese Halfway guy could visit America," I hypothesized.

"He could be sitting here in the car with us right now."

I glanced around instinctively. "We wouldn't see him," I said.

"And he couldn't see us," Zorba added.

We had strayed off topic. "And the different heavens can have wars?"

"The first skirmish that we know of happened during the time of Plato and Socrates, in fact. Heaven was preoccupied with invading Chinese Soldats, otherwise the great philosophers wouldn't have been left alone to develop their logical structures."

"Which works against recruiting," I surmised.

"Yeah. The big war started in the seventeenth century, and lasted decades."

"The Age of Reason!" I deduced.

"Yeah, when science—the great anti-heaven—established its roots."

I liked that. "Science really is the guardian against superstition, the shining light of truth."

"The truth is that Halfway and heaven are real. You can see that they exist. And you're making a judgment call that ascension is bad."

"That's true." I tried to imagine an existence loitering endlessly unseen among the flesh and blood, living mutely and invisibly inside the cracks of society. "Are you happy?" I asked.

Zorba hesitated a bare moment. "Sure! The goal, of course, is to get to heaven."

I had the impression that his enthusiasm was as much for his own sake as mine. "How long does it usually take? To get to heaven, I mean."

Now he looked uncomfortable, staring out the window and down at his hands. I had the sense that my question was hurtful, but I wasn't sure why, although I had a hunch.

He finally seemed to remember that there was a question waiting to be answered, and he looked at me with a wan smile. "It varies widely. The average is a few months, I guess. There's two parts: you have to be ready, meaning, you have to develop the skills and attitude, and Boney has to be ready for you. I've heard of second ascensions in as few as a couple of weeks—"

"The *expedited* ascensions."

"Exactly.

"What they're doing to Kirsten."

"What they're doing *with* her. You don't do an ascension *to* somebody."

"Jim Jones died in 1978," I commented before thinking how he might take it.

And he did, confirming my hunch.

"Yeah," Zorba agreed. "Even Jim Jones made second ascension before me, and my first ascension was nearly ten years before his."

I would have kicked myself, but I wasn't sure it would have been effective, since it might not have even hurt. "But he got bumped out again, right?" I said, hopefully implying that it doesn't pay to rush these sorts of things.

"That he did, but not because of any timing of his second ascension."

"Then, why?"

My host was watching our progress up Highway 101 as we came down the Torrey bluff to the lagoon preserve, and he threw me a glance. "He was . . . rogue."

"He stomped around destroying crops?"

"Ha, ha, very funny. Not like a rogue elephant. He couldn't take orders."

"Boney's orders."

"Of course."

"Er, no offense to Mr. Bonaparte, but that seems like a foregone conclusion. Why would he expect a guy like Jones to cooperate?"

Zorba seemed to contemplate this a moment. "Maybe Boney figured it was worth the gamble."

I was beginning to see a glimmer. "When you're trying to get people to believe in something outlandish as putting yourself into a coma to let your soul wander around behind the curtains of the world, a guy like Jim Jones could be just the ticket."

"You win a cigar."

One plus one should equal two. "It doesn't make sense. If Boney kicked Jones out of heaven, why not all the way out of Halfway as well?"

"He'd probably love to. Boney doesn't so much kick you out of heaven as makes it so uncomfortable that you leave on your own. But Boney's influence in Halfway is not nearly as strong. Once they've been to heaven, rogues like Jones can evade him pretty easily here."

I assumed that this wasn't the case for plebeians like Zorba—and me—but I didn't say that. Instead, I stuck my un-living foot into my un-living mouth again. "When do you think you'll be ready?" I asked, and then immediately followed with, "Oh shit, there I go again."

Zorba didn't flinch. In fact, he seemed to be completely absorbed in the ocean waves on one side, and the marsh lagoon on the other. "If you're talking about the skills, I've had those for some time. And I'm going to demonstrate one."

He climbed back up into the seat next to the elderly passenger and leaned forward, wrapping his arms around the driver's head. I caught myself from crying out, remembering that the man was looking right through Zorba's bizarre hug. The invisible Wop pressed his head sideways against the driver's and closed his eyes in concentration. I could see that he was talking quietly, as though consoling the man for being burdened with driving a comfortable car along the sunny California coast. This went on for maybe a minute until the driver suddenly turned his head to talk to the elderly passenger, tossing Zorba away like the Hulk might a clinging cat.

"Gramma," the man said, "do you mind if we stop at Roberto's for some lunch?"

"Isn't that the Mexican place?" she asked. "I thought you didn't care for those fast food grills."

He nodded his head. "Yeah, but I'm really hungry. It's quick and practically on our way."

We had come to the end of the estuary, and were starting up the bluff area of Del Mar. Instead of continuing north up the coast, our chauffeur turned East, inland on Carmel Valley Road. Within seconds we were parking behind the little restaurant—just an order counter with some outdoor tables.

"You want anything, Mom?" he asked, opening the door. I didn't hear her answer because Zorba was shouting for me to follow him as he climbed over the seat and exited close behind the driver. I was too late. The door slammed shut in my face. I sat, forlorn, in the driver's seat while Zorba stood just outside with his face pressed against the window.

"Get out when he comes back!" he yelled.

"What if I don't make it?"

He lifted his eyebrows. "Then I guess you're on your own!"

As Samuel Johnson might have said the same situation, "*Nothing focuses the mind like a hanging or being left on your own in Halfway.*"

Zorba glanced at the driver returning with a drink and a styrofoam lunch container. "If we get separated," he called, "I'll meet you back here later."

I crouched in the driver's seat like a sprinter ready to spring off from the starting blocks. The man placed the drink on the roof and opened the door. I hurled myself forward, but caromed back, bouncing off his shoulder as he leaned in to place the lunch box on the console between the seats. It felt like I'd just run headlong into a steam roller. He stood up to get his drink, and I repositioned myself, using the delicate styrofoam container as a launch pad. To me, the half-ounce box was as good as a metal platform cemented in place. I lunged just as my human obstacle bent over to climb in. Once again I smashed into the T-shirt-clad steam roller, and the world turned circles as I was sent flying.

I lay stretched out. That seemed good. I wouldn't have been stretched out inside the van. A hand grabbed my shoulder and I slid along face down on what was clearly pavement. The hand rolled me over. "Get up," Zorba said.

I sat up as the van backed away inches from me. If Zorba hadn't pulled me out, the front wheel would have run over me. "Thanks for your concern," I said.

"You're not hurt," he said in response to my sarcasm.

"How do you know?" I asked, but he was right, and he didn't need to answer. It hurt like hell when I was being ping-ponged around, but with no blood to pool or nerves to report damage, there were no bruises or lingering aches. Chalk one up for limbo after life. "What would have happened if the tire had run over me?" I queried.

"You would have been cut in half."

I blinked. "Like, into two pieces?"

"Yeah, like that in half."

"Would I have . . . died?"

"You can't die, since you're not alive."

Chalk up another for Halfway.

"But you would have dissolved," he continued.

"That doesn't sound good."

"It's the worst thing that can happen. It's the end."

I gulped. "Like . . ."

"The end. There's nothing after the end. That's why it's called the end."

I let it go, but I mentally removed both chalk marks for this new existence.

Zorba explained that he'd gotten us out of the van so that we could make our way east towards Rancho Sante Fe. "You convinced the driver to stop," I guessed.

He nodded.

"That's one of the skills you need to get into heaven?"

He nodded again. "First I tried to suggest that he needed to pee, but his bladder wasn't full enough to convince him. I moved on to the hungry button, and that did the trick."

I was impressed. "You can influence people, just like Boney."

He snorted. "No comparison. Subliminal suggestions only work on existing conditions. That man really was already hungry. That's light-years behind convincing a woman to hire a taxi and go to a hospital based on her imagined psychic powers."

The fact that we Wops—I was beginning to consider myself as such—could have any influence on the living at all was something of a revelation. I remembered the first person I came upon after ascending. "I think I had an effect," I offered.

"You mean, on one of the living?"

"Yeah. There was this woman that I tapped on the head—"

"Not possible."

"Why?"

"I told you. It takes months—sometimes years—to develop a skill like that." He looked at me. "I know what you're thinking."

"You do?"

"No, not that way. I can *guess* what you're thinking: you're wondering why I haven't second-ascended if I'm so skilled."

I was about to protest with some lie, but he cut me off.

"I'm still wandering around Halfway," he continued, "because Boney thinks I'm a doubter."

"Er, he thinks that you doubt that, what, heaven exists?"

"Of course not. No, he thinks that I'm not committed to the goal."

"Of him?"

"Heaven's goal, the purpose." He looked at me, but didn't say anything for a few moments. "Okay, it *is* his goal. They're one and the same. That's part of the problem. The story is that Boney is merely implementing the will of the Creators."

"The *story*?"

He lifted his palms in gesture of defeat.

"It's not supposed to be a story," I surmised. "It's supposed to be fact, right?"

He nodded. "But I do my best to be a loyal soldier for the cause. And right now that means hitching east to warn him."

I saw him looking over my shoulder, and I turned to see. A billow of smoke a few miles south along the coast was angling eastward with the onshore wind. It looked like it might be coming from the municipal golf course up on the Torrey Pines ridge, or even from the forest reserve. That could be devastating. Wildfires were the bane of southern California, and we couldn't afford to lose what few trees we had. Two fire trucks from Del Mar tore south on the 101, wailing their screaming alarm loud enough that I wanted to cover my ears. Somehow, I found this poignant. The men in these trucks dedicated their lives on the premise that the fire was consuming something precious and worth a great effort to save. And here I was, insulated from the world in a way that I would never have imagined. If a fire broke out right in front of me, if people's lives were in imminent danger, there wasn't a damn thing I could do to help.

No, that wasn't quite true. In all the world there was one person I'd promised myself I would help. It's why I was here in the first place.

We decided that a taco joint like Roberto's wasn't the kind of place to pick up a ride to an exclusive neighborhood such as Rancho Santa Fe, so we walked down the sidewalk and followed a couple into an upscale Italian restaurant.

It seemed strange that in a world swimming in cell phones, we couldn't just make a quick call, but without fingers able to push buttons or voices able to be heard, we might as well have been ghosts. That thought was a bit too close to home, and I shoved it away and concentrated on listening to the dining room conversations.

As I walked from table to table, eavesdropping, I experimented with the food. I poked at a plate of spaghetti, and my finger met a pile of frozen earthworms. I expected the tomato sauce to be slippery, but of course it had the texture of rough paint. I stuck my finger into a woman's glass of wine, and was surprised that it wasn't hard as ice. It felt slightly spongy, like foam padding. Curious, I pressed down, and gave a little shout when my finger began to sink into the red viscous semi-liquid. It didn't so much sink, as that it slowly absorbed the wine. This was a mistake. At that moment, the woman reached out and picked up the glass for a drink, but my appendage was still stuck inside like a Chinese finger trap. I tugged as hard as I could, but the exit was as slow as the entry, and the glass reached her mouth before I had fully extricated. My finger followed the slosh of wine into her mouth, and I was finally able to yank free just as her mouth closed.

"You could lose a finger doing that," Zorba said next to me.

"Really?" I felt flushed from the close call.

He nodded. "It happens."

A sudden thought loomed, threatening doom. "What happens if I get caught in, like, a car door when it slams shut?"

"If you're lucky you just lose a limb."

"And if not?"

He shrugged.

"I dissolve?" I squeaked.

"You learn to be careful," was his reply.

I gave up the food experiments and soon Zorba called me over to a corner table where a graying, handsome man in an expensive polo shirt was sitting with a young woman wearing a skirt and blouse. "He's paid the bill," Zorba explained, "and he's just about got this floozy convinced to come along with him. His wife is out of town."

"He lives in Rancho Santa Fe?" I asked, noting that the young woman wore a wedding ring as well.

"No," he replied, trotting off towards the front door, "but he's told her that he has the keys to his friend's house." He turned and gestured for me to follow. "We have to get out before they leave."

I saw what he meant. We had to grab at whatever opportunity became available. We couldn't assume that we'd both make it out with the clandestine couple when they left. Zorba demonstrated the preferred technique of exiting when two women came in, chattering away about some acquaintance's bad taste. The execution would have been ignoble if anyone had seen us. As it was, it was just slightly painful. Zorba stood ready next to the door and waited until both women had walked through. Then as the last woman stepped inside, he threw himself against her back, pushing away to bounce off of the door as it closed. The last I saw of him, he was sprawled on the small porch floor. But he was outside.

I copied the method when a man entered a minute later, and found it effective, if battering. My head bounced off the door, but Zorba was there to catch me, and at least I didn't hit the ground.

We didn't know which car belonged to Mr. Seducer in the small parking lot, so we sat on the steps and waited until the tryst-bound couple emerged. Zorba jumped up and fell in behind the floozy until he was practically stepping on her heels. He then wrapped his arms around her neck from behind her. He couldn't see her feet now, so he hung on and let his own feet just drag along the ground. It looked like he might be her desperate husband begging her not to leave him, but I could see that he was talking directly into her ear.

I had gotten up and followed along, assuming he had something cooking, and when Seducer opened the passenger door of a Lexus sedan, Zorba let go of his ride and waved for me to come close. "Get ready to get in," he instructed. "Climb into the back as fast as you can. I'll be right behind."

I eased up between the Lexus and the woman, who was still in the way, but she was hesitating, as though unsure whether she really wanted to go through with this. "Just a second," she said to her beau, and stepped away from the car, towards the back of the restaurant. I didn't wait to see what she was up to, but scrambled in and climbed over the seat as Zorba had instructed. A second later, he arrived on top of me, and I was getting the idea that a life in Halfway was one long, bruising tumble.

As it happened, our haste was unnecessary, since the woman took her time returning. "What was that all about?" Seducer asked as he got in the driver's side and slammed the door shut.

"It's silly," she replied, "but I had the strangest feeling that Doug was checking up on me."

"I thought he was working in Escondido all day."

"He is. In fact, he called me from there just an hour ago."

"Then it *was* silly."

"Don't give me a hard time, Ted. If he catches me, I'm done."

"Ah, he'll never leave you. He knows a good thing when he's got it."

"Just like you'll never leave Katie."

"Now, don't start up on that again. You know I have to play it right. I've worked way too hard building the business to walk away from it."

"She'd get half, and we'd still have plenty to live on."

"Come on! I'm not handing over even a tenth to her. Why should she get any?"

"Sometimes I think you care about your money more than me," she accused angrily.

"You're being obtuse. Can't we just drop it?"

But she wouldn't. They argued all the way to eastbound Highway 56. I asked Zorba if he'd planted the suspicion of her husband, and he confirmed; he'd guessed that the notion was probably already in her head, otherwise she wouldn't have acted on his subliminal whisperings.

Their arguing was too loud to compete with, so we sat back and enjoyed the ride. For the first time since arriving, I was able to just relax. Despite the inconvenience of having about as much access to the niceties of modern society as an infant, life in Halfway wasn't so bad: no job, no bills, no taxes. Heck, no teeth brushing, or even showers. Actually, I decided I might miss that one. And eating; I would definitely miss that. No, we had to get back. I would find Kirsten and we'd wait for Professor Clintock's sirens to bring us home.

At least, I was able to relax for a few minutes until Seducer paused the who-do-you-love-more debate and peered into the rearview mirror. "What kind of truck does Doug drive?" he asked suddenly.

The woman twisted her head around, but the fear evaporated, and she replied, "He drives a big Ford F350. That's not even a pickup."

Seducer watched the intruder in the mirror. "Whoever this guy is, he's been riding my tail for the last couple of miles."

Zorba and I exchanged alarmed glances and both turned around to look. An SUV hovered less than a car length behind us, so close I couldn't even see the bumper. The driver, a young man with glasses and a neat haircut, stared straight through me as if in a trance. Beside him sat an older man. His dark, handsome face broke into a smile as we turned around. Jim Jones slowly drew his finger across his throat.

PART II

BONEY

Chapter 5

"This isn't good," Zorba declared as Seducer threw an ineffectual middle finger into the air at the entranced SUV driver.

"How did he *find* us?" I asked a bit hysterically. I could feel the predator/prey instinct urging me to run-run-run.

"Not sure. Maybe he took a good guess that we'd end up coming this way. He probably knows that they took Kirsten to Rancho Santa Fe, but not exactly where."

"What'll we *do?*"

Zorba was already doing it. He'd leaned forward and wrapped his arms around Seducer's head in the Halfway version of a Vulcan mind-meld. I heard him mutter that no geek weasel was going to let him be intimidated. Zorba was obviously playing to the man's power ego. Seducer threw another quick glance into the mirror, knocking Zorba away, and stomped the accelerator. We surged ahead as the powerful Lexus engine responded to the order.

"Do you think we can get away?" I asked.

Zorba picked himself up. "No. It's stupid to try to outrun them. I just wanted our idiot chauffeur to ignore them until we could think of something."

The floozy didn't like it either. She demanded to know what he thought he was doing. "No geek weasel's going to intimidate *me!*" he responded.

I looked at Zorba who just raised his eyebrows.

"Ted! Slow down!" she cried. "You're going over a hundred!"

Ted stared straight ahead, his jaw muscles tight knots of perseverance. This stretch of the highway was just two lanes in our direction. Ahead were two cars in the right lane, one close behind the other. We were coming up on them fast. I'd been in this situation many times. Look out!" I shouted, but only Zorba heard me.

For reasons beyond me, a following car often waits for a third to approach from behind before deciding to finally pass. This one waited until the very last moment, perhaps miscalculating our extreme speed. I saw movement as it crossed in front of us, Seducer cursed, and the next moment the world was turning round and round as the Lexus spun off out of control. Centrifugal force plastered me flat against the door for what seemed like minutes, but was probably just a few full turns before the tires found an obstruction which sent the car tumbling and rolling. All was painful chaos while I bounced around like a pinball, colliding often with Zorba, which was obvious since he was the only soft object in the car.

The maelstrom ended as quickly as it had launched. One moment I was an ice cube in a drink mixer, and the next I was lying blinking at the back seat perched a foot above me. I lay across Zorba who seemed unconscious. After the tremendous bashing roar of the catastrophic tumble, the hiss of escaping steam and low groaning of one of the living victims seemed like deafening silence.

Zorba was not knocked out, however. I surmised that this was probably not possible without a brain to get bounced about. "Get off me," he demanded.

I expected that I would not be able to, convinced that my broken bones would prevent it. This was an irrational notion, of course, and I rolled away. The pain of being tossed around the interior had been intense and disorienting, but completely situational. No flesh, no nerves, no lingering pain. The excruciating suffering was now just a memory.

I looked around. The Lexus was upside down, resting on its roof like an upended turtle. The front of the car was smashed in and tilting upwards; I guessed that it was resting against whatever had brought the tumbling somersault to an end. The groaning came from the flooze, and I wasn't sure whether Seducer was alive. Both of their air bags had deployed, and were now limp, hanging in their faces.

A man's voice said, "Oh God, are you okay?"

It was the driver of the other car, the geek. He was on his hands and knees, talking through the broken window next to Seducer. He seemed to have come out of the trance that Jim Jones had put him under, and I could see why. The rogue heaven exile was walking around our wreck, looking for some point of access.

Seducer was indeed alive. Air bags were wonderful inventions. "You wrecked my car, you son-of-a-bitch!" he hollered. "Of course I'm not okay!"

"No, I mean are you hurt?" He seemed to consider a moment behind his thick glasses. "I didn't cause your accident. I wasn't anywhere near you."

"Well, you can talk to my lawyer about that. Now get me out of here." The stranded driver began yanking ineffectually at the draping air bag.

"I'll call 911," the geek decided, reaching for his cell phone.

"No!" Seducer yelled. "Get me out of here first!"

The geek hesitated, fingers poised above the phone. "I think we need help."

"You dial 911, and I'll break your fingers! *Now get me out of here!*"

"Er, what about the other passenger?" He peered through the back passenger window, looking through me, but the flooze's airbag covered her face.

"I'm okay," she said weakly, pulling aside her fabric veil. "Don't call Doug. Don't tell him."

I guessed that she was a little loopy from having her brains rattled.

A hand grabbed at my shoulder, and I batted it away and slid across the roof, pushing Zorba with me. Jim Jones had given up trying to find an easy entry, and was reaching through the passenger window. Having failed to grab me, he pulled his arm back through.

It retreated slowly, as though moving through viscous molasses. I recalled my finger adventure in the wine. He put his face to the window and called, "Where is she? Give me the address, Jordan. I can help her."

He moved around to the back and stooped under the upturned trunk, and then reached through the back windshield, but Zorba and I could easily avoid his probing hand by scooting forward. Standing behind Jones, watching closely, as though intent on serving as Jones's competent understudy, was the same middle-aged companion who had been with the charismatic cult leader when he'd first attacked us.

Seducer was still arguing with the geek. "Just yank at the door and open it," he directed.

The younger man reached for the door handle, but hesitated. "No. You're not supposed to move accident victims. I need to call for help."

Seducer's curses gained volume, and I saw Jones's feet walk around the car. I peered up through the window and saw him place his hand against the man's forehead a moment. The geek tilted his head, nodded, and said, "Maybe I should get the lady out first?"

"Fine," growled Seducer. "Just be quick about it."

Seconds later, the screech of metal against metal howled as the geek pulled open the passenger door, revealing the smooth white cement of a highway barrier beyond. This is what the Lexus was using as a pillow. The geek wasn't sure how to extricate the flooze, and in the end, he just undid the seatbelt buckle, and she tumbled headfirst onto the roof of the car. She was still immobile in an ungainly tangle, and he finally simply pulled her out by her ankles. Pantyhose and panties flashed freely, and I was going to avert my eyes, but figured that I was rendered harmless in any case by the sexless state of Halfway existence.

"Get out!" Zorba yelled.

I looked at him. "Jones is out there!"

"It doesn't matter! We'll be trapped in here."

I saw what he meant; this car was heading for the crusher. We might not have another opportunity once the tow truck arrived. I crawled over to where she had been dangling upside down, but the airbag still hung there, and to me it was as solid as a steel barrier. I tried to squeeze around it, but there just wasn't room. I felt panic boiling in my stomach, imagining the mighty jaws of the car crusher forcing our captive space smaller and smaller, like a James Bond scene.

A bang and squeak announced that the geek had gotten the driver's door open. Seducer was more agile than his mistress, and he scrambled out, pushing against the console with his foot. He irritably shoved the hanging airbag aside, and it blessedly wrapped around the steering wheel post. Our exit was cleared.

Zorba was closer, so he crawled under the driver seatback and into the open doorway. Jim Jones's hand reached down, grabbed my friend by the neck, pulled him out, and tossed him aside like he was made of cardboard. I guessed that one of the skills learned in heaven was extraordinary strength to bully lowly Wops. Jones's silent companion reached a helping hand to lift Zorba up.

I was next. I didn't mind if Jim threw me about like a doll, not if the alternative was the crusher. But as my head emerged into sunlight, the rogue from heaven grabbed my neck and held me firmly in place. I waited to be lifted neck-wise, but found myself being pushed inexorably backwards instead. "Where is she?" he demanded.

"I don't know—really!"

I heard a thump, and gathered that Zorba was hitting Jones. At the edge of my constrained vision I saw Jones swing his fist backwards, and then Zorba sprawled on the ground again. "Why did you come?" Jones pressed, staring intently into my eyes.

"To get her!" I cried. "To bring her back!" My voice was just a croak under his iron grip.

He didn't say anything for a moment. I wondered if this was news to him.

"You think you can return?" he finally asked.

I feared the crusher, but his incredulity at the idea of returning, the reinforcement of the assumed impossibility, was even more terrifying.

Before I could answer, though, I saw Zorba look up from where he was lying, and the expression on his face was astonishment. "Let him go, James," I heard a calm voice say. It was not delivered as an order, but the suggestion had the tone of unquestionable logic. It was a voice whose message you found difficult to ignore. It was the voice of reasonable authority.

Jim Jones did let me go, but with a parting shake that caused my head to bounce off the edge of the doorframe. I crawled from the smashed Lexus on hands and knees and got up. The newcomer stood watching me casually, but yet carefully. This was the hallmark that most distinguished him in my mind then and ever afterwards— the confusing (to me) contradictions of character. He could make a joke that was genuinely funny, yet simultaneously ominous; he would reprimand with convincing anger while placing a gentle hand of consolation on your shoulder; he complimented you with seemingly earnest conviction that at the same time conveyed criticism. I imagined what a dog might feel when its master pretends exuberant excitement over a tossed ball, followed immediately with stern rebuke when the play goes astray. The big picture is a mystery to the dog.

He stood now with the barest hint of a smile, as though amused at finally meeting me, but not quite enough to comment on.

"You're Boney," I said. The words spilled from my mouth before I hardly formulated the thought. This man wore no French Revolution napkin holder-shaped bicorne hat, nor double-buttoned waist coat, nor George Washington white button pants with matching knee-high black boots. In fact, he was outfitted like a businessman dressed down for the golf course, sporting chino slacks and what looked like a Casmir sweater. He wasn't all that short either, but I remembered reading that he had been of average height for his time—the British had invented the short myth in order to mock the man they so feared. The only visible clue was the pronounced widow's peak curling playfully between receding estuaries in a tossed sea of limp, black hair.

On the other hand, I reasoned, why should the man be stuck with the fashions that were popular in one slice of time? After all, there was a time when I wore—God forbid—pleated blue jeans.

"And you're Jordan," he responded. It was a simple statement of fact. He had a very slight accent, but I wouldn't have been able to place it.

Jim Jones had backed slowly away, as though thinking he might sneak off, but Boney held out his hand and pointed at the mass murderer. "Not yet," he said in the calm yet commanding tenor.

Jones froze. I assumed that this was out of obedience, but it had the sense of deriving from some supernatural power wielded by Napoleon's finger.

"Welcome to Halfway," Boney said to me. "We'll have to thank Professor Clintock for volunteering another recruit."

"I'm not staying," I replied.

He gave me one of those enigmatic smiles. "I'm sure that the professor sent you off with noble intentions," he continued, "but he's like a blind man groping around the feet of a great statue, trying to discern from the shoes the noble nature of the historic figure poised above."

"Like your statue *Mars the Peacemaker*?" I suggested.

I was surprised at my impetuous lack of savoir faire. I remembered reading that Napoleon had commissioned an Italian sculptor, and the result was a giant eleven-foot high nude likeness posed as the Roman god Mars. Napoleon had refused to accept the delivery on grounds that it was too athletic. I'd had enough experience to recognize that my faux pas was due to muddled thinking. A vague terror at being trapped here was overwhelming me, and although my usual anxiety is almost never situational, I could feel kindred tremors of its fateful call of doom. I sensed that this was a man to whom I'd never want to reveal my weaknesses, so I started the familiar suite of breathing and mind focus exercises that comprised my anxiety control.

If Boney recognized my unease, he didn't let on. Raising one eyebrow about a millimeter, he said, "I would perhaps prefer that if a blind professor were to grope, it would be about the hooves at Cherbourg."

I wasn't sure what he meant. "Er, this is a statue of a horse?"

Now he smiled fully. "I am mounted on a steed," he explained helpfully, "with my right hand extended as though I am commanding my troops, as an orchestra conductor might his symphony."

A Napoleon Bonaparte, hailed as perhaps the greatest general to ever live, joking good-naturedly might have allayed my fear, but instead, the casual familiarity seemed to just cement the finality of my predicament.

"You know Professor Clintock, then?" I asked. I knew immediately that this was a dumb thing to say, since he was obviously already very familiar with Kirsten, but the anxiety exercises were distracting.

"I know *of* the professor," he replied. "There's very little I don't know if the subject interests me. I am most grateful to the professor for recovering the manuscript of Exiguus. The monk is something of a legend around Home."

"You mean heaven?" I asked with the ten percent of my mind not occupied with the exercises.

His eyes flashed with anger and behind him, Zorba was wildly waving his fingertips back and forth across his throat.

I remembered that he had warned me that Boney didn't like the term heaven. "Sorry," I said simply. Then I remembered. "That's what Exiguus called it," I added defensively. I didn't want him to know that Zorba had told me that.

The great French general watched me a moment, and then nodded. "Forgiven."

It seemed an odd response given the informal tone up to then, but then again, he was once the emperor of most of Europe. Despite the collegiate cloths, the leader of heaven—AKA Home— did indeed convey a regal aura. I noted that the small crowd of living people that were gathering around the wreck avoided bumping him. If someone came to close, he merely threw them a glance, and they found the unconscious urge to step a different way. Nobody seemed to notice that there was a small spot among them that was continually empty.

I realized that he had said something. "Pardon me?"

"I said that Zorba will continue as your guide until we can find an assignment for you."

"I'm not staying," I repeated.

He shook his head sadly. "Yes," he said, "I'm afraid you are. There is no way back."

"Exiguus made it," I countered.

The shake of his head became certain. "That route was closed a long time ago, long before I ascended."

Those words struck a chord. There was something about time, about time passed. And then it hit me like a punch to my gut: the professor had told me that I would return in an hour, when I heard sirens. I had heard sirens—the fire trucks dashing towards the fire on Torrey Pines ridge. I caught a glance at the wristwatch of a man talking to a woman nearby. I couldn't breathe. It had been nearly an hour and a half since I had ascended. I had missed the professor's window.

Boney was studying me closely. "You are a strange case," he said. "Ascendees arrive ecstatic to be here." His eyes seemed to bore into my head looking for my secrets. "You will learn to be happy," he finally declared.

"And if I don't?"

He just looked at me. Words would be gauche.

"I'll be dissolved," I blurted the gauche fact.

He just raised one eyebrow in agreement.

My control exercises had been fairly successful up to then, but this revelation—this threat—released anew the terror. The fear came at me like Pacific waves, washing my fiber with dread unspeakable. I hadn't felt an intensity like this since the original anxiety onslaught years before. I was a different person now, though. I'd had a decade to develop techniques of mind and emotion control.

I closed my eyes and took a deep breath. The burden of my form of anxiety was akin to losing one's self, and the counteraction was a reaffirmation of one's self, one's core existence. I mustered my mental lenses and focused all my attention on *me*, on the me that lived deep in my chest and my head. I felt it working. I felt powerful and yet light as a feather. I was lifting myself up and away. I heard Boney shout in alarm and anger, but his cry came from a distance, as though receding at an accelerating speed.

And then I felt solid.

I opened my eyes and I was looking up at the roof of a car. For a moment I thought that Boney had perhaps pushed me back inside the wrecked Lexus, but in that case, I'd be looking up at the seats. I sat up, and I felt heavy, sluggishly full of mass. Outside, about fifty feet away, the professor was talking to some firemen. Beside them, smoke billowed from a copper fire pit—this was what I had thought was a copper ball in the back of the Explorer.

Hardly daring to hope, I reached out and pulled on the door handle. It moved.

Chapter 6

I felt very much real, but my head appeared to be filled with packed cotton. It had been little more than an hour before that I'd taken the Rohypnol, and the pills were still in command.

I yanked at the car door handle and then fell back, exhausted. The door had unlatched, though, and I kicked it open with my foot. The professor turned at the sound and ran over, abandoning the firemen. "Jordan!" he exclaimed, "You're late! I was . . . worried."

I sat up and let Clintock climb in next to me. "It wasn't wasted," I said.

"What wasn't wasted?"

"Your worry. I was afraid there for a while that I would never get back."

"You mean you—"

"Made it? Oh yeah, I made it to Halfway all right."

The professor just looked at me blankly.

"It's their name for what you call the overlay."

"Halfway," he mused. "Because it's halfway to—"

"Yeah, halfway to heaven. Listen, how was it supposed to work with the sirens? I assume that's what this is all about," I said, gesturing at the two fire trucks and the squad of highly trained fire fighters watching us from twenty feet away.

"You missed it," he said simply.

"I missed what? I barely noticed the fire trucks going by. What kind of abracadabra magic was supposed to happen? Whatever it was, it was a dud."

Clintock didn't say anything, but I could see that he was blushing.

"You flubbed it somehow?" I ventured. And then suddenly I understood. "It was all a fake!"

His blush deepened, and he still didn't reply.

"You were going to leave me there!" I cried.

"No!" he finally responded. "No! Exiguus never explained how he returned, but he *did*."

I waited, but he didn't say any more. "Did *he* have sirens?" I offered, not sure myself if I was trying to be sarcastic.

"No. I don't know. It doesn't matter. Belief is necessary to transfer—"

"Ascend," I corrected.

He smiled. "Ah, I like that better. From their perspective, of course, they would consider the overlay—*halfway*—to be in a higher position. Transfer implies something parallel, whereas to ascend is to rise—"

"Professor!"

"Eh?"

"The sirens."

"Er, right. As I was saying, belief is necessary to ascend, so . . . you know . . ."

"I *don't* know! What the hell are you talking about?"

The firemen had stopped talking among themselves and were watching us. I was getting loud.

He sighed. "Belief was necessary to return, just as belief was necessary to get there in the first place."

"And the sirens were just something to believe in?" I asked incredulously.

"They were a talisman," he said. I just stared at him. "An abstract talisman," he elaborated, "but a talisman all the same."

"A placebo," I challenged.

His brow wrinkled. "No. A placebo implies a malady, whereas a talisman is thought to have magic abilities—"

"I get it. The sirens were supposed to give me something to believe in. But how did you know that this was sufficient, that all I had to do was believe? Like Dorothy, clicking her heels together and simply wishing to go home."

He shrugged. "Belief was necessary."

"It was a first step," I said.

This time I was being explicitly sarcastic, but the professor didn't catch it. "Exactly," he agreed heartily.

I was fuming. I could have been stuck in that limbo land forever. It was like handing someone a pair of boots and expecting that this was all that was necessary for them to make their way to Alaska.

"What about that two-dimensional palindrome?"

"The Pater Noster palindrome?"

"Yeah. Was that also just an abstract talisman?"

His brow scrunched in contemplation. He shook his head. "No, I think that the Pater Noster does indeed hold some special power. Not magic. No such thing. But maybe the overlay—*halfway*—is somehow tuned to the pattern of the sounds, the intonations of the syllables—"

Clintock continued with his self-absorbed analysis, but I was thinking that there was one important question that he hadn't asked me: how *did* I get back? How, indeed. I replayed the scene. I had been fighting an anxiety attack. I'd amassed an extensive suite of mental tools, but in the end, what were they actually all about? Well, in a nutshell, belief.

"Kirsten," I said suddenly. Rational thoughts were slowly seeping through the packed cotton in my head.

He paused his self-intellectualization. "You found her?" he asked, his eyes popping with hope.

"Yes and no. I got a glimpse of her, but they've taken her away for special training."

The hope collapsed. "The Devil?" he asked darkly.

"No, Napoleon Bonaparte."

"I see." He thought a moment. "I'm sorry, I don't understand the metaphor."

"It's no metaphor. They call him Boney. But, who—or what—is this Devil you warned me about?"

"From all that I could gather, you would recognize him if you met him."

"What about a man who convinced nine hundred of his followers to murder a congressman along with his entourage, and then commit mass suicide? Including children."

Clintock stared, shocked. But then the horror morphed into interest. "You met Jim Jones? He's *there*?"

"More like he met me. So, what do you think?"

The professor reverted to furrowed brow mode. "Not sure. He sounds vile enough, but . . ."

"But what?"

"Remember, Exiguus made the transfer fifteen hundred years ago."

"And the Devil was there then?"

"Exactly."

"Which means that I might not have run across him yet."

"Exactly."

"Which means that he would presumably be an even worse bastard than Jim Jones."

"Precisely."

"Not exactly?"

The professor looked at me, confused.

"It was a joke."

Kirsten's plight was no joke. An inner struggle was tearing its way through the packed cotton. Even in my muffled, drugged state, I was thrilled—ecstatic—to be back in the land of the living, but I knew with even more assurance than before that I had to go back. And the very thought made me slightly nauseous.

"We have to go to Roberto's," I announced.

"I'm rather surprised," Clintock observed. "Rohypnol usually acts as an appetite suppressor. Plus, I have to deal with this sticky situation over the fire I made—"

"My contact may be there. It's my only chance to find Kirsten."

"Your contact," he echoed. "Er, Napoleon Bonaparte?"

"No. His name is Zorba, and he—" I saw that Kirsten's fantasy literature class instructor was watching me cautiously. "Look, professor, you can't discover a parallel universe populated by dead people, and then stop short of expecting that it would include a famous person from history."

He sighed and nodded. "You're right. This contact—Zorba—he can lead you to Kirsten?"

"He's my only hope."

"Well then, let's go!"

We moved to the front seats and drove off, leaving the firemen calling warnings to our rear end. It was a short drive, and we didn't have much time to talk, but at the professor's suggestion, we worked out a simple method to try to communicate. I didn't think it would work, but it was all we could come up with. By the time we arrived at the Mexican take-out joint, I was having doubts that I could ascend a second time. I began to think that the first time was just a fluke. The Rohypnol was still effective, though, and once I reclined the seat back and closed my eyes, it was easy to let my worries go and float in the drug's haze. Professor Clintock murmured away with his hypnotic drone, but I wasn't really listening. My attention fixed on his words, however, when he finally recited the Pater Noster palindrome, "Sator, Arepo, Tenet . . ." I could actually feel myself lifting up and away; or perhaps my flesh and bones were sinking away, like wet clothes doffed on the porch. My thoughts became clear and distinct as I left the drug-soaked brain behind.

"Welcome back."

I opened my eyes to find that I was standing outside, and Zorba was walking around the front of Clintock's car. Inside, the professor had his hand on my shoulder, and he looked about, clearly not seeing me standing there.

My Halfway friend was wearing a wry smile. "How did you do that?" he asked.

"I'm not sure—drugs, palindromes, and simple belief. How does anybody ascend?"

"No, I mean how did you get out of the car?"

I blinked. I hadn't thought about that. The first ascension had left me on top of the Explorer.

He stood looking at me admiringly, like a father might at his daughter's graduation. "You returned, didn't you?" he asked.

"To there?" I said, gesturing towards the professor. I meant the land of the living in general. "Yeah, but I came back for Kirsten. Thanks for coming back here, by the way."

His smile turned sardonic. "You may regret coming back. You're never going to get to Kirsten, and even if you did, it's not like she's being held hostage or anything."

I shrugged. "I have to try."

"That's not the worst."

"What could be worse than losing Kirsten?"

"Losing yourself."

"That used to happen every time I smoked pot. I do yoga now."

"I'm serious. I think that Boney has written you off."

I shrugged again. "I don't need his help. I'll find Kirsten on my own."

He shook his head. "You don't understand. When Boney writes you off, you're as good as . . . gone."

"You mean . . .?"

"Yeah. Dissolved. Obliviated."

That wasn't a word, but it was effective. I glanced around, expecting the Frenchman to appear suddenly out of thin air. "Why? I haven't done anything!"

"Oh yes you did. You returned to life."

"So what! Is he jealous?"

"Threatened. I don't know this for sure—nobody knows for sure what Boney thinks—but I have a strong hunch."

"That's crazy! I'm floundering here! I'm like a fish out of water. I can't even pick up a toothpick. I get knocked over if someone sneezes in my direction."

Zorba lifted his hands. "You're an unknown."

"Because I came back?"

"Because you returned to the normal world; because you ascended—twice—with no help from this end."

A sudden thought raised the imaginary hairs on my neck. "Did Boney send you?" If he did, then Le Petit Caporal might be right behind.

"No. I didn't tell him about our fallback arrangement."

I thought I detected hesitation. "Wouldn't he be angry?"

The hesitation settled into resignation. Zorba nodded. "He'll be furious. Boney demands complete loyalty." He must have seen the concern on my face. "I'm tired of waiting for heaven," he confessed. "They say that if you don't make it in the first couple of years, you never will."

"What will he do if he finds out?"

My friend just looked at me. The doom haunted his eyes. "Dissolve you?" I asked tentatively.

"If he catches me," he responded. His tight grin revealed little humor. "His people are pretty much everywhere."

"The Soldats?"

"Soldats are only sent to Halfway on specific missions. We Wops are either waiting for a pass to Boney's heaven, or part of a gang. If we still think we have a chance with Boney, we'll will do anything to curry his favor."

A sudden spit and hiss announced the automatic sprinklers turning on in the small grassy area between the parking lot and the street. I was surprised when Zorba ran twenty feet away and yelped as though they were rattlesnakes.

"What's wrong?" I asked, but then I was apparently hit by a bullet on my shoulder, which sent me sprawling in the dirt. I managed to get up on my hands and knees, but Zorba grabbed my wrist and dragged me away. When he finally let me go, I probed my shoulder, expecting to find a hole if not a flow of blood, but there was nothing.

"You okay?" he asked.

"I guess. What the hell happened?"

"You were hit."

"I know that, but by what?"

"A drop," he replied as though it was obvious.

"A drop of *water*?"

"Of course."

I thought about it, and it was logical, if bizarre. A drop of water might as well be a bullet to any poor Halfway citizen who happened to be in the way. "What do you do when it rains?"

"You stay inside."

"What if you get caught in it?"

"You make sure you don't."

"But what if you do? It must happen."

"You really don't want to let that happen. If it's just a little sprinkle, you are bashed to the ground, where you sustain more pain than you've ever imagined. The worst part is that you're essentially trapped, the droplets just beat you incessantly so that you can't move. I heard of one Wop who went mad."

"And what happens when it, like, pours?" I felt goose bumps just saying it.

He shook his head. "You just don't, is all."

I shuddered and moved a few steps more away from the spray of deadly water. "You mentioned that if you're not waiting for a pass to heaven, then you're part of a gang. There's Wop gangs? That sounds problematic when you can't lift a can of spray paint. I'll take a wild guess, though: Jim Jones?"

He nodded. "Southern California's pretty much his territory. He calls his gang The Flock. There are a few solo rogues. I might hook up with one of them."

"They provide protection?"

"Some. Boney could probably eliminate them if he really wanted to, but the bigger question is whether you can count on them in a pinch. After all, there's a reason why Boney kicked them out of heaven. I don't know—I might head out to Florida. I've heard that Malcolm has a foothold there."

"Malcolm . . . wait, you don't mean Malcom X . . ."

Zorba shrugged. "Yeah."

Malcom X was way before my time, but I had read about him. "Wait a second. He was assassinated. I thought that you had to be in a coma to ascend."

"No. That's backwards. Ascension leaves your body in a coma. You do have to be in a zen-like state, though."

"Well, that leaves the same question. Assassination sounds the exact opposite of a state of zen meditation."

"The story goes that he'd been dabbling in the idea of ascension; meaning, of course, that Boney had been recruiting him. He died in the ambulance on the way to the hospital, but I guess he had just enough time for Boney to grab him."

"I thought you said that Boney couldn't bring you up, that you had to do it yourself."

"I think I was talking about heaven, but a first ascension is basically the same. And yes, you do have to do it yourself. But a helping hand, so to speak, goes a long way. It's sort of like somebody giving you directions as you make your way through a dark room. You wouldn't start out in the first place if you didn't want to."

I remembered that the professor had said that you couldn't be forced, but you could be enticed. You might start out across the dark room on your own, but what if somebody was making promises that they had no intention of keeping?

I didn't voice these thoughts to Zorba. Instead, I asked, "Was Boney there to help you?"

He nodded matter-of-factly. "Of course. I don't know anybody who didn't have his help."

I just looked at him.

He tipped his head once in agreement, remembering. "Except you, of course. And that's exactly the exception that Boney doesn't like."

We both jumped when a car right next to us tooted its horn. "That's our cue," I explained.

Zorba watched Professor Clintock open the driver door and get out. "For what?" he asked.

"For us to get in," I replied, trotting around the car to where the professor was holding the rear door open. "Hurry!" I called to Zorba before climbing in the back.

My Halfway friend made it inside seconds before the professor started counting down from ten a bit louder than I would have liked. It was like a Cape Canaveral launch, but instead of a thunderous rocket liftoff, our chauffeur slowly closed the door, and then made sure it had latched.

"That was a pre-arranged signal," Zorba guessed as the professor pulled away from Roberto's and headed east, towards Rancho Santa Fe.

"You win back the cigar."

I explained the plan, that Clintock was going to take us. "How will he know where to go once we get there?" Zorba asked.

"That's where you come in. You'll tell him."

This gave him pause. "Interesting. I've never tried to influence somebody who was expecting it."

"Boney does it," I remarked, remembering the woman who'd brought the taxi that took Kirsten away.

Zorba snorted. "Like I would be allowed anywhere near candidates."

"But you can do it?"

He looked doubtful. "I can try." He thought a moment. "Sure. It should be easy."

During the short drive to the upper crust community, I asked Zorba about heaven, whether it was an overlay like Halfway. "Heavenites don't talk about it," he explained. "It's forbidden. Over the years, though, I've gathered that it is sort of an overlay, as you call it. But where Halfway is impressed *on* the world, the real world is more or less laid onto heaven. I think that the world you're used to is sort of a translucent shell around heaven. It's not easy to grasp if you've never been there—I certainly have a hard time—but it means that in heaven you can walk right through the walls of the real world."

"Like ghosts."

I had an epiphany. "Hey, is that where the myth of ghosts actually came from?"

"More or less."

"Is it more more, or more less?"

"The early church came up with the idea of ghosts to scare the congregation away from Boney."

"There wasn't a Boney back then."

"There's always been a Boney of some kind."

I filed that away for future study. "You're telling me that the Catholic Church knows about Halfway and heaven—the real heaven?"

"Not exactly." He looked uncomfortable, as though the whole subject was distasteful. "In fact, not really at all. The entire spectrum of myths about the Devil, and ghosts, and a brimstone-and-fire hell just kind of evolved over the centuries. People who believed in this stuff were immune to the succession of Boneys—"

"They were wary of any influence not sanctioned by the priest," I surmised.

"Right. So people who believed in the Devil stayed with the church, and the more the myths grew, the more successful the church was at keeping members. And the more successful the church was, the more the myths spread."

"A classic positive feedback loop," I observed, and upon seeing his reaction, I added, "Never mind. It's systems theory, a fancy way of describing evolution. But getting back to walking through walls, I can see how it would be difficult for a Wop to get away from Boney."

"It's not quite as bad as that. Once in Halfway, a heavenite can't just walk through a wall. They'd have to transition to heaven, and once through the wall, transition back to Halfway, and transitioning between heaven and Halfway isn't just snapping their fingers."

"But I can see how Boney could just appear out of nowhere."

"Yep. You can be sitting on a bench, and the next instant a Soldat is standing there in front of you. Scares the dickens out of me every time."

I related the professor's caution about locking us in his car before my first ascension. "It would have prevented Boney or Soldats that were manifested in Halfway from listening," Zorba confirmed, "but not if they were in heaven."

He must have seen my alarm. "Don't worry," he added. "Boney can't be everywhere, you know, and he's got a lot to deal with."

"Right," I agreed, very much wanting to be convinced. "He's not God."

"Not quite," Zorba concurred. He seemed to want to reassure himself of this. "For example, it's pretty much impossible for Boney to get at us now."

I considered this. "Because we're moving?"

"Yeah. Think about it; he'd have to be traveling along with us in heaven at the exact same speed and direction."

"Er, how *do* you get around in heaven?"

"Same as Halfway, I guess. You would hitch rides, but it would be easier."

"You guess? You don't know?"

"Well, my mistake; here I thought I'd already told you that it's forbidden for Soldats to talk about heaven."

"I'm sorry. I didn't mean to cross a line there. I don't know where the lines are."

"No, I'm sorry. I know you're just trying to understand."

Zorba continued to look troubled. "What?" I asked.

He glanced at the professor who was oblivious to what was going on in the back seat. "Look," he confided, "Boney's probably going to come after your professor friend—both of you, now."

I looked at the professor with alarm. I hardly knew Kirsten's teacher, but I had developed a liking the first time I'd met him. He was patient and inclusive. If you didn't know better, you might think him simple or naive, but the reality was that he just wasn't interested in using intelligence and knowledge as a club like so many other academics I knew. "What can Boney do to him?" I suddenly felt torn between a burning need to find Kirsten, and a sense of duty to return and warn Clintock.

Of course, I didn't really know *how* to return, so my dilemma didn't last very long.

"Boney can't directly harm living people, but he can affect their moods, instill impulses that would otherwise be bad choices. More directly, though, he has almost complete control over candidates that he's been fostering."

"The woman who brought the taxi."

"For example. Boney can direct them like willing puppets."

I wanted to ask about Oswald and even the Nation of Islam thugs who had assassinated Malcolm X, whether they too had been pawns of heaven's leader, but we had arrived in the vicinity of Rancho Santa Fe, and had to concentrate on the task at hand. That task was rather ill-defined. I had simply asked the professor to drive randomly around the neighborhood, waiting for some sign from us, where the "sign" would be what would appear as his own hunch or notion. He readily agreed. He seemed familiar with the method. For our part, Zorba and I would watch for ... I wasn't sure what—some indication of Halfway citizens; maybe people dressed in nineteenth century Victorian-era garb holding up two fingers as rabbit ears above unsuspecting living people's heads. Zorba had been careful to warn me, though, not to look directly into anybody's eyes unless I was sure they were living. This was how Wops recognized each other, just as I had recognized Zorba as another ethereal soul when I'd first met him.

Zorba suddenly sunk down out of sight. "That was it!" he exclaimed. "Don't look!" he warned, but it was too late. My reflexes were too fast for my brain, and I turned and looked back. We had just passed large ornate gates, and a young woman dressed in jeans and a sweatshirt was standing on the sidewalk nearby. Our eyes met.

"The jigs up!" I cried as I saw her run to the gate. "Pull over!" I called even as I remembered that the professor couldn't hear me. Desperate, I whacked him hard on the back of the head, and hurt my hand on his stone-hard hair.

He obviously felt something, for he did pull over to the curb. "Er, is this it?" he asked to the air. He put his finger to his lip. "Uh, what now?"

Zorba sat up and looked behind us at the girl, who was shouting through the closed gate. He leaned forward, wrapped his arms around Clintock's neck and pressed their heads together. The professor tilted his head in contemplation, breaking Zorba's communicating embrace, and then opened his door and got out. He stood there a moment considering, then opened the back door as well.

Zorba and I piled out past Clintock's unseeing gaze. The young woman was talking loudly through the gate to an older man who was limping towards her down the long inner driveway. "Distract her," I directed as I crouched down out of sight behind the professor and the car. Zorba hesitated only a moment before sprinting off, calling out to her, "Tanya! Wait, it's me!"

They obviously knew each other.

I waited until my Wop friend reached the gate and entered into a heated argument with the other two, then ran along the sidewalk until a slight curve in the high wall surrounding the estate hid me. I wasn't sure if the woman or crippled man had seen me, but I didn't wait to find out. The wall was covered in a curtain of dense, healthy ivy. I started climbing. Each leaf was a firm, steel hand and foothold. It was like climbing a ladder, trivial, until a very slight breeze shook the ivy ever so slightly. I lost my footing, and grabbed at a leaf that flopped sideways in the gentle puff of air just enough to pinch my fingers painfully against the wall. Wincing and cursing, I made the top, and jumped down on the other side, remembering how light-footed my leap from the top of Clintock's car had been.

Through the row of Ficus trees lining the driveway, I could see that the crippled man was making his way steadily back to the house. Just then the front door opened and a maid stepped out and stared at the sky wonderingly, then, shaking her head in exasperation, turned and re-entered. But not before a hefty man sprinted out past her. She seemed oblivious to him and he wore a smart beret, cocked to one side. I surmised that I had now seen my second Soldat.

I didn't wait to see more. I wasn't sure how I would get into the expansive three-story mansion, but judging from its size and sophisticated architecture, I guessed that there might be enough doors and windows for me to get lucky. I raced around to the back, and hopping over a small ornamental wall surrounding a back patio, I came up short upon finding a man dressed in sturdy cotton work clothes standing there. He looked me in the eye and nodded. I recognized him. This was the lackey in the company of Jim Jones. I glanced nervously around, but the man seemed to anticipate my fear. "Jones is not here," he assured me in a steady, deep voice, the voice of a man who was confident in his manhood.

The man's probing eyes were those of human insight itself. In a stunning flash, multiple recognitions collided in my head. I realized in an instant that, not only was this man the unacknowledged companion to Jim Jones, but also the commentator that had seemed to talk to me at the party while I watched Koyaanisqatsi in a dazed trance. It had never occurred to me until now that this cult film was famously unique in that it had no dialogue, no commentator. How had this man come to be in the film? He hadn't, of course. I had thought him part of the film, but he had been talking to me from Halfway.

But this was not the recognition that froze my breath. The receding hairline, the neat goatee so iconic that it seemed to support the chin rather than the reverse, the steady gaze that demanded truth and wisdom from the world, all this brought into focus the writer, the Nobel Prize winner, the spokesman for Depression-era America.

"You're . . ." I stammered, but my mind strangled itself on the improbability that I would ever speak the name to the man.

He smiled in sympathy at my consternation and held out his hand. "Yes, I am."

I slowly reached out and shook the firm grip of John Steinbeck.

Chapter 7

"You're . . . I mean, you didn't. . ." I stammered, tongue-tied at addressing the great American author.

He waited, grinning at my struggle. "Use words, man," he finally urged lightly. "They can often be useful."

I swallowed. "You didn't die," I stated simply.

He rubbed his scruffy goatee. "That would be most welcomed news indeed, but I think we can both agree that this is contradicted by the fact that my heart stopped beating in 1968 in a New York hospital. But I believe I know what you mean. I am, to be sure, one of the wraiths of this netherland."

"Are you . . . I mean, are you with—"

"Words, my friend."

"Are you with Jones or Boney?"

"I am my own man, as I've always strived to be. As far as it can be said that I am 'with' anybody, why I am with you; in purpose, not just in geography."

I felt a rush of joy. Now here was an ally I could get behind. "You're going to help me get Kirsten back?"

His fingers moved from massaging his chin to the side of his face. He looked torn. "Yes. But it would disingenuous of me to leave it at that, for that would imply this to be our immediate goal.

The truth is that we mustn't attempt to save your fiancée for a while longer. I am sorry."

"Why should we not?"

His habit of building full sentences with satisfying structure was infectious.

He took a few steps towards the house, turned around and walked back. He was pacing. "The answer is twofold: on one hand, we wish for Boney to keep his attention focused on her. She is, I am afraid to say, a very effective distraction. And should we actually be successful in enticing her to come with us, the very act would emphasize your latent abilities. This is to be avoided to whatever extent possible."

I shook my head, confused. Was he on my side or not? "Mr. Steinbeck, you don't understand. I have come for just one purpose."

"I know well why you've come, son. But you'll have to be patient."

"Why? If she makes it to heaven, I'll probably never get her back!"

"You are right. We daren't let her make the second ascension. But there's time. In any case, you're not ready to take her back."

"I am ready! I don't want to wait!"

He smiled a soft patience. "You don't know what you don't know. You're not even sure how to get yourself back to the living, let alone another."

He was right, of course. I hadn't thought past just finding Kirsten and convincing her to come along. I felt defeated, and the trembling doom of anxiety clawed at the borders of my consciousness.

My new guide was watching me with obvious sympathy. "Take heart, my lad. There is more to this than you realize, and with time, you will understand." He looked up at the sound of shouting from around the corner. "But now, we must get away."

"No!" I cried, louder than I meant to. More quietly I added, "I can't leave. Not after getting this close."

He glanced from the shouting activity at the front of the house to me. "I'll tell you what, if you see her, will you agree to then leave? You can't talk to her, understand. She might not even know that you were here."

The noise of the mobilizing Soldats was threatening, and pressed me with an urgency that precluded negotiation. "Fine! Let me see her."

John Steinbeck turned and walked briskly away around the far back corner. I was left wondering whether I was supposed to follow, but he returned almost immediately, strolling along with his arm thrown casually around the shoulders of a man who I took to be the gardener. I saw that he was talking quietly to the worker, who was ignoring him in a manner that would have seemed rude if I hadn't understood that this was the writer's more respectful alternative to Zorba's embrace of recipients' necks as though begging for mercy. The two of them walked to the patio door, where the gardener stopped, hesitating. The Nobel wraith reasoned with the man's inner, private rooms of logic he mistakenly thought accessible to just himself. Finally the worker reluctantly opened one of the French doors and peered guiltily inside. My Halfway guide waved energetically to me, and I ran forward and past the manipulated worker. Inside, I found a large kitchen, and was surprised to see a middle-aged woman walking along a hallway in my direction. She wore sweatpants and shirt, and her hair was matted against her forehead. She had obviously been working out, and was probably coming to the kitchen for a drink. "Manuel?" she called. "Is that you?"

"Si, Mrs. Steward! I . . . I thought I heard you call," he lied.

"No," she responded, stepping into the kitchen. "Not me."

"Okay, sorry," he murmured, and hastily closed the door behind him, but not before Steinbeck stepped through.

"A lucky coincidence," the Salinas author commented approvingly, walking along with the sweaty woman to the sink. "If I were of a religious inclination, I might think our intrusion was ordained."

As she drew a glass of water, he stood behind her, placed his hands gently on her shoulders and talked quietly into her ear. I could only make out a portion of what he said, but the gist was that the honor of Amy required a respectful visit. The dumpy woman paused, set the glass on the counter and walked off down another hallway and up a narrow flight of stairs. We followed close behind, as this was obviously the plan.

"Her teenage daughter was killed in an automobile accident a year ago," he explained. "She's kept the bedroom predictably untouched as a memorial shrine; untouched, that is, except by wraiths."

I didn't ask him to explain, because I was distracted by the shouting racket at the front door of the massive house. Zorba was apparently kicking up a real storm, and it seemed completely incongruous that such a ruckus could flare away so close, and yet this mother pattered up the back stairs hearing only her bare feet and the sparrows in the plum tree outside the window.

At the top of what I took to be servants' stairs, we turned down a long hallway, at the end of which stood a man who seemed surprised to see our small troop. Tellingly, he looked me in the eye. He stepped aside when the woman opened the door next to him, but began shouting a loud alarm which lasted only a second before Steinbeck gripped his arm, spun him around, and clapped a hand over his mouth. The man struggled, but my new celebrity friend clearly wielded an overpowering strength. "Don't go in!" Steinbeck warned, and I obeyed, although my anticipation was nearly as overpowering as his apparent strength.

Instead I leaned through the doorway and peered inside. The room was exactly what I might have expected a teenage girl's to be: posters, patterned curtains, and a pile of decorative pillows on the bed. A TV was playing a movie, and a young woman who sat on the bed watching it turned around when the owner walked in. My breath caught when I saw that the young woman was Kirsten. Her expression melted from surprise to joy. "Jordan!" she shouted, jumping up.

A firm arm wrapped around my chest and pulled me back. The Wop guard managed another abbreviated shout before Steinbeck repositioned his grip on him, now with just one hand. "This is not a visit," he warned, addressing Kirsten. "Let's consider it a live-action snapshot."

"Honey!" I called, even as Steinbeck dragged me back out of the room. "Are you okay?"

I wanted to follow with a plea that she come home, but I was pulled away from the open door. My last image of her was a quiet nod in answer to my question. That gesture, that peaceful acceptance of her prescribed fate felt to me like the end of the world as I cared to live in. I understood for the first time how utterly difficult it would be to convince her to change course.

Holding the Wop guard with his left hand, Steinbeck reached out and pinched the edge of the doorframe. Slowly, he pulled away a long strand that looked exactly like taffy, which he turned around and around the guards head, shoulders, and arms. When he finally let go, the wop was effectively incapacitated inside a loose web cocoon. Whereas the extracted strand was manipulated like soft taffy by Steinbeck, the Wop didn't seem to have the strength to budge even the thin sections. "It's called 'heaven's thread,' " Steinbeck explained to my surprised stare. "It will dissolve in a few minutes, but we'll be long gone by then. Now let's go."

As we followed the woman down the back stairs, Steinbeck explained that the mother of the dead teen was one of Boney's well-developed candidates, and her mansion home was essentially completely under his indirect control. Her grief had rendered her vulnerable to his subconscious advances. Tragedies and trauma were favorite open doors for the master of heaven and Halfway. Her lawyer husband had thrown up his hands by now with her occult obsessions and bizarre protection of the dead daughter's former bedroom. He spent a lot of time at the office and country club.

Disaster struck in the form of a beeping cell phone when we reached the kitchen. Steinbeck lunged, but she answered it before he could reach her. He cursed vivid images of sailors' woes, and then explained that it is nearly impossible to influence someone talking on a phone; the mind is too focused for acute self awareness. Meanwhile, the racket from the front seemed to be moving our way through the house.

I felt guilt over getting Steinbeck into this pickle just so that I could grab a glimpse of Kirsten. In frustration and panic, I gave the dame a whack on the back of her head. It was sometimes a distinct advantage to be able to smack people, knowing they couldn't feel it.

Astoundingly, she did, though. She paused in her conversation, told the other party to hold a second, and then looked around, perplexed. This was all the opening Steinbeck needed, and an instant later, he had his arm around her shoulder and his head pressed against hers as though they were fine old pals. The woman told the phone that she'd call right back, that she thought someone might be outside, and then walked over, opened the French doors, and stepped outside.

"Out you go, lad," my friend chimed, practically pushing me along behind her. Outside, I turned to find him still standing in the kitchen, even though there was a clear exit. As the woman finally stepped back inside, closing the door, he simply gave a nod towards the approaching trouble. "Get away!" he called. It was clear that he intended to hold off the approaching Soldats for my escape.

Leaving, however, would have been tantamount to betrayal. At least, that's how it felt. There was absolutely nothing I could do against a Soldat, but I remained, albeit trembling with fear.

Inside the house, I saw jerky motion, angry shouts, and flailing arms. After some lively moments, the movement condensed to just Steinbeck as he ran to the window next to the French doors. Holding his hands over his head like a diver, he leaned forward and . . . slowly slipped through the glass. As he came through the other side, he placed his hands on the patio floor and executed a slow-motion tumble as his feet finally came free from the window.

I now understood that Steinbeck was a rogue.

"Welcome to our little hideaway, gentlemen," a slightly accented voice said from behind me. I spun around, but I knew who it was before I saw him. The patio had been empty a moment ago. Boney must have descended into Halfway from heaven. As I stared in shock at the Casmir sweater-clad leader, a beret-topped man appeared out of thin air next to him. I heard a scuffle, and turned back to find Steinbeck swinging at two other Soldats who had joined us. Forearms came up sharply under my armpits and Boney's fingers entwined behind my head. "Careful!" he warned.

Steinbeck halted his struggle when he looked our way, allowing his attackers to step in and grab him, each to an arm.

"Greetings, John," Boney said pleasantly, although the utterance an inch from my ear dripped with sarcasm. "It seems that your stubborn devotion to the glory of anarchy still plagues you."

"If you mean the right of individual liberty, then I agree heartily."

"I mean the delusion that men by nature don't need to be led, that they're not begging to be told what to do."

I looked at the Soldats holding the rogue author, but their passive faces held no reaction. Some men perhaps did need Boneys.

"What happened to your own devotion to the Napoleonic Code?" Steinbeck challenged. "To the liberties manifest in the French Revolution?"

"That was another time, and another man, a naive man. But we won't open a debate that we put aside decades ago—"

"That you put aside when you gave me the boot."

"You had your fair chance, John. I have not come to argue, but to deal with this." At that, he gave my head a sharp jerk downwards. The pain was excruciating, and I feared for a moment that he might break my neck, before I remembered that I had no neck bones to break.

"Listen, man," Steinbeck urged, suddenly grimly serious. "Your shepherd is still safe. Let Jordan go. He won't bother you again; I'll make sure of it."

"Thank you, John, for your kind offer, but I think I'll see to that myself."

My captor quickly repositioned his hands so that they were interlocked around my chest, and then began squeezing. I tried to pry loose his fingers, but it was like pulling apart a steel cable. I remembered what Zorba had told me about getting caught in a closing door, and knew that Boney probably had the heaven strength to effect the same. Most terrifying, however, was Steinbeck's plea for mercy on my behalf. He feared Boney's abilities and inclination, and his concern was grounded in a history with the powerful leader of heaven.

Caught in a vise grip, unable to escape, and with oblivion looming, I panicked. With panic followed anxiety. And with anxiety followed the automatic response of calming exercises.

Suddenly—whether from the hyper-activated state of fear or a deja-vu of the previous encounter with Boney—as though I had lifted a cover off an elegantly set table, I saw with crystal clarity the method. It would be difficult enough to explain in words, but for those who have never had to struggle with anxiety, it would be practically impossible. Imagine reaching into a bassinet and lifting a distraught baby to cradle to your chest, cooing and stroking it in a calming cocoon of love. The baby kicks and fights at first, but you persevere until it senses your devotion and relaxes. Now imagine doing the same to your own troubled mind, to your own body. To your own soul. And like a calmed baby who becomes compliant to your wishes, so your very being. As Boney proceeded with his heartless execution, I closed my eyes and willed myself back to the living.

Distance was travelled, and time passed, but I knew there was no real travelling, and whatever time transpired would be measured in nanoseconds. I felt solid again, and I opened my eyes.

Once more I was looking at the roof of the professor's car, but this time I was still reclined in the passenger seat. I sat up, and it seemed as though I was pulling along sandbags.

"Yow!" Clintock was looking at me in alarm. "You took me by surprise."

I took a deep breath, filling my lungs with real air. My mind was not as dull as the last time. The Rohypnol must have been wearing off. Even though I knew perfectly well where I was, it took a moment to orient it all in my head. Instantaneous transportation was disorienting. "Steinbeck!" I cried, putting priorities in place.

"John Steinbeck?" the professor asked. "The author?"

"Yeah," I replied, trying to think what to do. I resented having to bring my chauffeur up to speed.

"Well, I'll be," he said, nodding in appreciation. "I didn't really believe it, I guess."

I looked hard at him. What he had said was sinking in. "You knew about him?"

The old face blushed. "Yes."

I remembered that the first time I had seen Steinbeck was at the party of one of Kirsten's classmates. When I had awoken—or returned—the professor was there next to me. Now *that* would be quite a coincidence. "You knew he was there—at the party!"

Clintock thought a moment, and then his face turned a brighter shade of red. "I didn't know it was him. Not exactly. I mean, I knew somebody from the overlay was there, but I wasn't sure it was actually John Steinbeck, even though he had tried to communicate that in the library by guiding me to his books—"

"*Professor!*"

"Eh?" he replied, looking startled.

I took another deep breath. "There's a lot you obviously haven't told me, but we don't have time now. I'll explain later—and *you'll* explain later too—but now I have to help him."

"John Steinbeck?"

"*Yes!* Steinbeck . . . and Zorba!" Where was my first Halfway friend? I'd left him arguing at the gate. Was he still there? Or had they captured him as well?

I opened the car door and jumped out, calling to Clintock to just sit tight. I remembered at the last second to close the door again. It wouldn't do to let invisible wraiths inside. I ran to the gate, calling to Zorba, then realized that this was rather foolish. I stopped a dozen steps from the large, ornate metal structure. Maybe it wasn't completely foolish. "Zorba! Come to me!" I called. Then, more quietly, "Let me know if you're here."

I waited. One second. Five seconds. Either he wasn't outside the gate, or he was not able to get through to me. The idea was brilliant, though. *He* wouldn't have thought of communicating across dimensions in both directions like this.

I blinked. Why did I think *that?* Was I suddenly so vain?

"Zorba! Are you hanging on to my neck?"

I tried to let my mind go blank, but I couldn't shake the image of him clinging to me like a drowning swimmer. I concluded that this was *yes*.

I held still, knowing that every movement I made was like the buck of a wild bronco to Zorba. This gave me an idea. "Listen," I whispered, "position yourself like you're riding a horse. Wrap your arms around my neck and hang on tight."

I waited, wondering if I would get some sign. The phrase, *Giddy-up cowboy!* came to mind. It could have come from my own subconscious, but I was already thinking about my next moves, so I took it as an affirmative. "Zorba, if you're not hanging on," I warned, "then you'd better jump back now." I brought my fists to my chest, and then began swinging my arms out and back as though I were performing a free-weight cardio exercise. At the same time, I slowly turned around in a circle. If anybody had been watching, I'm sure they would have thought me mad, but what they wouldn't have seen would have been any proximate Wops tossed aside like so many paper dolls. Of course, I couldn't see them either, so as far as I knew, I might just have been swinging at nothing but air.

Continuing to swing my arms about, mixing up the pattern now and then for good measure, I walked back along the property wall until I came to the vine-covered section I had scaled twenty minutes before. Giving a few good last wide swings to clear the immediate area, I proceeded to scale the wall. At least, that was my intention. What I actually did was pull down handfuls of vines off the smooth surface.

Shit.

I scanned up and down the wall, but saw no access, which made sense, since this was its purpose. Still swinging away like an idiot, I walked back to Clintock's Explorer. Time was slipping away, and I had no idea what was happening to Steinbeck inside the estate. Any chance at finesse had passed.

The professor watched me, a bit astonished, as I flapped my way up to his window, which he opened a few inches. "Ram the front gate," I told him.

"I'm sorry?" he replied.

"Break the lock on the gate with the front of your car," I directed.

"I can't do that! Why that's a criminal act—"

"John Steinbeck is inside and they may kill him ... or whatever."

"I see. Still, you can't expect me to just ram my way—"

"*Professor!*"

He stopped, frozen, gaping at me.

"You talked me into this whole thing. You can't bail on me now."

He continued to stare, but he seemed to look inward, balancing internal equations. He suddenly nodded, starting the engine, and pulled away from the curb, executing a U-turn, wheels squealing.

In my mind, I had envisioned him gently nudging the middle of the gate until the latch gave way. I hadn't imagined that he would take "ram" so literally. He must have been doing at least twenty miles-per-hour when the grill of his Ford Explorer blasted through. The two halves of the gate flew back like a batter swinging. One broke off its hinges and continued its flight onto the grass, the other rebounded, crashing against the Explorer's fender. I ran up as he backed away. The remaining gate caught the headlight assembly and yanked it off. Clintock sat inside smiling a triumphant grin. He was ready for another.

"Thanks!" I called, and ran through the ruined entranceway. From somewhere inside the mansion, I heard an alarm howling. I remembered my potential passenger and traded my bucking bronco, free sprint dash for a careful speed-walk. I expect it looked as though I had a load in my pants that I was trying to contain. Every few steps I swung my arms, sweeping away possible Soldats who might be trying to get at my cowboy rider.

"Zorba," I said, "I sure hope to hell you're still there. You need to guide me to Steinbeck." I realized that he probably didn't have a clue what I was talking about. "Crap, you may not even know what he looks like."

An image from my youth on my uncle's farm came to my mind, complete with jaunty tuft of chin beard.

"Oh, man. I hope that billy goat idea came from you, but I'll assume you know who he is. He's dressed like a farm worker. I expect that we're surrounded by Soldats. If Steinbeck is still here, he's probably with Boney."

What now? I'd come to the end of the circular driveway. A brick path led away around to the left, to the patio area where I had last seen my rogue accomplice. Warnings would have preceded me. I gambled that Boney had moved inside, and I continued on up the three steps to the double-wide front doors. The maid had left it open, and hesitating just a moment, I walked in.

I immediately felt threatened, sensing danger from all sides, even though I was standing all alone in a foyer with nothing but empty hallways leading away on three sides, and a wide stairway climbing up to the second floor. There would probably be Soldats for sure, but they couldn't hurt me—

"Sorry, Zorba!" I cried, swinging my arms violently, understanding the inexplicable sense of threat. I had forgotten for a moment my protector role.

Just then, the maid appeared at the top of the stairs, staring aghast at my bold intrusion. She took a frightened step back, but then paused. Her head twitched a little, as though she couldn't decide what to do. I could guess that her own mind was screaming to run away, but some wraith was urging her to do its bidding. Slowly, step by struggling step, she advanced and started down the stairs. She forced a smile that looked more a tortured grimace, and held out her hand in greeting. "Good afternoon," she offered, her voice quivering. "How do you do?"

Here I stood, a stranger who had broken into the house, swinging my arms around like an imbecile, and she was greeting me as a welcomed guest.

I guessed that only one wraith had that kind of manipulative power. I kept a poker face, though, biding my time. "Hello," I said, just standing there, waving my arms like I was drying my armpits. It occurred to me that Zorba was crossing a threshold; he was now an outcast, and there was no turning back.

I waited, forcing her to come to me. She held her hand out as she approached, hesitant step at a time. She looked as though her hand was some object that she was reluctantly offering me, and I supposed it was. Boney obviously wanted me to shake her hand, giving his waiting Soldats an opportunity to get at Zorba. I guessed that heaven's leader would have to keep very close to the young woman to countermand such primal survival instincts. When she was just a few feet away, her eyes wide with fear, I said quietly, "Hold tight," and stepped forward. I didn't know exactly where Boney was standing—if Zorba was trying to convey that, it wasn't getting through—so I wrapped my arms around the girl and then flung them wide, hoping that I was launching the French Emperor away.

Our heads were next to each other, and her hysterical scream seemed to burst my eardrum. I stepped away and the woman seemed to explode with terror, holding her head in her hands and shrieking one continuous wail. It was apparent that Boney was no longer in control.

He'd been upstairs, and so I bounded up the steps, keeping my motion as smooth as possible while swinging one arm ahead, and the other behind in case the Soldats were in pursuit. At the top, I had multiple possibilities in the form of two hallways, one to each side. "Zorba?" I asked.

My indecision just swelled to outright dismay. It seemed that Zorba didn't have a clue either. But then I jerked my head to the right. I had the distinct impression that I had seen movement out of the corner of my eye. There was nobody in the empty hallway, but the message had been received. I strode in that direction, towards the apparent Soldat who had shown himself. My arms were starting to get tired from all the exercise. I reached the end, where double French doors probably let into the master bedroom. These were closed, and I turned around. Where had he come from? All the doors along the way were closed as well. The notion that I was wrong nagged at me. I was looking down a hallway of latched doors, yet I began to feel foolish, stupid.

Zorba was talking to me. "What?" I asked. "They're all closed!" The nagging sense of error persisted. "I need more than just insults!" I complained.

I thought all the doors were closed, but he was telling me that I was wrong. Or maybe that I was missing the point. I turned back around to face the double French Doors, and realized that I was indeed foolish. The white painted doors framed large glass panels. Curtains hung inside, providing privacy, but one side was pulled away. There would just enough room for a determined Soldat to slip through the glass.

I opened the door and walked in, only to be met by another scream, this time from the mother who was backed into a corner, covering her face with her arms. I thought to try to make some sort of explanation or apology, but gave up, and just stood there swinging my arms around and around. "Is Steinbeck here?" I asked.

The woman's scream paused. She looked at me, confused. "There's nobody here but me," she replied tremulously.

"I'm not talking to you," I said irritably. To demonstrate that, I turned away so that I wasn't facing her. "Well?" I asked.

I tried to blank my own thoughts, clearing the board for incoming calls. The sense that I got was confused. I felt a sudden desire to sit down on the bed and just be quiet. I was hurting both Zorba and Steinbeck. Terribly. They were in agony, and would continue so until I just sat the hell down.

I almost did. But another sense conflicted with that. It was weaker, just a vague notion, but it conveyed that to stop swinging my arms, even for an instant, would be disaster.

It suddenly came to me what must be going on. I had been standing in one spot swinging away for some seconds. Long enough for someone—someone with a powerful influence ability—to glide in at a different altitude. I reached my right foot over the other and swept it in an arc in front of me. Instantly, all thoughts of sitting down ceased, and were replaced with the urge to flee.

It was time to escape.

Chapter 8

The professor was waiting when I returned, but he'd lost his glow of adventurous triumph, and he sat in the car looking forlorn. "I'll have to pay for that," he declared, nodding at the ruined gate.

"I'll take care of it," I replied. I could win that much money and more just in poker games. Invisible partners could come in handy. Actually, I never play poker, and never would have thought of that. Zorba was obviously thinking ahead for both of us.

Sirens were wailing their way towards us. Clintock suddenly looked alarmed. "We should leave," he warned.

There was one last small problem. I had no idea whether any Soldats—or even Boney—had followed us out. I was still swinging my arms, but I wasn't sure I could open the door and get Zorba and myself safely inside without an intruder coming along for the ride. I scanned the ground for a stick to use as a club, but then remembered what constituted a club in Halfway. I had already torn apart the ivy patch on the wall, so I pulled away a loose four-foot piece of vine and, standing next to the SUV, swung it back and forth in an arc, creating a Soldat-free zone. Whipping my impregnable one-ounce sword with one hand, I opened the back door and turned so that my back faced the opening. "If you're still there, Zorba, now's the time to jump down and climb inside."

I counted down from five, then gave my deadly vegetable mace one last good swipe before leaping inside and slamming the door. "Go!" I called to Clintock but the Explorer's tires were already screaming as he peeled away.

I realized that I had made a hasty and clumsy entrance. "Oh God! Zorba, I do hope you had enough sense to scoot over to the other side."

I waited, but could discern no extraneous thoughts. At least, none that I could identify as extra-Jordan. Suddenly, I felt an overwhelming need to confirm that my Wop friend was okay.

"Professor! I have to ascend!"

He broke his racecar driver concentration and glanced at me in the mirror. "Ascend?"

"Transition! Send myself to Halfway—to the overlay!"

His attention was momentarily consumed by a sharp turn that we fishtailed around, then he looked up again. "That seems problematic. I would think that we need to continue the getaway."

There were no police cars behind us, but they might appear at any moment. "Maybe you don't need to stop."

He looked skeptical. "How are you going to achieve the trance state? The Rohypnol will have been wearing off, and I can't very well perform the hypnotic process while driving." As if to demonstrate, he slammed on the brakes, throwing me forward, as we rounded another turn and almost rear-ended a slower driver.

"I have to try," I affirmed. I sat back and closed my eyes. The Explorer was swaying and bouncing around on the winding roads of rural San Dieguito. It was like riding a small yacht in a storm. I tried to remember how it had happened before. I had assumed that it was the combination of the sedative and the professor's hypnosis abilities. But there was the Pater Noster palindrome, the ancient Latin verse that people believed for centuries held magical abilities. Maybe it did. "Professor, recite that verse—that palindrome. Slowly."

He glanced in the mirror and gave a small smile. "Ready?" he called, and then started, "*Sator—arepo—*"

I took a deep breath and let my whole body relax, allowing myself to move with the motion of the car, trying to *become* the car, actually predicting and anticipating the motion.

"*tenet—opera—*"

I imagined myself rising, rising up and out of my body, but then a tiny corner of my brain suggested that this might not be a good idea in a moving car, and I envisioned instead my Halfway spectral self simply sitting next to me.

"*ROTAS!*"

I opened my eyes and was disappointed. Then I realized that I was sitting between two people. I glanced to my right and found Zorba grinning at me, and then, not without some trepidation, looked to the left to find me sitting back with my head lolling to the side and my mouth open.

"Did it work?" the professor called.

"Oh yeah!" I cried happily, before realizing that he couldn't hear me as he shrugged and returned to his task of keeping his SUV on the road.

"Oh, man," I said to my companion. "Am I glad to see you."

He didn't answer, but just sat grinning at me like he couldn't get over what he saw.

"Er," I asked, "did, um, everything go okay?"

Still he just sat there. Finally, he nodded and stated simply, "I'm here."

"Ah, I see. I guess that was not necessarily a foregone conclusion?"

He just shook his head slowly.

"You were able to hang on, though?"

He never took his eyes off of me, and he never stopped grinning. "Most the time."

"Zorba," I demanded seriously, "are you okay?"

He nodded, seeming to finally let go of his dramatic suspense. "You need to understand that a Wop doesn't get wounded or damaged in any measurable way. One either dissolves if the deformation is severe enough, or the soul returns to the original form."

"But you can be hurt," I confirmed. I knew this. I had felt it myself.

He didn't say anything, just nodded slowly.

"I'm gathering that our little foray caused you some, er, pain?"

He laughed now, getting some distance from what must have been quite an ordeal. "I never imagined there could be that much," he finally replied. "I thought you were going to dissolve me for sure when you bashed your way up the stairs."

"I tried to be careful."

"I thought you were trying to dislodge me."

"Sorry. But what happened to Steinbeck? Was he even there?"

"He was in the bedroom. I don't know what Boney was up to, maybe trying to get something out of him. In any case, when we came in he was being held down by two Soldats. But when you kicked Boney across the room, he managed to get free. The last I saw of him, he was sprinting out the front door with two of Boney's goons running after him."

"What about Boney?"

"He stood here at the car cursing you to hell. He vowed to spend eternity, if necessary, destroying both you and me."

"Today hasn't been going too great for you."

"When the alternative is sitting around watching TV—with somebody else picking the programs—a little pain isn't so bad."

"Only a *little* pain?"

"I didn't want you to feel bad. Listen, I'm worried about Kirsten, though."

"Join the club."

"I mean her corpus. This has never come up that I'm aware of, but on the other hand, nobody's ever tried to convince somebody to return, either."

"Oh, shit. You're right. See you later."

Fear over Kirsten rendered the descension trivial. I gasped as I woke up, jerking upright. Clintock glanced in the mirror. "You've returned?"

"We have to go back to the hospital."

"Back to the hospital—oh, my. Would Napoleon have that kind of power?"

"I'm not taking any chances."

"No. No, indeed."

I was suddenly thrown sideways as he spun the car around to head back. "Hey!" I yelled. "Let's have a little warning, there. We have an invisible passenger I could squash!"

He glanced in the mirror. "Maybe you should put on your seatbelt."

"Oh, yeah. We wouldn't want to get stopped by the police over a seatbelt infraction."

As I said this, the Explorer's headlight assembly banged about against the dented fender, dangling by an umbilical mass of electrical wires.

ж ж ж

I stepped out of the elevator, but then held my hand against the rubber bumper a few seconds as the door tried unsuccessfully to close, jumping back into its slot, irritated at being delayed. The three people going up watched me curiously. After I let the door close, I whispered, "Zorba, you here?" I stared at the blank wall until I sensed a feeling of success, then trotted off after Clintock. By the time I reached him, he was already in Kirsten's room. My breath caught when I saw her lying senseless in the bed, hands resting peacefully at her sides on the white sheet. It was difficult reconciling this insensible Kirsten with the smiling version I had seen less than an hour before. This one had a beating heart, but the other one had eyes that met mine. I needed to get them back together.

"Zorba?" I whispered.

Clintock glanced at me.

"He can let us know if there's any Soldats—Boney's soldiers—here."

I closed my eyes and thought of a yellow rubber duck. I had decided that turning my mind's attention to something concrete and random might be better than just staring at a wall, where it wasn't so obvious whether spurious thoughts were actually my own.

All I saw was the duck. That wasn't good. I realized that if there were Soldats around, Zorba wouldn't have a chance to cuddle up and press his head against mine. No response meant either that he was keeping away from Boney's thugs, or that I just wasn't getting his communication. On the other hand, Kirsten's room was at least a safe place to be right now.

On the *other* hand? What other hand?

"Zorba says we're alone," I conveyed to the professor.

He was gazing at Kirsten, with what I took to be sorrow. He looked up. "How fast can Napoleon . . . travel?"

"Exiguus never wrote about that?" I asked.

"No, not at all. Nothing in any kind of detail like that. Not at all."

It struck me as strange that the professor knew precisely how to aid in my ascendance, but was completely fuzzy—clueless, really—about almost everything else in Halfway, let alone heaven. During the ride to the hospital, I had asked him about his earlier contacts with Steinbeck, but his reply was vague. He pointed out that he hadn't even been sure whether it really *was* John Steinbeck. It seemed to me, though, that this would have been a paramount piece of information when he was showing me Exiguus's manuscript. Having been in contact with somebody from "the other side," no matter how vague, should have been prime evidence when trying to convince me to believe. I decided that I'd eventually have to press him about that.

He was looking at me, and I realized that he had said something. "Eh?"

"I said, can Napoleon perhaps fly through the air?"

"No. At least, I don't think so. Wops and Soldats in Halfway have to catch rides to get around, or walk. Zorba did say that Boney can go back and forth between heaven and Halfway, but I didn't have the impression that there were any shortcuts—no portals through space or anything like that."

At least, Zorba hadn't mentioned anything like that. That was another thing I'd have to follow up on.

"In that case, we should have a bit of time if he has to catch a ride here."

That's for sure, I thought. I was amazed that we hadn't been pulled over. I didn't think he'd dropped even close to the speed, not even at the traffic lights.

"So, what exactly are we going to do now that we're here?" he asked.

I sighed. "That's the million-dollar question." I hadn't really thought beyond speeding here to be by her side. But even when Boney did get here, if he even did, what could he do? Tickle Kirsten with insubstantial dreams in her coma sleep? Zorba would know, but that wasn't the kind of concrete information that could be impressed between snuggled heads.

Just then a nurse's aide came clattering into the room pushing a wheeled contraption consisting of a cloth bag hanging inside an open metal frame. From the lumpy contours at the bottom, I guessed that she was collecting laundry to be washed. She jerked to a halt and stared at us, seeming at a loss.

"Let's step outside," I suggested, figuring we should allow her to get her work done.

Once out in the hall, we waited until some visitors walked past. "I should have asked Zorba what harm Boney can manage on a corpus," I observed.

"A corpus?"

"That's what they call us living versions." I glanced around, feeling apprehension. I knew that I wouldn't be able to see Boney if he arrived, but it was instinct. "Zorba might not even have a chance to tell us if Boney shows up. He'd have to run away or hide before he had a chance to snuggle with me."

A passing nurse gave me a look at the mention of "him" snuggling me.

My sense of unease was aggravating. I shouldn't be so fearful of Boney. Sure, in the long run he could cause a lot of trouble, but it didn't seem possible that there was any immediate danger.

Still I couldn't shake the sense of intense disquiet.

Suddenly, understanding about my unease slammed home, and I jerked my head around to stare at Clintock.

"What?" he asked.

I realized that I had been hearing muffled grunts from inside Kirsten's room. "Damn!" I cried, running back inside. "Zorba, where is he?"

Any thought of tuning into ideas implanted by my wraith friend vanished at the sight before me. The nurse's aide was on the bed, straddling Kirsten, her knees hugging my fiancée's waist. The woman seemed to be struggling to pull a blanket off of Kirsten's head, grunting at the difficult labor. I tried to comprehend how Boney could be fighting with a corpus like this. More importantly, how could I help the woman?

In an instant I realized that she wasn't grunting, but whimpering in anguish, and she wasn't *pulling* a blanket off, but *pushing* a pillow down! *"What the hell!"* I yelled, jumping forward and grabbing the aide by her shoulders. She didn't resist, but let me pull her away, almost falling back into my arms. She gasped and covered her mouth with her hands, then began sobbing.

In the meantime, Clintock had yanked away the pillow and was checking Kirsten's neck for a pulse. "She's okay," he declared.

I helped the aide off the bed as a stout nurse came running in, demanding to know what happened. "It's okay," I assured. Instinct told me to hide the truth. "There was a misunderstanding, and I frightened the woman," I lied.

The nurse wasn't buying this so easily. "What sort of misunderstanding?" she barked, checking Kirsten for herself as the aide backed away towards the door, crying quietly. "And what's this?" she accused, pointing at the pillow on the floor.

"Well," I started, "it's like this." My mind whirred, searching for an actual story. "The woman had the pillow in her hand, and I thought that it was a bag."

"A bag," the nurse confirmed.

I nodded.

"A bag of what?"

"A bag of . . . dirty socks. Kirsten has this thing about dirty socks, and even though she's, like, insensible, I thought, you know, that she might, I don't know, remember . . . or something."

The nurse looked like a boot camp drill sergeant, standing with her fists planted firmly on her thick hips. "Are you daft?" she asked simply, then, shaking her head, she shooed away the aide and straightened Kirsten's blankets. She shook her finger at me. "You behave yourself, or you'll have to leave." Then, throwing a suspicious glare at the professor for good measure, she stormed out.

Clintock was by my side a second later. "What happened there?" he asked quietly.

I felt flushed, and my heart thumped in my chest, but all sense of apprehension was gone. "I'm not sure. I think that the woman was being influenced. Boney obviously wants to kill Kirsten—her body—so that she can never return."

"They can influence people like *that*? My God, they can make a person want to *kill*?"

He seemed horrified at the idea. It *was* horrifying.

"I don't think that they can make just anybody do something like that. That woman was probably a candidate; Boney would have been working on her for some time, preparing her for ascension."

I was confident that any normal Wop or Soldat wouldn't have that kind of influence on a non-candidate, but I wasn't so sure about Boney's limitations. But I didn't want to talk about that, or even think about it, if possible.

"Does that mean that Napoleon—Boney—was here?" Clintock asked.

"He couldn't have been. There's no way he could have gotten here before us. It must have been one of his soldiers, a Soldat."

"Are you sure?"

"No. We'll find out later." I realized that Boney's thugs might still be in the room, and I didn't want to give anything away. I cupped my mouth over the professor's ear. "Zorba will tell us," I whispered.

Clintock nodded, then frowned. "What if they try it again?"

I took a deep breath and let it out slowly. "We can't leave her here," I declared.

"That would indeed seem prudent, but we can't exactly just check her out."

"No," I agreed rubbing my chin. "We'll have to sneak her out."

"That's why you let that puppet nurse's helper go without a fuss, isn't it?" he surmised. "You wanted to keep things quiet in here, avoid a lot of attention."

I nodded. That hadn't been my conscious intention, but sometimes instinct and the subconscious are two steps ahead of slogging logical analysis.

The grizzled old face looked at me skeptically. "You can't exactly just put her in a bag and carry her out, you know."

I glanced around, and my eyes fell on the laundry cart that the aide had abandoned. "Why not?"

He saw what I was eyeing. "You can't be serious."

"Do you have a better idea? If not, then, make sure nobody's coming while I unhook all these tubes and wires from her."

Handling limp bodies looks so easy in movies, but I can tell you that it was very nearly impossible for Clintock and me to lift an inert Kirsten, and then fold her butt-first into the bag-cart. Part of the problem was that the professor spends all his time on academic activities at the expense of fitness and struggled mightily lifting his half of my fiancée's 110 pounds. The bigger dilemma was that the cart kept skittering away at the slightest nudge, so that we were chasing it around the room like a hockey puck with my girlfriend as the stick. Finally, we cornered the reluctant container between a chair and the wall. The professor's strength was depleted, and he dropped his end, leaving her headfirst inside, with her legs hanging out, crooked over the edge. Pulling her head up to arrange her into a folded position was almost more difficult than getting her inside in the first place. When we finally had her safely out of view inside the laundry bag, we were both panting, sweat stinging our eyes and matting our shirts to our chests. It was a veritable miracle that nobody had happened into the room while the first stage of the kidnapping proceeded. The machines she had been connected to were beeping away like crazy, and I unplugged them to shut them up.

Kirsten was out of view only if you stood ten feet away, so I piled towels on top, but then I worried that I might suffocate her after all, so I pulled them out and placed a lampshade over her to provide a cavity, then put the towels back on top.

The wheels squeaked and groaned under the unnatural load as I tugged the love of my life across the room, telling Clintock to go on ahead and pull the SUV up to the outside exit. When I reached the door, I looked out but immediately jerked my head back at the sight of a doctor walking briskly down the hall towards me. I held my breath, waiting for him to either walk by, or send me to jail by coming in to check on Kirsten. I waited, but nothing happened. When I finally peeked back around the door frame, the doctor was standing ten yards away staring at the floor, deep in thought. Then he shrugged, turned and hurried back the way he had come. I knew what had distracted and redirected his plans, and I made a mental note to thank Zorba when I had a chance.

I didn't so much roll Kirsten down the hall, as drag her makeshift buggy along. Visitors threw quick glances at my struggle, but it wasn't until the drill sergeant nurse called from behind me that my heart tumbled and I thought my jig was up.

"What's this?" she demanded, pointing at the bulging bag.

I looked at the overstuffed cloth container dumbly. "This?" I asked, joining her in pointing.

Her eyes narrowed as she studied me. "You really are daft, aren't you? Yes, this laundry cart. There's something other than laundry in there."

"No there isn't," I countered. My mind circled, frantically searching for some kind of credible explanation.

"Well, let's just take a look," she said, stepping forward.

I put out my arm to block her. "No!"

She stopped short and looked at me, surprised, but it was obvious that she wasn't going to let me push her around.

"It's an experiment," I blurted.

An experiment could be pretty much anything. Now I just needed somewhere to go with this tack. "I'm a graduate student at UCSD, and we're . . . well, this is going to sound a little weird, but—" *Think! Think!* ". . . but, we're studying how much DNA can be pulled from dirty laundry." I winced internally at my own lame attempt. "You can't touch any of it, or you'll, you know, taint the samples."

The nurse's skepticism was palpable. "DNA," she repeated.

"Yeah."

"From patients. Patients who clearly haven't given permission."

"Right. You see . . . in order to be an unbiased analysis, the donations need to be anonymous." This obviously wouldn't even have convinced my ten-year-old niece. "Zorba!" I called.

"Who's Zorba?" she demanded, her outrage building by the second.

"It's part of my fraternity's motto," I explained. "Zorba is Greek for 'good fortune.' " Once the flood gates opened, the fantastic lies flowed of their own accord. I held out my arms in a gesture of begging, even though I knew that my invisible co-conspirator might have been bullied off by Soldats.

"Hogwash," the drill sergeant nurse barked. "Show me what you're hiding in there." She waited just a second, and when I didn't jump to her command, she said, "Well, I'll just see for myself."

She stepped forward and grabbed the metal rim, and I held my breath, but then she paused and looked around at me. She seemed to be mulling it over. She just stared a few moments, then stepped back and shook her finger at me. "You wait right here. I'm going to get the supervisor." She bustled away down the hall, turning halfway to shake her finger again in warning.

I waited until she disappeared around the corner. "Thanks," I said quietly to no one visible as I considered my next move. The elevators were just twenty feet away in the other direction, but the kidnap vehicle made a terrible racket. I gambled. I ran over, pushed the 'down' button, and hurried back to Kirsten. I waited, wishing for the old-fashioned elevators with the dial above the doors showing the progress. When I couldn't bear it any longer, I grabbed the cart and hauled it over, squeaking and groaning with enough Decibels to wake every patient on the floor. Luck was with me. The elevator door opened just as I arrived, and just as the bull nurse came running back calling to "Hold that elevator!"

A young woman, barely out of her teens, stepped aside in the elevator to give me room. Obeying the commands of the approaching pounding steps, she reached out to press the <| |> button, but I grabbed her wrist. She looked at me, shocked, her wide eyes with fear. "It's okay," I assured her as the doors slid together, cutting off the nurse's bellowing commands. I let go of her wrist. "She's having a bad day." The next lie stepped up and volunteered. "We get credit for how much laundry we collect. She thinks I stole some from her." The young woman just stared at me. "I didn't," I assured.

The ground floor was busy with bustling visitors, doctors, and nursing staff. Nobody gave me a second look as I manhandled my banshee-wailing load to the front doors. The professor was waiting, the SUV parked with the engine running at the curb. People coming and going gave no notice of two men struggling to jimmy an incongruously heavy laundry cart across the jams of the double outer doors, but glanced with obvious dismay at the wounded SUV with its entrails hanging out. Sympathies track priorities.

We were stymied when we got Kirsten and the laundry to the car. The cart was too clumsy to lift, so in desperation, we finally just tilted it up and dumped the contents into the rear cargo area, being as careful as possible with the unconscious human load that rolled out and lay clearly visible among the towels and sheets. A young couple happened to be passing by, and the woman yanked on her husband's elbow, and they stood gazing at Kirsten. They watched as I held the rear door open, calling for Zorba before counting down and then slowly closing it and jumping in the front seat. I looked back as the professor pulled away, and saw the woman poking at her phone, and then putting it to her ear. I feared that she might be calling the police, but decided that she was more likely just sharing the bizarre event with her friends on Facebook.

When we came to the parking lot exit, two young men stepped in front of the car, holding their hands up for us to stop. Their black pants and white shirts were pressed Army regulation smooth, and their hair was trimmed and neatly combed. "I don't trust them," I declared.

"I can't just run them over," the professor reasoned, and slowed to a stop.

One of the young men remained in front of the SUV, while the other walked around to the side. Clintock opened the window a crack. "What's the problem?" he asked.

"Good afternoon," the dapper young man said pleasantly. Then his face and voice became serious, and he asked "Do you realize what you're doing?"

The professor glanced at me, at a loss, and replied, "Er, we're attempting to leave the hospital."

The interrogator took a couple of steps back along the car, peering through the windows.

"Let's get out of here!" I urged quietly.

The professor lifted his shoulders and indicated towards the other man that was still blocking our way.

I looked back and shouted, "Shit!"

The man had pulled a gun from somewhere, and was holding the tip against the glass of the rear window, tilting the barrel around, trying to find just the right angle. The angle he sought was clearly the one that contacted Kirsten. The fact that this guy had probably never fired a pistol before, and was as likely to shoot his own foot as my fiancée failed to contain the scream that issued from my mouth.

"You don't understand!" he called, seeming to settle in on just the right position. He could have been correcting our misconception about the next day's weather. "This woman was sent by Belial."

I remembered that Belial was another name for Satan, but it was just a flick of a thought, as I was straining mightily and uselessly against my seatbelt, trying to reach back to do ... something, anything.

I was suddenly thrown back against the seat as the professor surged forward, and the man that had been standing in front of the car was now lying face-down on the hood staring at me wide-eyed. I jerked forward as Clintock slammed the brakes, sliding the man off the car. He waited exactly five seconds before flooring the accelerator again. I had a glimpse of the man on his hands and knees beside me as we sped away.

"Minions of Bonaparte?" the professor asked above the squealing tires as he fishtailed onto the street.

I hung on while centrifugal force tried to squash me against my door. "Or Jones."

For being invisible and intangible, willful forces of Halfway and heaven had disturbing ways of exercising visible and very tangible effects.

PART III

OVER THE WALL

Chapter 9

"Apostles of Irenaeus?" I repeated. "It sounds like a fantasy novel."

"Saint Irenaeus was a second century bishop in the early Catholic church," Zorba explained. "He was formative in the early development of Christian theology. He helped establish the primacy of a centralized authority in the Pope."

"You sound like Wikipedia."

"I should. I was looking over a corpus shoulder when he read the article."

My Halfway friend was talking about the two gun-toting evangelists who had attacked us. I had ascended shortly after escaping the hospital, and was dismayed at first to find myself alone, until Zorba called to me from the back of the SUV. The professor sat parked on a side street in Del Mar, patiently waiting for me to return to the living.

"I never heard of them," I said. "Maybe they should call themselves Apostles of Jim Jones instead."

"They're Boney's candidates, not Jones. He concocted the whole cult, but he keeps them under wraps. He knows that public scrutiny would distract them from his mission."

"Which is?"

"Two days ago it would have been simply to quietly recruit other candidates. Religious fanatics by definition are already in the mode of believing outlandish ideas, so it's easy for Boney to steer them towards ascension. Now, though, I imagine that he's massing them against us."

"To kill Kirsten," I guessed.

"Boney would like nothing better than to eliminate the possibility of her returning to her corpus. This has never been an issue before; you're forcing him into unfamiliar territory."

"Was the nurse's aide an Apostle?"

"I imagine. Boney might have been able to make a regular candidate do something so extreme, but not a Soldat. She had to be already brainwashed."

Zorba had explained that there had been just one Soldat with the aide that had come to assassinate Kirsten. Zorba had kept out of sight, and the Soldat hadn't recognized Clintock and me; word hadn't yet reached him from Boney. Which meant. . . .

"Boney must have decided to do away with her corpus before we stormed his Rancho Santa Fe stronghold," I said.

He nodded. "Otherwise the Hardy Boys would have tried to shoot you and the professor first."

I just stared at him. Brainwashed religious fanatics with guns were after me. It was like running from zombies; you could at least outrun a waddling zombie, but not a bullet.

"You understand that you are now Boney's enemy," Zorba added. "He's going to do whatever he can to kill both you and the professor."

"Or dissolve me in Halfway, which is the same thing."

"Along with me, if he can," he noted.

Zorba stated this matter-of-factly, a simple matter of fact.

"I'm sorry I got you into this," I said. I wanted to say more, but couldn't think of the words.

He shrugged it off. "I love stirring up Boney's pot. I feel alive for the first time in decades." He grinned and switched to a mock British accent. "Devilish good fun, don't you know."

"I'm not sure I'd mix 'devil' and 'fun' in the same sentence."

That spurred another thought. "The professor warned me that Exiguus had written about meeting the devil. I would have guessed that would be Boney, except that he was born a thousand years after Exiguus."

"Before Boney, there was another Boney."

"You mean, another leader in heaven?"

"Oliver Cromwell."

"You're kidding."

"No. It was Oliver Cromwell. They say that he was a real son-of-a-bitch. Boney was a welcomed replacement—at first."

"So Napoleon Bonaparte finally got to conquer Britain after all."

"Before Cromwell, it was Charlemagne. He had the longest reign, over eight hundred years."

"Wait a second," I objected. "How does it just so happen that famous leaders from history end up as heaven's leaders?"

"Why not? Whatever characteristics brought them to prominence as corpus would serve them afterwards as well. You'll note that heaven's leaders were all ambitious and often ruthless conquerors."

"Makes sense, I guess. So, Charlemagne takes us back to the ninth century," I continued.

"It was Nero before that."

"Which would have been during Exiguus's time. That monster executed his own mother and poisoned his brother—"

"Half brother," Zorba corrected.

"Is that only half as bad? I read that he also captured early Christians to burn them for light in his garden at night. Actually, that doesn't even make sense, since a body doesn't burn—it's almost all water."

"Maybe he was being efficient. If he had to use a lot of wood to burn them, he figured he might as well have the bonfire where it suited him."

"In any case, Nero certainly sounds like somebody Exiguus might have mistaken for the Devil."

We were interrupted in perusing the historical scorecard of heaven's leaders by the professor, who asked the empty air if I was going to be much longer. He was afraid that either the police or some spectral scoundrels would find us, and he also had to pee.

"What *do* we do now?" Zorba asked.

I looked at my fiancée lying next to me. Her hair was a jumbled mess, and somebody at the hospital had removed all her makeup, but she was still the most beautiful woman I'd ever met. My heart pained at the thought that this body might never awaken. "The goal is the same as when I first ascended; we have to convince Kirsten to return."

"So, it's back to Rancho Sante Fe?"

"But this time we have a package ready for the contents. Listen, do you think we can get any other Wops to help?"

Zorba shook his head doubtfully. "Wops want to get to heaven. You'd have a hard time convincing them to go up against Boney."

I waved it off. "It was a dumb idea; we don't have time anyway."

We debated our next move: how to get back into the mansion. I asked Zorba whether we could somehow use heaven's thread. He looked at me oddly. "How do you know about heaven's thread?"

I told him how Steinbeck had used it to immobilize the Wop guard.

"You're sure it was heaven's thread?" he asked.

"That's what he called it. He sort of pinched it off of the door sill and pulled it out like taffy."

"Huh," he mulled, "it sure sounds like it."

"You've never seen it?"

He laughed. "Everybody assumes that only Boney can do that, and I'm lucky if I even get a look at him once a year. Let me re-phrase that: 'unlucky.' "

We resumed our brainstorm about getting back into the mansion. It seemed an intractable problem, and our ideas progressed from the desperate to the outlandish as we racked our brains. When we'd finally exhausted all but the fantastic, we sat back and crossed our arms, both contemplating the insane risk I'd be taking. "I guess we'd better be going," I finally concluded.

Zorba didn't say anything. I think that he didn't want to take responsibility by agreeing, but was unwilling to protest since he had nothing better to offer.

I closed my eyes and tried to descend back to my corpus sitting dead to the world next to the professor. I opened my eyes, but Zorba was still watching me. I needed something to make me anxious. Closing my eyes once more, I imagined Kirsten never waking up; I imagined her dead. At the same time, I willfully pulled my comatose body to me, not with my arms, but in my mind. Zorba had started to say something about moving closer to the front seat, but his voice flew off into the distance, getting smaller and smaller as though he was speeding away on a silent rocket. I knew before opening my eyes again that I once again inhabited 160 pounds of lumbering flesh.

The professor was whistling Beethoven's *Fur Elise*, a little nervously, it seemed to me, and jumped when I spoke. I explained the origins of the Apostles of Irenaeus, and the plan that Zorba and I had worked out. "It sounds like a scene from Loony Tunes," was his response. "You're going to be killed."

"I would be dissolved, but my corpus would then die, so I guess it's the same thing. In any case, that's all we came up with."

Clintock sighed, then started the engine. "I'm beginning to regret ever listening to Steinbeck," he muttered. When I asked him what he meant, he simply replied, "All in good time."

ж ж ж

"I'm having second thoughts," Zorba confessed.

"Too late," I declared. I was only half listening, as I kept my attention on the professor. I had to be in position when he swung. Earlier, I had used a thin vine as a fearsome sword, and now a stick was going to serve as my launch vehicle. We'd parked the Explorer a block away, and after some searching found a suitable branch, heavy enough to overcome wind resistance, and forked sufficiently wide to provide me a seat. I'd then ascended, leaving my corpus lying next to Kirsten, and Zorba and I had followed the professor to the estate perimeter wall that faced a side street, out of view of the mangled front gate. "You'd better go," I told Zorba. "Looks like the professor is just about ready."

Shaking his head skeptically, my wraith friend trotted off around the corner. He would provide the initial distraction.

Clintock laid the stick on the ground and stepped back, waiting the agreed thirty seconds. I stepped up and sat down facing forward, placing my butt in the fork crotch, and grasped the fork ends with my hands behind me. It didn't seem right. My center of gravity was too high. I imagined myself tumbling off under acceleration. At the last minute, as my launch engine reached his hand down for liftoff, I spun around so that my belly was in the crotch, and I was looking down between the forks. I was going to fly blind, facing backwards.

Not that I'd have any control.

"Here goes," I heard the professor say, and a moment later, the angled forks of the branch pressed against my shoulders as he carefully lifted it by the very bottom. From outside the wall, we could see the balcony attached to the second story bedroom where I had last seen Kirsten. We could also see that the sliding glass door was open, implementing the common form of San Diego air conditioning. The professor was going to launch the branch capsule on a ballistic path, with the balcony as the journey's goal. The total distance was perhaps fifty feet, and Clintock was confident he could hit it.

The larger question was whether I would still be riding along when it did.

He counted down, "Three, two, one," and the branch jammed into my gut and shoulders as he swung the limb in a long, arm-length arc, letting go at just the right point to send us on our way. I had hoped that my capsule would maintain a stable orientation, but the expectation proved naive, and I found myself spinning somersaults with the world whipping past like the view from a loop-to-loop roller-coaster.

My life depended on my next move. If I hung on to the very end, the branch might well land on top like a log on a salamander, dissolving me in an instant. If I abandoned my ride too early, however, wind resistance—for there was a small amount affecting my spectral essence—would drag me down to miss the balcony wall. Spinning like the ball on a roulette wheel, I wasn't able to gauge my progress, and I had to guess when to push away. My guess was way off. Before I even knew we had topped the balcony wall, the world seemed to explode as the forked branch made a crash landing among the patio furniture and I was sent tumbling over the top of a glass table to come to rest crumbled against the sliding glass door. The pain was immense. It felt like I had just been dismembered by a machine programmed for expediency at the expense of finesse. I finally appreciated what Zorba must have endured riding on my back the last time we were here. The saving grace was that the pain did not linger, other than as a disturbing memory.

"Jordan?"

She must have heard the racket, and come to the door. "Kirsten!" I cried, scrambling to my feet, the excruciating pain pushed aside. A moment later she was in my arms. I would have done anything to have her there in my embrace, but now that I had her, the touch was cold, like hugging cloths stuffed with socks. I held her face in my hands, but I was holding an essence of her face, lacking the flesh and blood and nerves responding to another's nerves. I wasn't sure it wouldn't have been better to go back and hug her senseless, comatose body. "I've come to take you back," I said, glancing through the open sliding door, but finding no Soldats inside.

"Back?" she asked surprised.

"Back to the world of the living. Back to your body, to your corpus."

"You can . . . do that? They told me it wasn't possible."

"Boney would like you to believe it. It serves his purpose."

I knew this to be true; as to how confident I was that I could actually take her back, that part I chose not to answer.

She shook her head in confusion. "I wasn't sure if it was you at the hospital when they took me away. I thought so at the time, but Boney convinced me that it was my imagination. It wasn't until you came to me, here, that I knew you had ascended, and what a terrible, terrible mistake I had made."

It was my turn to look surprised. "You *want* to go back?"

"More than anything—as long as you go with me. I believed everything Boney told me, that God had planned that I ascend, and that you would follow in your time to join me. It was after your visit here, when Boney said that you were sent by Satan and that I should avoid you at all costs, that I knew he could lie, that he had probably been lying about everything."

I smiled. "Because my love for you is so pure, it could never be used by evil?"

She smiled in return, the mischievous little smile I so adored. "Because you are too much a thick-headed engineer to believe in God or Satan in the first place."

As though dissatisfied with the little repartee, she pulled me to her and hugged my sock-filled sack of clothes.

The rattle of a doorknob from inside broke up our tender reunion. I pulled Kirsten to the side, away from the glass door, putting my finger to my lips to indicate silence. I heard voices in Kirsten's room, surprised and angry at her absence. A patio umbrella, closed and folded into a column of tan cloth, stood against the wall, and I moved us to the other side, out of view of the open door. An instant later, the beret-clad head of a Soldat popped through and glanced around as I peeked through a crack behind the umbrella. "No one here!" he called. "Maybe she jumped over the wall," he suggested, and walked out to peer over and down.

I held my breath and pressed my hand cautiously against Kirsten. We were looking directly at the wraith heaven soldier. All he had to do was glance around to see us hiding in plain view.

Someone called to him from inside. We had a fifty-fifty chance which way he would turn, and luck was with us as he spun away from us to sprint back through the door. After a moment, I was astonished to hear the glass door sliding closed. I wondered for a anxious moment whether the Soldats had some unrevealed power to manipulate the material world, when I saw in the reflection of the glass that it was the maid, probably under the controlling influence of one of the Soldats.

The voices of the Soldats were now muffled, but after a few more minutes, they disappeared completely. I risked a peek through the glass, and saw that the bedroom was empty and the door to the hallway was closed.

I took a deep breath. "We're safe," I declared, putting my arm over Kirsten's shoulder, happy to be looking into her eyes, even if they weren't real eyes.

"I would agree that Kirsten is safe."

It was Boney! He had appeared out of thin air, or perhaps from a very great distance, arriving at some phenomenal speed, light photons straining against their Einsteinian limit. Heaven was both impressed on the world we know, yet at the same time unimaginably distant. For a moment he seemed drained, as though weary from the travel. He recovered quickly, and glared at me in anger. I thought that he was going to immediately attack me, but he glanced at Kirsten, and I could see that he restrained himself.

"She's coming with me," I declared, realizing how lame it sounded, yet meaning it completely as I moved in front of her.

Boney took it as lame as well. He grinned, his initial rage seeming to subside under the calm of assured dominance. "Kirsten," he said with paternal patience, "you realize that this is a grave mistake. Your destiny is to work beside me to fulfill the Creator's plan, not wandering Halfway, aimless and destitute with this engineer."

He made it sound as though engineering was essentially cleaning sewer systems. I remembered what Zorba had told me when I'd first arrived. "Would the Creators have agreed that their plan was for heaven to make war on heaven?" I taunted.

His eyes flared a moment. "I would dissolve you for that alone," he stated flatly.

Meaning, I thought, *that he intended to dissolve me already.* "So you admit it," I concluded. "You want Kirsten so you can recruit an army."

The hate emanated like heat waves. "I admit nothing. You are no more than a toad to me, and I acknowledge no demands from toads."

He seemed to realize that this was not endearing him to Kirsten. "The Creator's plans for Home span millennia, and ultimately benefit all mankind."

"Just as your own plans were once going to benefit all of Europe?" I countered.

He looked at me, the toad, and decided that this was one of those demands he needn't acknowledge. To Kirsten, he said, "You understand that I could eliminate your boyfriend in an instant. Come with me now, and I will spare him."

To my surprise, she stepped forward. I grabbed her arm, but she looked me in the eye, shook her head solemnly, and gently lifted my fingers away. "It's okay," she assured.

"No!" I cried. "Don't you see? He's lying."

She shook her head. "It's okay," she repeated. "I trust him."

I could only gape in horror as she walked the few steps to where he waited at the balcony wall. She turned as though to say farewell one last time to me, but then spun and lunged at him with open palms. He tumbled over the edge of the balcony and was gone an instant later.

She stood grinning at me in triumph, and a grin of my own slowly spread across my face. "That's my girl," I said, holding out my arms to her.

Chapter 10

Our grins faded fast as the shouts of Soldats bubbled up from below.

"What now?" Kirsten asked.

"You're asking me? You're the one who pushed him over."

"Jordan," she protested, "there's no time for joking. We're trapped up here."

I went to the wall and confirmed her assessment. One Soldat stood in the grass below, keeping an eye on us. Boney was nowhere to be seen. I wondered if he'd already returned to heaven. Zorba had said that it wasn't easy to transition between heaven and Halfway. Still, I couldn't shake the apprehension that he might appear again right in front of us at any second. I told myself that even if he could flip back and forth between the layers, he still had to make his way back up the stairs inside. He couldn't *fly* in heaven.

Could he?

"I guess we'll just have to jump and try to make a run for it," I concluded.

I looked down, and the Soldat stared up at me, a dare to go ahead and try it. I sighed.

Just then I heard shouting from the bedroom.

"Professor Clintock!" Kirsten shouted, amazed and overjoyed.

Through the glass door I saw that she was right. I also had a chance to see how I must have looked an hour before. He stood uncertainly in the middle of the room, swinging two three-foot pipes, one in each hand, in long, intersecting arcs. Zorba clung to his back, and I could now understand the trauma he had previously endured. Each time Clintock swung both arms backwards, my spectral friend was squeezed between his arms. When he saw me through the glass, he flashed a quick smile that was immediately replaced by a grimace of pain.

Zorba pressed his cheek against the professor's, and the old head turned to look at the balcony door, causing the rider to cry out at the jostling this caused. Three Soldats, invisible to the professor danced around just beyond the reach of the pipe clubs, watching for their opportunity.

The professor backed slowly to the door, and Kirsten and I huddled close on the other side, ready. I realized that Clintock, intent on sweeping his perimeter, seemed to have forgotten that he carried a delicate package on his back. I saw with horror that he was about to crush Zorba against the glass door, and I shouted, "Professor! Behind you!"

"He can't hear you!" Kirsten cried, but Clintock jerked to a stop, and glanced backwards. His eyes went wide in alarm when he saw how close he'd come.

Kirsten looked at me in amazement, but we had no time to debate. Using his left hand to continue the security sweep, Clintock reached around with his right and slid the door open.

"Thanks for coming to our rescue," I said to Zorba who still clung to his riding position. "What now?"

Interrupted by grunts of pain, he replied, "I was hoping—ow!—you'd take it from here."

"You have no plan to get us out?" I asked, incredulously. "How did you get the professor to come this far?"

"It was—ouch!—his idea."

I looked at Kirsten, but she just shrugged.

"Boney will be back any minute," I warned. As I said this, I saw the professor glance around, as though he too was anticipating the Little General's return.

Was it just a coincidence? One of the Soldats was inching his way around to the right, where the far perimeter of the professor's swings didn't quite reach the edge of the sliding door. I remembered that Jones and Steinbeck were able to slip through glass, and guessed that Soldats might have the same ability. My guess was confirmed when the assailant slowly pushed his hand through the door and grasped the aluminum frame in preparation for pulling the rest of himself through.

I considered trying to beat the soldier back with my fists, but remembered how strong heaven's hordes were. Instead, I stepped up close to Zorba. I was going to try to talk to the professor, and imagined in my head what I was going to try to get him to do. But before I could utter one word, as though by magic, I watched him stretch his arm out and tap the end of the door, exactly what I had envisioned.

The result was appalling and vastly out of proportion to the casually executed action. The tip of the pipe caught the Soldat squarely in his midriff. He bellowed a blood-curdling scream that evaporated into a sickening gurgle as his chest, sides, and groin expanded in grotesque distortion, like a squeezed balloon. For a fleeting moment, missed by a blink, he became transparent, as though formed from Plexiglas, and then was gone; not a trace remained other than the memory of the heart-stopping shriek still ringing in my ears. Zorba had not exaggerated the risks of being dissolved.

The professor knew nothing of this, of course, and he continued his careful rhythmic sweeps, probably wondering if there was even anybody else around, other than the poor distraught maid watching him nervously from the bedroom doorway.

The remaining two Soldats moved more cautiously now, but were joined by another who squeezed past the distressed maid. I heard grunts from behind, and looked over the balcony wall to find the Soldat who had been watching from below now laboriously climbing the decorative facade of the wall.

"We've got one coming up from behind," I informed Zorba, and as I said this, the professor threw a quick glance backward, looking through me.

"I don't know what to do!" Zorba pleaded. "I can't maneuver him to protect us all!"

"No, you can't," I agreed, but I had an idea. "Get down," I instructed.

He looked at me, not sure what I meant.

"Step back, away from the professor," I reiterated.

"But, then he won't have—"

"Just do it! There's no time to argue."

Grumbling about dire consequences, he put his feet on the floor and let go of Clintock's neck. I stepped up until my chest was touching the stone-hard clothes of the professor's back. He tilted his head slightly, as though listening to music in the next room. "Okay," I said softly, "let's dance." I lifted my arms and moved them to match his swinging motion, placing my hands lightly against the back of his wrists. Once I had the rhythm down, I departed from the pattern, lifting my right hand on the out-swing. It seemed to me that the professor followed suit, but so slightly, I couldn't be sure.

"What are you doing?" Kirsten asked.

"Connecting the strings," I replied.

"What strings?"

"Puppet strings." Into the professor's ear, I whispered, "Follow me." This time, I tried to ignore my own hand, and concentrated on imagining the professor's instead. As though finally deciding to go along with the pre-planned choreography, Clintock lifted his hand to mimic mine. On the next swing, we did a little loop, like a symphony conductor cueing the string section. The professor smiled, pleased with his little innovation.

"Are you doing that?" Zorba asked incredulously.

"Shh!" I admonished. The distraction caused the professor to miss my next trial exercise, a downward flip of the pipe. I again focused, and we completed that maneuver on the next swing.

"Uh, oh!" Zorba said at the same time that Kirsten gave a sharp squeal of surprise. I glanced behind us, and saw that the climbing Soldat was pulling himself over the balcony wall. Zorba was beating at him with his elbow, but it was like holding off a wolf with a straw.

"Time to deploy," I muttered into Clintock's ear, then more loudly, "Follow me inside!" I called to the other two. We hadn't practiced walking yet, but the gentle old man obliged, and we took a step forward, then another. I heard a rustle and felt the bump as Zorba and Kirsten pressed through the door behind me. "Move to the left," I instructed to them, as I stepped Clintock forward and rotated us to the right. This left a wide opening off to our left, and I had to lean us and reach the professor's left hand quickly to tap the Soldat who had sprung forward to take advantage of the opportunity. Although the motion was a mere flick to Clintock, the tap sent the Soldat flying back to crash painfully against a dresser. The other two hovered well beyond our reach, now visibly more cautious.

The Soldat outside appeared at the sliding door, and not realizing what was going on, rushed in. Before I could maneuver Clintock to react, Boney's soldier was behind me. From the grunts and shouts, I gathered that Zorba was struggling with him, and judging from all previous evidence, futilely. Something knocked me painfully between my shoulder blades, and then I felt hands groping for my neck. I remembered that Wops don't actually breathe, and I wondered for a brief second why the Soldat was trying to choke me, but then with a jolt I understood what he was after. My neck made a good handle, and he used it to yank me back, away from Clintock. His heaven strength was irresistible, and after the world stopped spinning, I was on my back, and his face hovered above me as he landed one mind-shattering blow after another to my head. Between punches, I saw both Zorba and Kirsten pulling at his arms and landing their own fists on his head. They might as well have been whipping him with string.

Above and oblivious to it all, the professor continued his pipe sweeps, free from my control, but unaware of the fact. The other Soldats, though, had caught on to my game, and were taking advantage, moving around to each side, just beyond the sweep perimeter.

"Professor!" I called, knowing he couldn't hear my voice, but hoping that he'd hear my plea. His head tilted slightly to the distant music. "To the sides!" I yelled as another punch knocked the last word from my mouth.

He glanced back and forth at invisible beings, and for good measure, in what to him was an empty room, reached first one way and then the other, swinging the pipes so that they nearly touched the opposite walls.

For those of us in Halfway, the result was dramatic. On our right, two Soldats were sent sailing across the room in front of Clintock. To the left, the third Soldat was caught in his back-sweep, and flew past me to land out of sight with a thump and groan. That was bad news, as now there were two soldiers on our side.

"Professor!" I called again, and he turned his head a tiny notch in response. I gave up the verbal directions, and concentrated on what I wanted each hand to do. I say concentrated, but the reality was snippets of urges between teeth-rattling punches. I may not have had blood vessels to bruise in Halfway, but the creators had deemed it useful, for purposes beyond knowing, to incorporate what served as pain nerves. Each blow felt no less severe than if I had been a flesh and blood body. It seems a miracle that I was able to think of anything other than pain.

Somehow I did, though, and I brought Clintock's hand around for a quick little backwards flick. My assailant flew away like a scrap of paper in a gust. With a spinning head, I pushed myself to my feet. The two Soldats on our side were also picking themselves up. Zorba too was helping somebody that my re-focusing eyes recognized as Kirsten. For a brief moment I thought that one of the Soldats had hit her, but I realized that my last flick of Clintock's pipe must have caught her too.

No time for apologies. One of the Soldats pushed Zorba away and grabbed Kirsten, and the other came after me. I had no time to think, so I did what non-thinkers have done throughout history—I grabbed my weapon, which, of course, was the professor. I stepped up behind him and turned us around. Why he would have thought that this would be a good thing to do at that moment was beyond me; I was just glad that he did. Our windmill turn swept away the Soldat that was nearly upon me, but left me now exposed to that side. I didn't attempt to look behind me, but simply had the professor direct his swings to the back so that his arms came nearly together behind us. This was effective at keeping the three Soldats there at bay, as evidenced by a bump and cry as one apparently tried to get at me, but it was also squeezing me like a lemon in a juicer. The pain was almost beyond description, what I would imagine it would be like to be crushed between two colliding cars, but over and over again. I began to appreciate Zorba's ordeal while riding me, the corpus me.

Through the fog of excruciating torture, I peered around Clintock's neck to find the sole remaining Soldat on "our" side with one arm wrapped around Kirsten's neck, while holding Zorba off with the other. "I'll dissolve her!" he warned when he caught my eye, giving her a quick, painful jerk for emphasis.

My mind and the thoughts seemed like so much mush, but from somewhere in the tossed salad a kernel of truth found its way to the front. "If you do, then Boney will dissolve you," I replied, my voice rising to a squeak with each backward swing of Clintock's arms.

I could see by his hesitation that he knew this to be so, and he reached out to grab Zorba for additional hostage bait, but my friend was too nimble for him. I stepped the professor forward like a zombie showing Frankenstein how to dance, and yelled, "Zorba, duck!" which he managed to do as I brought one of the professor's arms forward. The Soldat was holding Kirsten on his left side, and I brought the pipe around on his right. He too tried to duck, but Kirsten was in his way, and I managed to adjust Clintock's swing downward to fall squarely against the side of his head.

I expected that this would send him tumbling, hopefully releasing Kirsten in the process, but the blow must have caught his head against the wall, squashing it, for he went momentarily translucent, and then was gone, leaving Kirsten to fall to the ground. I hadn't meant to dissolve the former human man, and I had no time to gauge how I felt about it.

"Stay down!" I called to my two comrades as I spun the professor around again to face the three remaining Soldats. They seemed shaken by the demise now of two of their own, and shied away from aggressive risks.

It seemed a long, long way through the door, down the hall and stairs, and out the front door, all the while keeping Boney's troops at bay with a tool that I only indirectly controlled. And even if we made it outside, what was to keep them from continuing to hound us?

We needed a plan, and now that the professor was only swinging his arms forward again, I could think without interruptions of searing torment. Unfortunately, the renewed thinking produced no useful thoughts. All I could do was continue with what had worked.

Another Soldat arrived, and he waited out in the hall, anticipating our escape. I realized that what had worked so far would not be viable outside the contained space of the bedroom. Despite my miraculous ability to direct Clintock's pipe wands with a surprising degree of accuracy, it seemed impossible that I would be able to shepherd all three of us to freedom without one, or maybe all, being grabbed.

To us wraiths of Halfway, the professor was a man of steel. What we really needed was for him to wrap us in his mighty, impervious, thin old arms and carry us away.

It was a fantasy thought, but it gave me the idea I was hoping for. It would be risky. In fact, the image made me flinch, but I saw no alternative.

"Zorba," I said, "get Kirsten and move in front of the professor."

"In *front*? Where the Soldats are?"

"Yes. No time to explain. Duck under his left arm," I directed while simultaneously holding Clintock's arm out straight.

That seemed to ease my friend's mind, and he hustled my fiancée under and forward until the professor was looking through their heads. "Jordan," Kirsten said, turning to look at me, "what are you doing?"

"Putting you on the bus," I replied. I didn't want to be too specific, since our attackers were standing there listening.

One of the Soldats decided the bait was too tempting to resist, and he started forward, but a warning waggle from the professor's right hand stopped him short.

Now came the part that froze my figurative heart with fear. A misinterpretation by the professor—hell, even a sneeze—and my new friend and my girlfriend would be gone forever. I instructed them to raise their hands above their heads. "Easy," I whispered into Clintock's ear as I brought his left hand slowly around, keeping his elbow cocked outward, until his arm and extended pipe formed a protective semi-circle around the two. The professor looked down quizzically, and I wondered if he somehow sensed the two cradled inside with their arms dangling over his. I closed my eyes a moment in concentration and willed him to feel the fragile peril of his invisible cargo.

"Indeed," someone said.

I opened my eyes and realized that it had been the professor. "Can you hear me?" I asked, but he made no response, apparently still deaf and blind to the world of Halfway.

"Hang on," I warned the passengers. "You might want to lift your feet." I took the first step with Clintock slowly, letting Zorba and Kirsten adjust to their new mode of transport. Despite the professor's instilled sense of extreme caution, inevitable jostling produced grunts of pain from the delicate riders. Step by cumbersome step we moved towards the doorway to the hall, and I saw before we arrived what the next hurdle was going to be. The professor couldn't swing his weapon arm around on both sides of the door as we squeezed through. I considered having us turn around and go out backwards, allowing the professor to fend off the inner three Soldats from getting at Zorba and Kirsten, but decided that the outside Soldat would just drag me away, and leaving the professor to fly solo and blind would probably be even more dangerous to the two.

Instead, we just pressed forward with Clintock's right arm extended backwards, swinging the pipe back and forth behind me with his wrist. This squashed me between his upper arm and the doorframe, and I returned to the world of excruciating torment. Through the pain, I saw the Soldat in the hallway grab Kirsten around the waist and pull. Her hold on Clintock's arm was pitifully weak compared to the heaven soldier, and she slid down and out. I had no hand, or rather no professor hand, in front to stop him, and without thinking, I willed Clintock to launch the only weapon available. He seemed confused by his own rude behavior, but he complied with my subliminal wish and he spit. The discharge was wimpy, a mere spray of spittle, not at all the lugee projectile I had envisioned, but the effect was impressive. Several large droplets must have caught the Soldat square in the face, for his head whipped back so hard, I imagined it would have broken his neck had he a neck bone. He let go of Kirsten, and she pulled herself back up into position.

The stricken Soldat was somewhere on the floor where I couldn't see, but I had the professor step high and long. This produced distressed cries from Zorba who was closest to the uplifted knee, but a piercing shriek when it stepped back down. I couldn't be sure, but my bet was that we were minus yet one more Soldat.

Once through the door, my own distress was relieved, and we proceeded with good speed to the stairs. The maid stood well out of the way of this very strange old man who walked along so carefully, holding his arm out as though dancing with an invisible partner. She didn't realize that in a way he actually was—with two, in fact.

The stairs posed the next hurdle. Going down either forward or backwards would cause Clintock's knees to become pistons threatening to crush Zorba and Kirsten, plus his free hand would only provide protection in one direction. Instead, I had our human Humvee go down sideways, bending the uphill knee far to the side, out of the way. This way I could also watch both directions.

I was gratified to see the three Soldats pause at the top of the stairs, allowing our descent unmolested. Downhill, the large foyer was empty. It seemed we might make it after all. I guessed that Boney had perhaps only posted six Soldats at the estate, and we had already dispatched half.

We reached the bottom and had taken a step into the foyer when I saw that my optimism was disastrously misplaced. A tall, muscular policeman stood just outside on the porch talking to the mother I'd seen earlier in the kitchen with Steinbeck. Between them, invisible and unnoticed, Boney stood with a hand on each of their shoulders, as though a mutual pal who'd brought them together. He was glowering at us, and had obviously been following our progress down the stairs. If he hadn't actually seen three of his Soldats dissolved, he'd probably heard their final screams. He tilted his head toward the policeman and said something, all the while keeping his eyes locked on mine. The cop dutifully glanced over in our direction, and his eyes went wide.

"Perhaps I should be impressed with how you've trained your monkey," Boney said, nodding at the professor, "but that would be much like a Mozart finding inspiration in a musical doorbell." To the subconsciously connected policeman he said, "I think it's time to make an arrest."

Chapter 11

The professor looked stricken as the policeman walked over with a dour Bonaparte Napoleon by his side, his chino slacks and Casmir sweater unsoiled from his fall from the balcony. Kirsten and Zorba crawled out from under the professor's extended arm, and I let him relax it. For good measure, I had him drop both pipes as well. We three Wops instinctively huddled behind Clintock for protection. The three Soldats stood at the top of the stairs, waiting direction from their leader.

"What do you think you're doing?" the policeman demanded.

"Yes, er," the professor stammered, "that's a reasonable question."

"Do you have some identification?" the cop asked as Boney stepped wide around the professor to get at us. Clintock reached into his back pocket for his wallet and I pulled Kirsten behind me as I faced the French general. It was a noble gesture perhaps, but futile. I lifted my arm in defense as Boney reached out, and the next instant I was flying through the air with such intense pain in my shoulder that, had I been material, it would have meant dislocation at least.

I scrambled back to my feet to find Zorba doing the same, while Kirsten screeched and clawed at her abductor. Boney could throw her across the room, could hurt her with intense pain, or maybe even dissolve her, but if he wanted her eventual cooperation, his retaliation against her furious counterattack was limited. The brilliant military leader had his hands full.

The professor stood massaging his hands, looking most distraught as the officer read him his Miranda rights while pulling handcuffs from his belt. I felt terrible that I'd gotten him into so much trouble. I knew that it had been he who had pulled *me* into the whole multi-dimensional fiasco, but he was now just helping to get Kirsten back. "It's not his fault!" I yelled from twenty feet away.

My proclamation was a cry of despair, addressed to the universe, not anyone in particular, but the policeman glanced in my direction, looking through me for a moment.

Well, well.

Boney was still busy with my feisty fiancée as I ran over to the two corpora. I looked from the miserable, defeated professor to the cop who seemed almost bored with an accused trespasser who was nothing but a compliant old coot. "You don't want to arrest him," I stated clearly, peering into the policeman's eyes. The man pursed his lips slightly, as though resisting a foolish thought.

I understood that I couldn't make him do something he wouldn't ordinarily do, just as a hypnotist couldn't induce an otherwise uninterested woman to have sex, or as Zorba couldn't convince our first hitch driver that he had to pee with an empty bladder.

"Look," the cop said to Clintock, putting his handcuffs back. "Will you promise to leave quietly and pay for the damages?" The professor nodded enthusiastically. "Okay," the officer continued, glancing back at the matron, "let me see what I can do."

I turned and gaped at Zorba, who just shrugged. Turning back, I said "Tell her he has Alzheimer's."

The professor wrinkled his brow and shook his head. "I don't have Alzheimer's."

The policeman raised one eyebrow. "Well, make up your mind; do you, or don't you?"

"I never said I did."

The cop waved it off and turned to go to talk with the woman, but suddenly Boney gave me a bump that sent me sprawling and moved in next to the cop, all the while struggling to contain a flailing Kirsten. By the time I had recovered, the policeman had turned back to the professor, looking confused. "No!" I called. "Let the old man go!"

The cop flinched, but Boney was right by his side talking to him continuously, and I had no chance to get a telepathic word in edgewise. "I don't know what I was thinking," the cop said to the professor, "but I'll need to take you in."

"He committed a very serious crime," Boney reminded, and the policeman repeated the accusation, but dropping the "very."

We were back where we started. I moved in, keeping just out of Boney's reach. I noticed that he kept close to the officer, protecting his influence. But that put him right between the cop and Clintock.

Well, then.

To his utter surprise, I made the professor reach his arm out and slap it against Boney. Heaven's leader was holding Kirsten by her waist, and she was bent over, leaving her abductor's upper half open. He was quick, though and leaned back. But not quite far enough. Clintock's fist caught Boney on the bare patch of forehead inside his receding hairline . . . and flattened his head against the cop's shoulder. I saw it with my own eyes, or what I used as eyes. His whole head wasn't squashed, just the forehead, but it caused his eyes and cheeks to bulge for a brief second. It was absolutely the most disturbing thing I had ever seen, or even imagined seeing.

Napoleon Bonaparte gave a little *oof* sound, and collapsed. The policeman, though, only saw a suspect detainee accost him. Harmless little tap or no, you don't touch a policeman. In one swift motion, the cop twisted the professor's wrist so that he was spun around with his arm locked in the classic painful detained position. "Now you did it," the cop growled, reaching again for his cuffs.

I stepped over the motionless nineteenth century general to get close to the policeman. Out of the corner of my eye, I saw Zorba pull Kirsten away. "He wasn't trying to hurt you," I urged. As I said this, I placed my hand on top of the policeman's, willing him to put the cuffs back on his belt. He didn't comply, but he did hesitate, holding the steel bracelets poised. "He's a harmless old man," I persisted, "probably somebody's dear grandpa. You'll ruin his life and make all his little grandchildren unhappy. They'll cry," I added for good measure.

The burly cop sighed. I needed help, and noticed that the woman owner had moved inside and was watching from the entrance. "Just wait," I directed firmly to him. "There's no rush."

I noticed that Boney was moving. I'd assumed he was dead, but remembered that people in Halfway don't die, they dissolve, and since he lay there, he was still "alive," even though his head was still horribly misshapen, although seeming to slowly resume its original iconic shape. I don't consider myself mean, but I must confess; I convinced the cop that he felt a twitch in his leg that could be relieved with a little kick, sending the recovering French emperor sliding across the foyer to crash against the far foyer wall.

With that little bit of satisfaction, I ran to the woman. "You're doing this harmless old man a grave injustice," I pleaded. "He doesn't deserve that." To optimize my influence, I draped my arms over her shoulders and placed my head next to hers. This caused her to jerk, as though a bug had crawled into her ear. I backed off and she seemed to relax. "Tell the officer to let him go," I demanded, trying a forceful approach. I grasped her arm and gently pulled, and she obediently came along, step by hesitant step.

The cop noticed her approaching. "Stay back, ma'am," he instructed.

She obeyed, and stopped, despite my continued pulling. I tried another tack. "See?" I urged. "He's just a big bully. Who knows? He might have *you* in an arm-lock someday."

That did the trick. "Officer! Please let that man go."

"You sure?" he asked. I had the sense that he was relieved.

"Of course I'm sure. You're hurting the harmless old man. He doesn't deserve that."

The policeman hesitated. His training told him to follow through with the apprehension and arrest, but his heart, now invaded by me, urged pity. He compromised, buying time. "Are you saying that you do not want to press charges?"

"You never wanted to," I instructed.

"I never wanted to," she echoed.

"But you called him a dangerous maniac just minutes ago," he reminded her. That would have been Boney's doing. "If I let him go now, he's free to go. I can't apprehend him twice."

I guessed that this wasn't true—he could apprehend a suspect as many times as necessary—but it was a good way to put his heart at rest.

"You're completely sure," I prompted.

"I am completely, one-hundred percent sure," she responded, going off script, but in the right direction.

"Okay, ma'am. Have it your way," the cop said, finally letting go of the professor's arm. He was pretending professional caution, but I knew the truth: my influence had won the day. The guy had to deal with a never ending stream of unredeemable criminals, and my nudging had convinced him that leniency where it would do no harm was a respite from dragging degenerates off the street.

Now I could turn my attention to the broader perimeter, and I saw that trouble had already arrived. The three Soldats had come down the stairs and were holding Zorba and Kirsten. I noted with grim satisfaction that while one held Zorba by the neck, it took both of the others to hold my girl who clawed and twisted like a cat in a cold shower.

There was nothing I could do directly against soldiers from heaven, but I had already indirectly nearly destroyed their leader, and I considered how to apply my impervious fighting machine against them. The consideration went nowhere, as I couldn't imagine how to keep the Soldats from simply dragging Zorba and Kirsten out of the professor's way. After all, my indestructible human robot was blind to the world of Halfway.

But there was one heavenite who couldn't get out of the way. I ran to the professor, and took him by the elbow. "Come along," I directed, and pulled him towards the wall where Boney sill lay senseless.

He looked at the policeman and shrugged sheepishly, but came with me, all the while glancing back apologetically at the cop and woman.

"Tell them that you think you dropped your keys over here," I impressed on him.

He did, and the policeman apparently believed him, telling him to be quick about it.

I stopped him just in front of where Boney lay. I noticed that the leader's head was almost back to normal, and he opened his eyes and looked up at us, but he seemed dazed, barely aware of us.

To the Soldats, I yelled, "Let them go!"

They glared menacingly, but complied. My threat was obvious.

"Now go back up the stairs. If I see any of you thirty seconds from now, Boney's going *poof*."

They hesitated, looking at each other for direction.

"*Poof?*" I reiterated, and they took off up the stairs like scared rabbits.

I told Zorba and Kirsten to run away, that I'd meet up with them at the car, and watched as they high-tailed it out the door, which the woman had fortunately left open.

I took a step forward, intending to yell a final warning to watch for Soldats outside, and this probably saved my life, for the next instant I was sent tumbling to the floor. Above me, the professor was clutching at the air where I had stood. The policeman was demanding to know what the hell the professor thought he was doing now, but I didn't care about him, I saw that Boney had grasped Clintock's ankle. The bastard had commandeered my battle robot!

I scrambled up and approached the professor, but he swung his arm at me, and I had to jump back. "Professor!" I called. "That's not me!"

He looked confused, but swung again.

At the periphery of my consciousness, I heard the cop telling the woman that he might have to take this guy in after all, for his own safety. "Professor!" I yelled. "Boney's at your feet. He's controlling you."

He blinked, a man presented with an idea that doesn't make complete sense.

"Professor, please! Just step forward, and you'll understand."

He started to, but stopped, as though pulled back by bungee cords.

"Do it, professor! For Kirsten!"

He blinked again, but this time as though waking up. He took a confident step, and Boney tried to hang on, but lost his grip. Risking a chance, I stepped up and placed my hands on both sides of his head, thinking thoughts of congratulations, images of Kirsten sitting in his class. I felt his whole body relax. To the policeman and woman he said, "I'll be going now. I'm very sorry for the bother, but I'll make it up."

And with that, he strode away towards the door, nearly knocking me off my feet. I had to run to catch up.

It was my turn to be confused. I hadn't even told him to leave. He'd somehow understood.

We marched out the door, down the long driveway, and through the wrecked gates undisturbed. As we made our way along the sidewalk, I thought about the Soldats that we had dissolved—that I had caused to be dissolved. I wasn't sure if I felt guilty or not. On one hand, they were thinking, feeling (at least I assumed they had feelings) entities who had once been living men. They were no different than Zorba, who I considered my friend. No, I decided, they weren't like Zorba. He had resisted giving in to Boney's plans at conquest. They were soldiers who had tried to destroy us, would try again given the chance. Soldiers die in war.

I put those uncomfortable ideas aside and turned my thoughts to Kirsten. Thank God, I thought, that she'd come around so easily. She could be naive and impressionable sometimes with subjects that tickled her childlike fascination with things fantastic and magical, but she was no dummy, no sheep to be led around by a nose-ring.

Well, okay, she did almost become Boney's head sheep, but she didn't have a chance against a master puppeteer, a puppeteer who's had two centuries to hone his manipulation skills.

But now I was running up against the greatest hurdle, one too high for me to even see over. I had no idea how I was going to get her back into her corpus.

We rounded the corner and I saw that Zorba and Kirsten were sprinting up the street towards us. Zorba looked worried, but I detected a terror in Kirsten's eyes that I'd never seen before. Zorba was yelling something I couldn't make out. It sounded like "Tassels of your anus." As they got closer, I recognized that he was yelling,

"Apostles of Irenaeus!" It took a moment to remember that these were the clean-cut fanatics with the gun.

"They took her!" Zorba wailed as they reached us.

"Who?" I asked, glancing at Kirsten who stood right there looking terribly frightened.

"Her!" he shouted, pointing at her.

Like an unexpected slap across the face it came to me, and the terror in her eyes became crystal clear.

"Her corpus!" Zorba explained impatiently, interpreting my look of shock as incomprehension. "They broke into the SUV and stole her!"

It didn't matter how high that hurdle was after all, as it had now disappeared.

Chapter 12

The professor had proceeded unawares on to the car, and was calling out softly but urgently to the invisible me about his own discovery of the missing body, but I ignored him for now. A new thought, equally as terrifying as losing Kirsten, had occurred to me. "What about me? I mean, my body, my corpus?"

"It's still there," Zorba assured. "The Soldat that was guiding them saw us, and they all left in a hurry. They were putting Kirsten's corpus in the trunk of a Camry when we came around the corner."

"They put her in the *trunk*?"

Kirsten nodded dumbly, still horrified at the thought that the human part of her was maybe suffocating or being poisoned with carbon monoxide.

"My body's there," I repeated, "but is it . . . alive?"

Zorba looked at me with the same question in his eyes. "I don't know. Actually, as the Soldat was getting it through their skulls to leave, I heard the Apostles arguing about who should finish taking care of 'the other one.' I thought that they meant taking you away as well, but—"

"One of them was holding a knife," Kirsten added almost in a trance. The trauma was saturating in her.

I didn't ask if the blade was bloody, I just took off as fast as I could, racing to get to the car, but dreading arriving. The doors were closed, and I peered through the window. I sat in the passenger seat, my head lolled to the side. There was a glare on the glass that I couldn't shade with an invisible hand, so I couldn't tell if I was breathing. I was so intent on getting an angle to see that it shocked me when suddenly my view became perfectly clear . . . and I was looking down at me. My head had passed right through the window. This shocked the hell out of me, and I pulled back in a panic. It was like dragging my head away from a hundred grasping fingers.

When my head finally snapped free outside, Zorba was standing watching me with what seemed like awe. "How did you do that?" he asked.

"As with too many things in my life," I answered, distracted, "by dumb luck. Professor!" I called, running over to him. His brow furrowed. I was going to tell him to open the passenger door, but I didn't get a chance. He'd already gotten the message, and stepped towards me, knocking me backwards so that I did a little dance to stay on my feet. After he opened the door, I had to mentally remind him that he also had to step out of the way so that I could get through. I put my hand on my own comatose chest, maybe the first time in human history, and felt the fear melt away as it rose slightly with an intake of air. "I'm alive!" I announced, maybe a wee bit too ecstatically.

I sat down right there on the pavement, letting relief flow over me. I was alive; Kirsten's corpus had been kidnapped, but we had no reason to believe it was not also alive. No permanent doors had yet closed. I realized that the professor might inadvertently step on me, and moved to safer territory near the rear of the car.

A sudden thought occurred to me, completely tangent to the emergency at hand, but irresistibly calling for an answer. "Would I even know if my corpus had died?" I asked Zorba.

"Maybe," he replied, sitting down next to me.

"Maybe? It doesn't seem like a trivial change of state of my universe."

"The feeling is slight. You could miss it if you were busy. It's like when an elevator starts going down. You feel a little bit lighter."

"You sound like you're talking from experience."

He looked at me a moment with a grim little smile. "That's right."

This was an experience you could feel exactly once. "I see. You felt your own corpus . . . die." It was hard talking to somebody about their own death.

He nodded. Forty years was probably long enough to get over the squeamish feelings. "I was in transition for an hour or so—"

"Transition?"

"When your corpus is still alive. Both you and Kirsten are still in transition."

I didn't like thinking of it as 'still,' as though moving on to full Wopness was inevitable. "Sorry. You were saying—"

"If my transition had been shorter, I would have still been adjusting, and wouldn't have noticed it."

My curiosity bested me. "How did you . . . you know—"

"Do myself in? Drugs."

I thought about what he'd told me earlier. "That seems risky. I mean, your goal was to put yourself into a coma, right?"

"That wasn't so much the goal as the end effect, but yeah."

"And it takes some amount of time to ascend. It doesn't happen the instant you go into a coma."

"Yeah. So?"

"Well, how would you know what was just the right amount of drugs to put you in a coma, but not, you know, like kill you too quickly?"

"Doctors know these things."

"You found a doctor to help you? An early version of Kevorkian?"

He smiled. "A very close family member."

Not that it really mattered, but, "Like your . . . father?"

He shook his head, smiling widely now.

"Brother? Sister? What? I give up."

He just smiled, enjoying my consternation.

It came to me. "No! *You?*"

He nodded. "I was still in residency."

I don't know why it made a difference, but we're so used to thinking of the value of our lives as measured on career success. "But you had so much to—"

"Live for?" he finished, his smile never wavering.

"Sure, I guess."

He shrugged. "I was young. It was the sixties."

"But, you didn't have a wife?"

He shook his head. "A girlfriend, but we'd broken up a couple of months earlier."

"So, you were . . . despondent?"

He laughed. "No."

"What's so funny?"

"All my friends thought I'd committed suicide, and in a way I guess I did, but not for the reasons they assumed. 'He seemed so normal—you never know what pain is hidden inside.' By the way, this is how the Catholic Church's dogma that suicide leads directly to hell evolved. What my friends didn't know was that Boney was calling me hither with promises of heaven."

"You knew that Napoleon Bonaparte was talking to you?"

He seemed to blush, which wasn't technically possible without cheek blood vessels. "I thought it was God calling."

"I see."

We let it go at that. It *was* embarrassing to admit.

Something else occurred to me, though. For a while, I had been fascinated with early television. "Your name is unusual," I said. "Even for the sixties."

"It's a nickname," he explained. "In high school I knew I wanted to be a doctor—"

"Ben Casey!" I exclaimed. My guess had been right.

He grinned. "Not many people remember that TV show anymore."

I pointed. "Your hair."

He ruffled the mop that remained behind the receded hairline. "I couldn't argue the resemblance to Doctor Casey's mentor."

Kirsten sat down between us. "Doctor Zorba was old," she observed. "You don't look anything like him." She patted his head reassuringly as she said this.

She seemed recovered. The fear of being separated from a body she had just decided to re-inhabit—or try to—had ebbed. I figured that now was not the best time to bring her up to speed on our incident at the hospital, where members of the same cult had tried to kill her body.

"We should leave before Boney comes to find us," Zorba observed, getting to his feet. He reached down and offered a hand to hoist up both Kirsten and me.

"Boney will recover?" I asked.

"Oh, he'll be back to his old domineering self in no time. We should be so lucky. I've heard of this sort of thing happening before." He paused a moment. "I don't think a lowly Wop could survive that, though." He looked at me and laughed, apparently seeing the discomfort on my face. "Oh, come on now; you don't feel guilty, do you?"

Did I? I had already offed three Soldats, but I hadn't come to know them, hadn't talked to them.

Zorba recognized my inner debates and put his hand on my shoulder. "Believe me, he wouldn't hesitate to take you out if it served him. Look, who do you think gave the order for the cult to kill Kirsten's corpus in the hospital?"

The thought of that whisked away whatever regret lingered over the rude humiliation I had visited on Napoleon's head.

"It had to hurt like hell, though," he added.

"He's going to be pretty mad, eh?" I guessed uneasily.

"He's going to want to get even, that I can predict. Which is all the more reason to get this circus on the road."

ж ж ж

I had already worked myself into an artificial state of minor anxiety in order to descend, so when I opened my eyes and found myself sitting in the passenger seat of the professor's SUV paralyzed, my induced fearful state exploded into bona fide panic. I cried out in something between a whimper and a wail before I realized that I had been sitting on my hands and they'd gone asleep.

The professor had been pacing up and down the sidewalk, and came running over. "Are you all right?" he asked, seeming worried about me, but also relieved that I had returned. Since throwing a branch, which may or may not have flung me over the wall and onto the balcony, the notion had come to him to invade the mansion swinging two pipes around like an imbecile, then had followed the dictates of some inner insistent voice to tap the pipes precisely this way and that, before descending the stairs to confront what would have appeared to be a confused and wishy-washy policeman and owner before finally returning to the car.

"I'm fine," I replied, shaking my hands, which only induced little bombs of tingling pain. "Kirsten and Zorba are around somewhere."

"You convinced Kirsten to come along?" he asked excitedly, but then his face sagged. "They took her body," he informed, pointing to the back.

"I know. Professor, what are we going to do? At the hospital, they tried to—"

I remembered that Kirsten was probably listening. "We have to find out where they took her," I finished.

His brow furrowed. He was back where he was most comfortable: thinking. "They had definite incentive to kill her body there at the hospital—"

"Er, professor, she's, uh," I tilted my head vaguely.

"Oh, yes! She would probably be hearing us now." Into the air, he said in a loud voice, "Hello, Kirsten! It's good to have you back. Or, somewhat back. Don't worry. We'll have you back in one piece in no time." To me, he said quietly, "I'm not sure that their goal regarding the killing of her body would have changed since then, but we can't take any chances. We should try to find her—her body."

I stared at him a moment. "Professor, she's probably sitting right there in the back seat."

He glanced back, at the empty air. "Of course. Hmm, you're probably distraught, my dear, but take heart. Your body's not dead until we confirm it so."

I rolled my eyes. "Never mind. Do you have any ideas? Zorba has no clue where the Apostles would have gone."

He tapped his chin. "Perhaps it's time," he muttered.

"What?"

He looked at me, and his confidence had returned. "Perhaps it's time to go to the meeting place."

"What are you talking about?"

"Steinbeck didn't explain?"

"No, not at all. What meeting place?"

"Steinbeck had suggested a place to meet in case there was trouble, in case we found ourselves—"

"Steinbeck told you this?" I interrupted, shaking my head in confusion.

"Well, he couldn't actually speak to me. He induced it through my subconscious, like you did back in the house. Of course, I didn't exactly know it was John Steinbeck at the time—"

"Professor."

"Yes?"

"Let's go."

"Right," he agreed, starting the engine.

The meeting place was a coffee shop in Del Mar, which made sense, since Steinbeck would have wanted to stay close to my launching point. He wouldn't have known at the time where they were taking Kirsten. As we drove, I asked the professor yet again about his original contact with Steinbeck. He glanced at me, and nodded his head a little, as though he too had decided that it was time to talk. "I think that Steinbeck must have been watching me. I wondered about this at first, but then realized that it might have been my research into Exiguus. People in the overlay would have understood the importance of those documents, and would have noticed anybody that showed an interest in them. I think that it may have been him who put the original idea in my head that a modern-day transfer was possible in the first place—"

"They call it Halfway, and it's an ascension, not a transfer," I reminded him.

"Oh, yes. I've been thinking about it in my own terms so long, it's hard to change."

"But I still don't understand. Why would Steinbeck go to the trouble of maneuvering you into believing that ascensions were possible in the first place?"

The professor looked at me so long, I was afraid he would have an accident. "Because of you," he finally said, turning his attention back to the road.

"Me?"

He just looked ahead.

I remembered what the Nobel laureate author had said when I first met him behind the mansion. He had talked about my latent abilities. "Steinbeck told me that there was more to this than I realized. He said that with time, I'd understand. Do you know what that was all about?"

"You remember the party where you first met him?"

"Of course. The Koyaanisqatsi party, but I didn't know it was him."

"He had been following you. He had suspicions about you, but I think that was the moment when he decided that you were special. It was not too long after the party that I started to get ideas—his ideas—about the possibility of transfers . . . of ascensions. I would expect that by now you would have noticed a difference between yourself and others in Halfway House."

"It's just Halfway, not Halfway House," I said, not sure if he was joking. I hadn't had a moment to think about the bigger picture, but I began to see just how odd I was. "I can influence living people," I observed.

He looked at me and raised an eyebrow.

"Even strangers, people who aren't waiting for direction like you. It takes a long time for Wops to learn that, and even then, their effect is weak until they've spent time in heaven. Zorba has to smash his head against a person just to infer a vague notion."

Clintock nodded. He was expecting exactly something like this.

"I stuck my head through the window," I added, remembering that as well.

"When it was closed?"

"Yeah, right through the glass. Only heavenites can do that."

"Don't forget that you can return," he reminded me. "Nobody's done that in over a thousand years."

"Huh," I concluded. That about summed it up.

But then. . . . "I guess it was good luck that Kirsten ascended when she did," I observed. "For Steinbeck, that is."

The professor's brow furrowed. I figured that this was an unpleasant subject, since he probably felt guilty about her.

"Here we are," he said brightly with what could have been relief.

As he pulled onto a side street to find a parking spot, I suddenly felt an odd sense of foreboding. "You feel that?" I asked.

The professor pulled into a spot and thought a moment. "Ah, there. Yes. Your friend must be communicating something. The feeling portends trouble."

I sighed. "I'd better go see what's up."

This was becoming second nature. Less than a minute later, I opened my eyes to find a face staring at me from a few inches away. The head was protruding through the window next to me, and it belonged to Jim Jones.

Chapter 13

Jim Jones's eyes went wide, and he pulled away, sliding partway back through the window. He seemed as surprised as I was.

"That's a good trick," he observed, regaining his composure.

I was sitting on my own comatose lap, and had no room to move. I looked behind me, and Zorba and Kirsten sat staring at us. Without saying anything, Zorba pointed out towards the sidewalk. Standing there in a small group, were three men and two women. They seemed perfectly normal, except that they hadn't been there when I closed my eyes, and more telling, they were looking me in the eye.

"I see you brought some of your gang," I observed, a little surprised at my own boldness.

"You mean members of the Flock," he corrected waving vaguely in their direction. "They're ready to help. Others are on the way."

"Help with what?"

"Regain her flesh," he said pointing. His hand was outside the window, but it was obvious he was indicating Kirsten who sat silently staring, waiting to find out what this charismatic intruder was up to. Zorba would have told her who he was in the minutes before my ascension.

"You're going to help us," I challenged skeptically. "The last time I saw you, you wanted to steal her body."

He shrugged, and it was a gesture in slow motion, as the glass resisted his movement. "Circumstances change. John asked for a favor."

"John? John Steinbeck?"

"None other."

"Wait," Kirsten interrupted from the backseat. "Are you talking about *the* John Steinbeck? The author?"

"I'll explain later," I said.

"This isn't exactly comfortable for either of us," Jones suggested. "Why don't you come outside?" He pulled his head all the way back through the window and stood waiting.

I looked at Zorba and Kirsten. "What do you think?"

Their replies tripped over each other. Kirsten remarked that Jones seemed like a nice enough man, and Zorba suggested waiting until hell froze over.

I'd obviously have to break the tie. "How would he know to come here if John hadn't told him?" I challenged. Kirsten agreed and Zorba argued. I was wishing that Kirsten be a little less sympathetic towards the mass-murdering SOB. "Oh hell," I finally concluded. "We don't know where they took the corpus, and Steinbeck's not here. I don't see that we have much choice."

I was going to have the professor open his door, but he was already on top of it, apparently tightly tuned to my every wish. He got out and held the door, waiting. I climbed out, and Kirsten and Zorba followed, but I "told" the professor to wait for my go-ahead before climbing back inside.

Jones didn't miss this last. As the three of us walked around the back of the car, he said, "You don't trust me, do you?"

"Do you blame me?" I asked.

He smiled, and it seemed genuine. "No. I would do the same. And I understand that it's up to me to change your mind."

Jones introduced the five members of the Flock, and we shook hands all around. They had normal Bob-Dave-Jane names that I failed to tag permanently with a face. It was like meeting colleagues of a friend at a social lunch, except with a surrealistic bent, as the bodies of these smiling people had been dead for over thirty years, and they were here to help gain back another that was still alive. At least, I hoped it was.

I noticed that Jones continued holding Kirsten's hand as he introduced himself. I didn't catch what they said, as Zorba pulled me aside. "You're not serious," he scolded in a whisper.

"What do you suggest?" I challenged.

He wagged his head in consternation. "Anything but teaming up with Jones."

"But that's the problem: there *isn't* an anything."

He glared at me, searching for an argument.

"Look," I said, "I'll ask him exactly what Steinbeck told him. Maybe we can get an idea if he's lying."

When I asked him, he glanced at Zorba, who cringed and took a step back, as though expecting a blow. "The esteemed writer told me that you might show up here in need of help. You'd probably be hitching with an elderly man. I was to give you the message that he would try to meet up with you later. He wanted to thank you for coming to his aid."

He stood waiting with his arms folded across on his chest. Except for the last part, he could have made it all up just by looking at us as we arrived. "That was all?"

"Just that you had stomped on Boney's toes when you rescued him, and now we are all going to have to keep an eye out for you."

I glanced at Zorba. It sure sounded legitimate. "His toes weren't the only casualties; I also squashed his head. But, why would you want to help us?"

He held out his hand towards the small group of his Flock who stood listening, as though offering them up as a best example. "You're either under Boney's thumb, or avoiding it."

The unspoken logical connection was that if you were avoiding it, then you were in league with others who were as well. I didn't have a chance to confirm this, as a car came in to park behind the professor, unaware, of course, of the small mob scrambling to get out of its way. Jones and I ended up standing together on the sidewalk. "We should go," he said. "Every minute counts."

It seemed that every minute had counted since I got the call from Professor Clintock. "Where to?"

"The lair," he replied impressively.

"Whose lair?"

"The Apostles of Irenaeus, of course."

I looked at Zorba, but he shook his head and shrugged. "They have a lair?" I asked. "Does it include a pit full of snakes?"

"You joke, but they're not to be taken lightly. There's nobody quite so dangerous as those deluded by promises of metaphysical salvation."

I looked to see if he was serious, but his eyes were earnest; if he caught the complete irony of what he, of all people, was saying, he hid it well.

On the other hand, I thought, if his followers were deluded, it was only about the nature of the after-world promised them. "Okay. Where is it?"

"Wait here," he instructed, and took off at a trot down the sidewalk and around the corner.

"Where's he going?" I asked the Flock as a group.

"Probably to get the bus," one of the women said that I thought might be named Janet.

"He has a bus?"

"Of course not. It belongs to a dropout."

I was trying to imagine the connection between Jim Jones and somebody who never finished high school when Zorba explained, "A dropout is a former candidate. For one reason or another, Boney decided to stop pursuing them, and sometimes a rogue will pick them up. They're already tuned in, so to speak."

Janet pointed, and I saw an ancient, decrepit VW bus come around the corner spewing black exhaust. As it got closer, I saw that Jones was inside, squatting next to the driver, who actually did fit his own label. The man must have been at least sixty, and most of his long hair was pulled back into a white ponytail. Most. The rest hung about his head in a frizzy aura of unacknowledged aging.

"That could have been you," I said to Zorba. "He's about your age."

My friend snorted. "Maybe if I had fallen off my bike and suffered brain damage."

"I don't know. I think we're maybe looking at forty years of smoking pot. You smoked pot."

"I never said that."

"You grew up in the sixties."

"True."

I could see Jones talking to the aged hippie, and the van stopped in the street, double-parked next to the professor. The dropout got out, opened the rear door, and then began slowly waving his arms up and out with cupped hands. It looked like he was maybe trying to whoosh out the smell of his pot smoke. "What's he doing?" I asked.

"It's probably a ritual that Jones taught him," Zorba explained. "Candidates and dropouts need some rationale to justify in their minds the things they do that benefit us. In this case, his little ritual gives us time to get into the van."

"That's rational?" I asked.

"In his mind it is," Zorba replied as we watched the Flock file inside, while the dropout stepped back, placed his palms together in front of his chest, and closed his eyes for a moment of meditation.

"He refers to Jim as 'Noshi,'" Janet explained as she climbed in, the last of the Flock.

I realized that we were now expected to climb into the far-out-van as well. That felt rash. Professor Clintock still sat in his car, patiently awaiting instructions.

I walked over and called through the open door to Jones. "Zorba and Kirsten will go in the other car."

Jones turned and looked at me. "Still don't trust me? Have Zorba direct your driver to go to Encinitas. If we get separated, have him meet us at Moonlight Beach."

He thought that Zorba was still the communicator. Steinbeck had apparently failed to tell Jones about my abilities. "Wait for me. I'm coming with you," I said, waving Zorba and Kirsten towards the professor's car.

"Where did he say we would meet?" Zorba asked.

"Moonlight Beach, but it doesn't matter. We'll be in contact."

"How can we be in contact—"

"You'll see." I turned to Kirsten who stood silently taking it all in. "I have to leave for a bit, but Zorba will be with you until I return."

Her brow scrunched in concern. "Where are you going?"

"Not very far, but a world away." I hugged her, and she held me tight for a moment. It was the same familiar shape I had grown so used to cuddling, but this sack stuffed with socks just wasn't the same as when we had been corpus-to-corpus. This was disconcerting, and I used the discomfiture as my handle.

I gasped and opened my eyes, instantly realizing that I had just left Kirsten hugging empty air. "Sorry, love!" I called as I got out and opened the back door. I waved for the invisible two to get in, and then waited. If anybody had been watching, they would have thought me no less daft than Hippie Dropout.

Slowly, slowly, I closed the back door and leaned into the front. Professor Clintock was watching me curiously. "How's it going?" he asked. "Is John Steinbeck here?"

It was impossible to explain in five seconds. "No, but there's somebody else who's going to help us find Kirsten. Do you have your cell?" I asked, patting my pocket to make sure I had my own.

He lifted it off its cradle on the dash to show me what had been in front of my face.

"Okay, you're going to follow this van next to us," I said. "We'll stay in contact with the phones. By the way, Zorba and Kirsten are in the back seat."

"That van?" he said, pointing. "Oh, my. I'll have to put my air on re-circulate. He has a nasty emissions problem."

"Fine. Just keep your phone on."

I trotted around to the van, and opened the passenger door. The dropout looked at me with surprise. "We're going to Encinitas," I said, shooing a possible Jim Jones to the back. For good measure, I warned Jones, "I'm getting in."

"That's cool," the hippie agreed, "but how did you know I was going to Encinitas?"

"We're tuned to the same vibes," I tried.

He bought it. "That's cool . . . er, are you hip to Algonquin spirit aura?"

"Sure." What else do you say to a question like that? I tried to remember what Janet had told me. "Noshi sent me," I added.

The dropout's bloodshot eyes spread wide. "Far. Out."

On the short clap-rattle ride up the coast, I learned that the dropout's name was Tod, that Noshi was Algonquin for "father," that the spiritual guide had been talking to him for something like three years, and that about six months ago Noshi had become a lot more patient with him, but also a lot more demanding. Tod believed that this meant that his spiritual awakening had achieved a new level, but I guessed that this was when Boney gave up on him, and Jim Jones stepped in.

I also learned that Tod had lost his job as a courier a few months before. He had missed too many calls because he was servicing Noshi's bidding, mostly just driving around from one place to another. He had been sharing a small house with two other people, but they'd kicked him out when he stopped paying his share, and he now mostly lived in his van. His former house-mates did let him store most of his stuff in a shed out back, though, so he was thankful for that. Tod believed that this was a benevolent intervention on the part of Noshi.

We rumbled along in silence for a bit as we crossed the land bridge separating the San Elijo lagoon from the Pacific. Scores of surfers plied the waves on our left. San Diego's climate was benign, but only relative to the rest of the country. In winter, it regularly dipped into the forties at night, and occasionally even near freezing. Life in an ancient VW bus bordered on desperate.

Hell, it was desperate.

"You're pretty confident that Noshi exists?" I asked.

"Totally, man." He glanced at me, a wondering, almost hurt look. "You're not?" Then he remembered. "Wait, you said that he sent you. Duh, of course you believe."

I suddenly felt a pang of ominous anxiety. Watching Tod to make sure he didn't see me, I held my right hand up, middle finger extended; a communication to Jones. "But are you sure that the voice you hear is always his?" I insisted. "What spiritual purpose is served by just driving around?"

The anxiety heightened. I suddenly had an image of me standing on the sidewalk and Tod driving away in the van. Jones's message was clear. It was true, I was at the rogue's mercy.

I realized that Tod was talking, an urgent rebuttal. ". . . you have to have faith, man. You can't let the Makadewà get to you. Listen, if you're having doubts, I can hook you up with a really cool guru guy who—"

"What's that, 'Makadewà'?"

The anxiety was getting to me. I was having a hard time concentrating.

"Makadewà! Evil! I think it means black in Algonquin. This guru I know, he explains it all. It was him who got me connected with Noshi. He lives in Pacific Beach, sort of a commune, only everybody has to swear allegiance—"

I stopped listening. My head was hurting. I hadn't realized how powerful a rogue's effect could be. I hated to think what it would feel like if Boney set his mind on me. Under his thumb indeed. "Tod!"

He stopped short, staring at me.

"It's okay," I went on, trying to be more calm. "I was just . . . testing."

"You were testing me?"

"No! I was . . . testing myself. You know, every once in a while you have to reaffirm your faith."

He watched me a moment, and I could see the acceptance relax his face. "Cool. Nothing wrong with a little tune-up."

The anxiety evaporated immediately. It was like stepping from a loud, smoke-drenched room into the clear, star-filled night. I lifted my right hand and middle finger again. Just because an interrogation torturer lifts the water bucket before you completely drown doesn't earn him gratitude.

"Do you know where we're going?" Tod asked.

We were coming into Encinitas, passing the onion-shaped architecture of the Swami's yoga compound on our left.

"Not specifically."

Not specifically, as in no clue.

I looked over and was alarmed to see Tod driving with his eyes closed. "Er, are you okay?" I asked, ready to grab the wheel if he started to drift.

He opened his eyes, then stopped the van in the middle of the street and closed them again. In the rearview mirror, I saw the professor's SUV stop as well. It was pretty easy to spot with its entrails hanging out.

"All the way past Encinitas Boulevard?" Tod asked.

I started to explain again that I didn't know where we were going, before realizing that he wasn't talking to me.

A car somewhere behind us tapped its horn.

"The first right? The second? That's Third Street. The second left is . . . uh, yeah, Sylvia. That sort of turns into Neptune. Got it."

He opened his eyes and drove on.

"Noshi talks to you?" I asked. "I mean, with actual words?"

Tod had to think a moment. "Not really. It's like, if I wasn't familiar with Encinitas, we wouldn't have got it ahead of time."

"What about when you take him places . . . I mean, when he wants you to go places you've never been before?"

Tod shrugged. "He just directs—now left, now right, now park."

I imagined Tod driving around with his eyes closed waiting for Jones-cum- Noshi inspiration, and decided that I needed to watch oncoming drivers more carefully in the future.

I stopped talking. I didn't want to distract the old hippie any more than he already was. Just before we got to Neptune Avenue, though, Tod suddenly hit the brakes again. He looked puzzled, then turned to me. "There's a car following us."

"Er, yeah. It's, uh, part of Noshi's plan."

Tod didn't question this. "The parking is limited on Neptune. That driver should pull off and park on a side street."

"Noshi told you this?"

He nodded.

"What kind of trick is this?" I said to the air.

I had a vision of me getting out of the van, and Tod driving away. I wasn't sure if this was instructions, or a threat. I decided to call his bluff, and I opened my door. "I think I'll stay with the others," I announced.

Tod winced. "Hmm, anger. Not cool."

"I have Kirsten's soul," I reminded.

Tod shrugged. "Who's Kirsten?"

"That wasn't for you, it was for Jo—for Noshi."

He closed his eyes. "Noshi has your body." He opened them and looked at me, confused; he was looking at my body.

"He's referring to Kirsten's body," I explained, and then to the air, "and he doesn't *have* her body, he just knows where it is."

But he still had a point. I got out, ran back through a cloud of burned oil and unburned gasoline, and told the professor to pull off and park. I wanted to say something to Kirsten, to reassure her somehow, but to my corpus eyes, the backseat held just empty air.

I made my way back through the petrochemical fog holding my breath, and Tod drove two blocks, but there were no parking spots, so he too pulled off onto a side street. Even then, this close to the beach, he ended up squeezing into a spot too small for the bus so that his bumper partially blocked a driveway by a foot or two. When I pointed this out, he said, "Ah, this is Encinitas. They won't call the cops."

"What now?" I asked.

"We wait."

"For what? Some sign from heaven?"

I realized that this would actually be true if Jones hadn't been kicked out of heaven.

"Dunno, we just wait."

I looked around, wondering what a lair of religious fanatics looked like. To Buddhist monks, it might be a Pentecostal church. To Pentecostals, it might be a Mosque. One man's devout worship is another man's fanatic delusion.

It wasn't all relative, I decided. A thousand people who would commit mass suicide were fanatics in anybody's book. I had to remember who I was dealing with, here.

"What was Noshi like before he changed six months ago?" I asked. Any insight into both Jones and Boney was worth plumbing. I wasn't sure how much Jones was going to let Tod expound, but it was worth a shot.

Tod hesitated. I could see that he wasn't sure if he wanted to gossip about a superior entity who could be listening at any time. He gave a little shrug. "At the beginning, like three years ago, Noshi was cool . . . I mean, he's still cool, of course, but back then he was a different cool. Real gentle, man. Patient. But I think he got, like, frustrated. I'm not a sharp blade. I was in my younger days. I went to Berkley for two years. I just got moldy with age."

He went silent, exploring his own world within.

"Pot will do that," I offered. I knew that I wasn't in a position to criticize, but hiding from a simple truth seemed almost worse than bad manners.

"I know," he agreed. "Some wines improve with age, but some just turn to vinegar."

I tried to understand what he was saying. "You think you would have . . . gotten moldy even without smoking a lot of pot?"

He seemed to contemplate that. "Yeah. Maybe, maybe not. But what I do know is that I had a satisfying life. Pot has been a good friend. We've gotten through some rough times together."

I wondered how many times the pot was the instigator as well as the solace, but this time I held my tongue.

"In any case," he went on, "Noshi let up on me a few months ago, and we've been laid-back pals ever since. Man, it's like he's two different dudes."

I looked at him. The words were right there, ready to roll off my tongue. But I didn't. Instead I poked at Jones in a different way. "Maybe the first Noshi was trying to groom you for some purpose," I said. I expected some punishment, but my skull contained only me.

"If he was, I sure disappointed him."

"Maybe Noshi isn't right all the time," I offered. Still no retribution.

I wasn't sure if Tod's expression was alarm or epiphany.

I checked the time. We'd been sitting there for over five minutes. "Any status update?" I asked.

Tod closed his eyes. "Nope."

"Can we get an update?" I said to the air.

Tod just watched me. He was getting used to my direct verbal approach to Noshi.

"Well?" I asked.

Tod closed his eyes and shook his head.

So. If he was going to be that way. "Tod, Noshi isn't who you think he is."

I braced, but there was no response.

What the hell. "Noshi was indeed two different entities," I continued, "and neither of them were ever an Algonquin native."

Tod was staring, open-mouthed. "Further, in the future, you should question every notion you get from him. Ask for a reason."

Nothing. Damn.

Something was restraining Jones. There was only one person who could do that. And it wasn't even really a person. Whatever was going on, I needed to get back to the others.

"I don't like this," I said, giving him my cell phone. "Call the contact named Clintock if Jones—damn! I mean if Noshi re-surfaces."

"Where are you going?"

"To check on the others," I replied, opening the door.

"Hey!"

I turned back.

"I don't even know your name," he said.

I smiled. "I'm Jordan," I replied, shaking his hand.

"Glad to meet you, Jordan. Listen, you be careful, man."

"Why would you say that?"

He didn't know about all the crap that was swirling around in both worlds.

"I don't know. Just a sense. You're the first person I ever met that understood about Noshi, and something tells me that you and him aren't the best of buddies."

"We'll see. If he follows through on his end of a bargain, I'll be his devoted friend."

He looked me in the eye. "You know, Abrahamic tradition teaches that, other than the covenants, God doesn't make bargains; they're the tool of the devil." He winked. "On the other hand, I don't buy into the literal Bible."

I nodded. "I'll keep that in mind."

You can't judge a hippie by his blood-shot eyes, I decided as I closed the door and ran down the sidewalk.

Chapter 14

I felt relieved to find the professor peacefully dozing in his violated Explorer, but realized that this sense of ease was not warranted, since the trouble would be invisible to my corpus senses. He jerked awake when I opened his door. "It's you," he stated, surprised.

"We parked a couple of blocks away. I just came back to check on things. You thought I took off and left you here?"

"No. I just thought that you had transitioned into the overlay and already came back."

I gave up trying to teach him the proper terminology. "Why would you think that?"

"I thought you told me to open the back door. I assumed you were back there with Kirsten and your friend."

Uh, oh. "How long ago was this?"

"Not too long after we parked here. I figured that you must have transitioned as soon as you left. In fact, it was a little strange that you would have returned so quickly. I remember thinking that your skill at moving back and forth between the overlay and normal space must be progressing, since—"

"Professor!"

"Eh?"

"I don't want to be rude, but I'm worried. The person who had you open the door must have been Zorba, and he wouldn't have left without a good reason. I think I should check it out."

I ran around and climbed into the passenger seat, what was becoming my standard launch pad. As soon as I settled in, though, I was draped in a sense of alarm. Something was very wrong. I could tell it was Zorba, nothing so specific as the sound of his voice, but the general sense was the essence of *him*, the Zorba I had come to know.

Just as I got a handle on the source, however, the alarm faded, and was gone. In its place was a new sense, an insistent notion that I should go back and be with Tod. Maybe Zorba knew something. Maybe Tod was in trouble. He couldn't be harmed by anyone from Halfway—at least that I knew—but if Jones was right, then the Apostles of Irenaeus were somewhere close by, and they could most definitely be a danger to a corpus.

No. I didn't trust it. This new warning was not Zorba, in the same way that I was confident that it was him initially, I was equally confident this new imperative was not from him.

Oh, hell. I closed my eyes and tried to relax, tried to let my spirit rise. Instead of calming quiet, though, my head was filled with a turmoil of apprehension. I decided that it must be Boney, and this just inched up the volume of distress.

I needed an anchor, a safe haven in the storm to focus my attention. Kirsten. My beautiful fiancée. I let my imagination go back to the times we lay together in silence, just floating in each other's loving grace. Quietly, almost humming to himself, I heard the professor intone the ancient palindrome: s*ator—arepo—tenet—opera—rotas.*

I knew I had ascended. I opened my eyes, preparing to scramble into the back to defend against the leader of heaven, but there was a face hovering just inches from mine. It was so close, it took a moment to realize who it was. Again.

"Jones!" I shouted.

He pulled away, back to the rear seat from where he had been leaning forward.

I was sitting on my corpus, hard as a rock, and uncomfortable. Struggling within the tight space, I crawled into the back seat, where

Blaine C. Readler

Jones and Kirsten made room for me. Zorba was squatting in the luggage area, scowling and angry.

"What the hell are you doing here?" I demanded of Jones.

His smile was condescending. "Take it easy, there, friend. Just checking on the troops."

"How did you get here?"

"He got out of the sheep bus when you stopped to talk to us," Zorba informed sourly.

"What happened to the big mission to the Apostles' lair?"

"Haste usually creates delay. We need a coordinated plan."

"What am I? Chopped liverwurst?"

His condescending smile broadened into a grin. "I think you mean chopped liver."

"What-*ever*!" I exclaimed, realizing that I sounded hysterical. "How can you make a plan without *me*?"

"I would have brought you up to speed. You weren't really available, you know."

"You had returned to your body," Kirsten explained, trying to be helpful.

I didn't want her to be helpful. I wanted her to be mad at Jones, like I was.

"It was you who wanted our very special comrade here to be isolated in a separate car," he reminded me.

"I don't think he's talking about me," Zorba observed sarcastically.

I ignored Zorba's remark. "For good reason, apparently," I concluded. "I'm surprised you didn't bring the Kool Aid."

"That's unfair," Kirsten said.

"Un-*fair*!"

"And mean."

"Do you know who this *is*?"

"I know perfectly well. This is the man who shepherded over nine hundred people to Halfway."

I just looked at her, my mouth hanging open. I didn't even know how to begin to respond to that.

Jones relieved me of my burden. "We should be going. Boney's reinforcements will be arriving soon."

"So, now we're in the haste mode?"

162

"No. My own reinforcements should be here by now, and there's no need to wait any longer."

"I still don't know the plan," I protested.

To Kirsten, he said, "Can you explain it? I'll meet you at the bus."

He leaned forward, and Clintock jerked upright, got out, and opened the rear door for the invisible guest.

Kirsten explained that Jim Jones was gathering his flock, both spirit and body. The Halfway followers would create a distraction and lure away most of the Soldats that would be guarding the lair. We would go in, find Kirsten's corpus, and Jones's flesh-and-blood followers would then come in to carry her away.

"What about the Apostles?" I asked. "They have guns."

"He's not concerned," she replied. "He believes that his followers can handle them."

"Like he wasn't concerned in 1978 about the congressman that was murdered, or his thousand followers who might have been ending their existence as far as he knew," I observed.

Her eyes flashed anger. "That was a long time ago. You don't know that he even had any involvement with that politician's death, and as for his followers, well the proof is in the pudding."

"Hey! Who's side are you on? He tried to kill me!"

Kirsten turned to Zorba who seemed amused by our spat. "Did he? Did Jim really try to kill him?" she asked.

"He had him by the throat twice."

"But did he actually try to kill him?"

Zorba looked at me and gave a little apology shrug. "If Jones had wanted to kill Jordan, he could have done it instantly both times."

"He was going to let me be crushed in a wrecked car!" I protested. "And since when did he become 'Jim'?"

Kirsten didn't answer. As far as she was concerned, there was no point.

"He's just a philandering playboy," I lobbed, embarrassed even as the words left my mouth.

Normally Kirsten would just ignore further jibes once she crossed the no-point line, but this one was so outrageous that she threw me a scathing sidelong glance.

"Maybe we should go," Zorba offered as an arbitration.

"You two go," I groused. "I'll bring the professor up to speed and follow in a few minutes."

I was frustrated and angry with both myself and Kirsten. But she leaned over and gave me a kiss. "You're the one I'm going to marry," she said, climbing out the door that Clintock still held open.

The anger washed away. She had a way of healing wounds instantly and effortlessly. I only wished that the kiss had been flesh-on-flesh instead of what served as an ethereal token substitute.

I thought that I might have to muster back some of the contentious feelings to descend, but I found that after I closed my eyes, I simply willed myself back, and instantly felt the heavy mass of a molecular existence.

I told Clintock what had happened and realized that, not only did Jones not talk about the professor's role in the pending assault, but I didn't even yet know the actual location of the lair. I concluded by simply suggesting that he stay tuned for more updates. He looked at me solemnly and put his hand on my shoulder. "You know why Napoleon has kidnapped Kirsten—her body, I mean."

I shrugged. "She's a hostage. He wants her spirit."

"That may be, but I wonder if there's more? After all, he had his Apostles take her body even before you'd freed her spirit."

"I don't understand. You think he's trying to get at Jones?"

He just looked at me with one eyebrow riding high.

"What?" It came to me. "*Me?*"

He lifted his shoulders at the implied possibility.

"I know I've pissed him off, but why would he go to all this trouble just to get at me?"

"Steinbeck recognized your special talents. That's why he enlisted you. Why wouldn't Bonaparte?"

"I can understand why he wants Kirsten recruiting for him, but why me? I'm a terrible people-person. I couldn't sell my own mom on the idea of ascending."

"Bush nearly ruined the US economy trying to get at Saddam Hussein, but I don't think he had in mind offering the Iraqi leader a cabinet position."

I blinked. I felt like an idiot. I could feel the chill on my face as the blood drained away. "Bush dragged Saddam out of a filthy hole and hanged him."

Clintock nodded in resigned agreement. "At some point, Bonaparte was bound to realize the extent of your abilities. He wants Kirsten on his side, but there's a crossover threshold where killing you is worth losing her cooperation."

"And she becomes bait," I finished for him.

He sighed.

ж ж ж

I arrived back at the hippie bus to find that Jones's Flock had swelled. Eight bright color polyester-clad people milled around the ancient vehicle, five men and three women. Kirsten and Zorba came over to meet me. "Glad to see you made it back," Zorba said.

I knew what he meant. "The ascension was pretty easy."

In fact, with all the practice I was getting, the back and forth was becoming old hat. "Do we know where the Disciple's lair is?" I asked.

"Jones has gone ahead to scope it out. He hasn't told us yet."

I walked over to the bus where Tod sat listening to music, oblivious to the Halfway activity. I was surprised to hear that he was playing Pat Metheney; I was expecting the Electric Prunes or Strawberry Alarm Clock. Smoke swirled out of the open window, and I saw that he was holding the last remnants of a joint between thumb and forefinger. I also noticed that I couldn't smell the pungent odor, even though my face was framed in the opening. Apparently functional olfactory nerves weren't part of the Halfway plan.

Bummer.

I wondered if he remembered the injunction I had delivered about questioning Jones's commands.

He nodded.

I stepped back in surprise. I wasn't sure if he'd reacted to my thought, or was just moving to the music. I moved closer and directed a thought to him to change the music. He started to reach forward in compliance, but stopped and pulled his hand back. "Why?" he asked the air.

Good lad! I was pleased to see that he might no longer be Jones's unquestioning slave.

He tilted his head, as though he'd heard something.

"What's going on!"

It was Jones. He was striding towards the bus, obviously upset. I saw that the Flock had stopped gabbing and were staring at me.

"Listening to Pat Metheney," I replied.

His glare moved from me to Tod. "Turn the damn music off!" he directed.

Tod looked puzzled. He started to reach forward again, but stopped. "Noshi?" he asked.

Jones threw me a menacing glance. "Of course. Now turn off the racket."

Tod seemed to consider this. Maybe he was just sorting out the intrusive thought. He finally lifted his chin and said, "Why?"

His erstwhile master clenched his jaw and gave me a withering stare. "Laugh now, funny boy, while you can." He looked around at his Halfway followers watching the disruption, seeing their leader of decades, the man who had convinced them to abandon their flesh, now tussling with his heavenly powers perhaps compromised. His face softened, and the smile he gave his Flock was the very meaning of confidence and grace as he launched into a little speech about the imminent test and ultimate proof of their resolve and commitment to him.

I had to hand it to him, the man had the gift of the preacher and politician.

Their instructions were simple: wait five hundred—I learned later that this meant counts, since Wops didn't have watches—go to the address up the street that he gave them, and try, however they could, to break in. Ideally, the Soldats on guard would chase them, in which case they should entice the soldiers on, making sure they didn't give up and return to the lair. I had witnessed the strength of the Soldats, and I was thinking that it was rather naive to think that the Halfway Flock members could get away from them in the first place.

Jones waved to me to follow him. He told Kirsten to come as well, but Zorba should remain at the bus.

"Isn't that backwards?" I asked. "I think Kirsten should stay here where it's safe, and let Zorba come along."

The Flock leader looked at me as though he hadn't thought about this. "It will be easier if we can get Kirsten back into her corpus right away—you can *do* this, right?"

"Of course," I lied. I couldn't bear telling her the truth yet.

"Also," he added, "Boney could show up anytime, and you wouldn't want her here unprotected."

No arguments over that one. "What about Zorba? Why does he have to stay here?"

"Because I said so."

He was getting impatient, and I knew that I had to pick my battles. "Sorry," I said to my friend.

Zorba laughed. "Sorry that you're not dragging me into Boney's lair full of both Soldats and Apostles of Irenaeus? You can owe me."

Jones led us out to the main street, and half a block south to a set of beach access stairs. The coast from the San Diego harbor north to Oceanside is a series of fifty-foot bluffs cut every few miles by estuaries, Moonlight Beach being one such. Here, north of the city park, the "beach" houses on the west side of Neptune Avenue sat perched at the edge of the bluff, some even hovering over the edge on spidery bracings. Besides Moonlight Beach, the city of Encinitas provided half a dozen public access points down the bluffs to the beaches, consisting of steep stairs, some wood, some cement. Jones took us down a seemingly endless series of switchback cement steps. Stairs are usually punctuated periodically by the distance between average floors, so descending the fifty feet seemed endless, like we were descending into the bowels of the Earth. After learning that there is a very real place called heaven, this feeling proved disquieting.

We finally stepped out onto beach sand, though, and followed Jones north past surfers in various stages of preparation or departure. I wondered what we would have done had we happened to meet some surfers on their way up. Their boards would have been effectively solid steel plows to our insubstantial Halfway forms, and we would have had no choice but to scramble back up in full retreat. Life in Halfway was perpetually tenuous and fraught.

It was strange in the extreme to walk on sand that my whole life had been soft and accommodating, a virtual foot massage, but now met my shoes with a surface as hard as granite bedrock. The expectation of penetration was an illusion that I couldn't shake. I could only imagine that I was perhaps in Greenland where the sand had been saturated with water, and then frozen solid.

I was so enthralled with the illusory phenomenon that I bumped into Jones when he stopped. Here, an outcrop from the bluff forced us to move closer to the water, and Jones hesitated, watching the ocean as though expecting a submarine to suddenly surface.

"What's wrong?" Kirsten asked next to me.

I shrugged, but Jones pointed at a particularly large wave that was beginning to recede and he then sprinted forward, around the jumble of boulders blocking our path.

Kirsten started off, but I grabbed her arm. "No, wait."

"What for?"

The next wave plowed into the one receding, and the two wrestled themselves into a chaos of foam and random spray, like spittle from the flummoxed sea. I remembered what the droplet from the sprinkler in front of Roberto's had done to me. "We don't want to get hit with spray," I explained.

"Hmm . . . ah," she murmured, absorbing some implications of a fragile Halfway life.

The memory of the water bullet was still painfully fresh, and I waited as one, then two, and then three more waves climbed up the sand and retreated. I realized that I didn't know exactly what I was waiting *for*. When the next wave began retreating, I took off, waving for Kirsten to follow. We crossed a small pool of tidal water, not even an inch deep. At first, I thought that the water felt spongy, but when I stopped a moment, I saw that it was more like quicksand. I slowly sank until my soles touched the sand beneath. Lifting my feet to move on was like pulling boots from deep mud. I imagined that I could run right across a calm lake, but I wouldn't want to stop for even an instant.

We caught up with Jones, and soon after, he stopped. I followed his gaze upward, and saw that one of the houses above had added a private stairway down the face of the bluff. Ten feet from the beach, though it stopped. The last section was folded up and back. The residents could let it down from above, but random members of the public were denied access from below.

"This is it?" I asked. "The lair?"

Jones nodded without looking at me.

"It's a house," I objected.

Now he looked at me, and the look wondered if I was an idiot. "What did you expect? A cave with bats streaming out?"

"But it looks so . . . normal." In fact, compared to the multi-million dollar custom architected neighbors, it looked downright plebeian. A screened porch extended a couple of feet over the cliff's edge facing west, but the paint on the window frames was peeling, and two screens were torn, one hanging out like a gasping tongue.

"It's not normal," he replied. "It's Boney's San Diego base."

"I thought that was the Rancho Santa Fe mansion."

He sighed impatiently at my endless questions. "That was a resting place for her," he said, gesturing at Kirsten who stood listening.

"Why not bring her here?"

He glared at me menacingly, as though to intimidate me into silence. "You're not impressed; why would she have been?"

"Boney was trying to impress her with luxury living in a swanky neighborhood?"

"What the hell do you think?"

Suddenly the sound of shouting dribbled down from above. Jones's Flock was launching their attack.

"How do we get up?" I asked.

Jones didn't answer. He stood staring up at the rickety stairway. He lifted his arm and pointed. I looked up. One of the Apostles had opened a door and stood on a landing far above gazing down. I saw that he had a gun, and was pointing it at us.

"Shit!" I cried, pulling Kirsten behind me. It was reflex. If a drop of water could knock me to the ground, I sure as heck wasn't going to stop a bullet.

"Take it easy," Jones admonished. "He's under control."

The Apostle put the gun down and started down the stairs, and that's when I saw the Soldat behind him, speaking instructions. He waved when he saw us, and Jones waved back.

"What's this!" I exclaimed, spinning to face our guide.

"I said, take it easy. He's with me. You didn't think we were going to just waltz in on our own, did you?"

I had thought about it, and had worried about the waltzing part. I was actually relieved.

The Apostle—he looked barely old enough to be out of high school—hesitated when he came to the folded-up stair segment, and Jones's inside mole had to work on the boy with elevated urgency before he undid the latch and let the stairs down using a rope. The boy came down and stepped out into the sand, probably wondering why his god had brought him out onto the beach.

"Thanks, Donald," Jones said to the Soldat who followed behind. "I owe you."

"Damn right you do. You're going to start by having your people watch over my niece." To the Apostle who had turned to start back up the stairs, he said, "Pray."

The boy turned back and fell to his knees in the sand, head bowed, hands clasped at his chest.

Donald looked at me and then Kirsten. "That's her, all right."

"Let's go," Jones urged suddenly, waving his hands for us to climb the stairs. He seemed to want to curtail discussion about Kirsten.

When Kirsten and I got to the porch landing, we waited for Jones and Donald. The view of the ocean was spectacular, but my attention was drawn inside. The screened porch was small, just enough room for some lounge chairs. Through the windows on the inside, I saw a large, open area that was once a kitchen, dining, and living room combined. Now, however, it looked like an upscale sports bar, because high along the walls on three sides were mounted half a dozen large-screen TVs, and each was alive with the shifting, flashing scenes targeted for the attention-deficit generation. Unlike a sports bar, though, none of the channels were sports. Instead, each screen contained a talking head time-multiplexed with scenes of war, natural disasters, and either happy or outraged citizens. Underneath it all, like a continually unfolding verdict of our race, scrolled ticker-information.

"The world's news," Kirsten whispered, awed by the unexpected flood of visual data.

"They can't open a book," I remarked. "They can read the front of a newspaper but the rest is buried inside an impenetrable block of stone."

I marveled at the perseverance that must have been required of Boney's Soldats to convince the Apostles that God wanted them to build a cable news equivalent of NASA's ground-control center. Arrayed around the perimeter were what appeared to be simple altars, but I guessed that these served as viewing posts for Boney's Soldats, front row seating where they were safe from an inadvertent crushing by a blind Apostle.

Jones led us through the room, past a handful of unaware Apostles who sat in chairs staring at the screens. We were closer now to the Flock's attack out front, and it seemed surrealistic that the Apostles could remain so completely oblivious to the battle raging.

As we were leaving the news arena, Kirsten clutched my elbow and pointed out a window where a Soldat had grabbed a Flock member by his wash-n-wear polyester shirt and spun him around, causing him to trip and fall to the ground. The Soldat then pounced on him, wrapping his arm around his neck. The hideous look on the man's face as it began to expand like an overfilled balloon testified to the Soldat's intention to dispatch him. Jones's attention was drawn by our diversion, and he yelled a curse, as though he could countermand the Soldat. At that moment, though, another Soldat, apparently of higher rank, sprang into view and rapped his knuckle across his comrade's head, sending his beret flying. An instant later, the Flock member rolled away clutching at his bruised throat.

"Come on," Jones ordered, sounding disgusted.

He took us down a short hall, and stopped in front of a closed door, then waved impatiently for us to move to the side. Following behind us, Donald was shepherding the same Apostle who had let down the stairs. The boy opened the door, and he and his puppeteer walked in. Jones held out his hand for us to follow. I took his grand smile to be a celebration of victory; he had indeed gotten us in. As I stepped across the doorstep, I had a fleeting moment of doubt, but inside, the bedroom held a single-sized bed, and lying on the bed was Kirsten's body. Another moment of panic passed once I saw her chest rise perceptively with a breath.

I heard a soft sigh, like air escaping from a tire when the valve-stem is removed. I put my arm around Kirsten's shoulders to steady her. "You didn't see it at the hospital?" I asked.

She shook her head, entranced at the sight of herself. "They led me away before I could look back."

The moment had come that I had been dreading without realizing it. I might be expected to wave my hand and somehow merge Kirsten with Kirsten. But the plan called for Jones's flesh-and-blood followers to storm the house and carry her away. I was desperate for them to arrive before either Jones or Kirsten asked me to perform my magic.

Jones's smile had melted, and he was frowning. "Where the hell is he?" he muttered.

"Are they coming up the back stairs as well?" I asked, assuming that he was referring to the leader of his corpus followers.

He shushed me, and waved to Donald. The accomplice Soldat led the boy, who had been staring at Kirsten with a little too much admiration for my taste, out to the hall. "Have him close the door," Jones called, and the boy's hand reached in and swung the door shut.

That seemed unnecessary. "Aren't we, like, trapped in here?" I asked.

"Shut up," Jones retorted, and looked up, as though entreating God.

Kirsten and I exchanged alarmed glances.

"Where's your other followers?" I asked, but Jones ignored me.

I was in full blown panic mode now. I knew better, but I turned to the door and yanked at the doorknob. The Apostle boy hadn't even latched it, but it might as well have been cemented in place. A little scream from Kirsten spun me around. There in the middle of the room looking us over was Boney.

PART IV

BULLETS AND KNIVES

Chapter 15

"Well done, Jones," the little colonel said.

The truth slammed home. "You bastard!" I cried as I tried to grab the traitor Jones by his shirt, but he knocked me away with one sweep of his arm.

I bounced off a dresser, and Kirsten helped me get up. "You sold us out!" I spat. "Why? What could Boney give you that's worth that much? You can't use money!"

"He wants to return home," Boney explained, watching Jones.

"Back to heaven?" I asked.

It actually made sense. It made so much sense, I hated myself for not seeing it earlier.

Boney glanced at me darkly before returning his attention back to Jones. He didn't like it referred to that way.

"Not only back," Jones stated carefully, returning Boney's stare, "but with my own domain."

"The city limits of Houston," Boney agreed. "For fifty years."

"Autonomous," Jones added.

Boney's eyes narrowed.

"Your Soldats enter only by permission."

"Only by prior notice. That was the deal."

They were staring each other down, sparring the last details of the negotiation. Intent on their battle of wills, they seemed to have forgotten about Kirsten and me. I whispered to her that I would create a distraction, but Boney heard me and turned his attention our way, which was just as well, since I didn't know what Kirsten could have done anyway.

"But to the business at hand," he said, looking me in the eye. He glanced at Jones and said, "But first, a little housecleaning. Don't go away."

He took a breath and his eyes seemed to go unfocused as he shivered a little. His body became indistinct, like someone walking away into the fog, then transparent for just an instant; I could see the poster on the wall behind him and a spray bottle of window cleaner on the dresser. And then, as the concentration pulling his brow together tightened, he disappeared.

"You worm!" Kirsten suddenly yelled, and ran at Jones, fists flying.

I wasn't able to catch her, but the Flock leader took her rage in stride. He grabbed her left arm and waited a moment as she covered him in meaningless punches before grabbing her other wrist as well.

"Let her go, Jones," I demanded, walking over and putting my face up to his in an attempt to be threatening.

He smiled, and then quickly tipped his head forward, which sent me falling backwards against the dresser. My back slammed painfully against the spray bottle and I fell to the floor. Before I could pick myself up, Kirsten landed on me, and we helped each other to our feet.

A loud discussion rumbled just beyond the door. One of the voices was Boney's and I thought the other might be Donald. This was confirmed a moment later when they both appeared out of thin air in the middle of the room. The Soldat didn't look happy at all.

"Come on, Boney," Jones pleaded. "You got what you wanted."

The French general shook his head. "You and I had a deal. This man, though, has betrayed me."

"It was all part of the plan!"

Boney wasn't buying it. "He didn't know this. Loyalty isn't the important thing; it's the only thing. Without it, there is no honor, and chaos reigns."

Donald's eyes were wild with terror now as Boney grasped him by the neck with one hand. With the other hand, he pinched the corner of the dresser and pulled away a length of the taffy-like strand that Steinbeck had called heaven's thread. Donald began thrashing, but Boney quickly wrapped the otherworldly extrusion around the Soldat, binding his arms against his sides. The poor man pleaded for mercy, but Boney ignored him and calmly continued turning the seemingly inexhaustible material around and around until he had formed a veritable cocoon from his waist to his shoulders, rendering him completely bound. Boney then reached over and pulled away a second string, and Donald began screaming. Working methodically and precisely, as a doctor might while suturing a wound, Boney wrapped this second thread around the Soldat's neck twice, and then, taking a couple of wraps around his hand for a better grip, he gave one forceful yank. Donald's scream terminated instantly, and I had a brief, horrible image of his head falling away. It never reached the floor, though. His head and the rest of his body disappeared, dissolved. The coils of heaven's thread, that had a moment ago bound him, fell limply to the carpet.

Kirsten fell against me sobbing, and I put my arm around her for comfort, but I could feel myself shuddering at the horror.

I had dispatched three Soldats at the mansion, and I could argue that I had had no choice, that this had been done in self defense, but the truth was that there had been no personal connection. They were just nameless opponents, adversarial fighting units that appeared and disappeared at will. Donald, though, had a name and a personality, and both Kirsten and I had come to understand at a gut level the difference between transitioning between Halfway and heaven, and dissolving.

"That was murder!" Kirsten cried, the words catching in her throat.

"That was justice," Boney corrected calmly.

"Justice? How could it be justice when you were both the judge and jury?"

Boney's smile was condescending. "I should have perhaps tried him in front of a jury of his peers?"

Kirsten didn't answer. She was smart enough to know that he was just baiting her.

He continued anyway. "You Americans just love your jury of peers, peers that pass judgment based on forensic evidence they can't possibly understand. How many prisoners on death-row have been exonerated after decades because their false verdicts were based on common, uneducated prejudice? How many innocents have been executed?"

Kirsten still didn't rise to the bait. She knew he was just soap-boxing. "And who appointed you the infallible judge?" I asked, partly to take the heat off her.

He studied me, as though deciding whether it was worth responding. He gave a little nod, deigning to consider my offer to spar. "The thousands of subjects who accept my rule."

"They voted?"

He smirked at my naiveté. "One votes for the president of the PTA; one casts a ballot to send someone hungry for power to Washington to reap the benefits of that power. A vote in selecting a leader of men is the simple acceptance of his authority."

"That's just a truism. You might as well say that a wolf pack has 'voted' for its leader because nobody's willing to challenge him."

Boney just looked at me a moment, letting the veracity of that analogy settle into place on its own. He glanced at Kirsten before continuing, cautious about how she was taking all this. He still wanted her as a shepherd. "You know, the Creators' plans for Home span millennia. It will ultimately cradle all of mankind."

"You mean, the aliens."

I was fishing, probing among the hints that the professor had found.

"Since 'alien' refers to any being not of this world, then it is you who are now offering a simple truism."

"Unless Halfway and heaven were somehow created by men."

His brow pulled together. He really hated hearing it called that. "Who? The Egyptians? The Babylonians perhaps? Home was built with horses and rope? Home was built *for* man, not *by* man."

"That may be, but whoever made it, they made more than one heaven—one for each cultural heritage on Earth."

I wanted to hear him say it.

"For now," is all he said.

I'd have to pull it out. "Meaning not forever. Meaning that one of the heavens will absorb the others."

"Don't call it that!" he suddenly shouted. "Don't be an idiot!"

His outburst took me by surprise. But I pressed on. "If the-place-above-Halfway will ultimately cradle all of mankind, then somebody's going to have to pull them all together. If you don't, then some conqueror from one of the others will."

His anger eased, or he managed to hide it, and he smiled. "You've been talking to Steinbeck."

That didn't make sense. "Steinbeck wants you to conquer the other . . . places?"

"Of course not. He says this sarcastically, like you did." To Jones, he said, "You've been keeping company with my greatest disappointment. He's still dead set on thwarting me?"

"I thought I was your greatest disappointment," Jones said.

"Don't flatter yourself. One must have expectations to be disappointed."

"Steinbeck is Steinbeck," Jones replied curtly. He was obviously smarting from Boney's insult.

"The socialist hero still fantasizes that the common man has the wherewithal to manage his own affairs?" To Kirsten, he said, "The average man eventually has trouble with the perfection of Home. He is used to a world of limited resources, where he had to elbow others for his place. He gets restless. If I didn't wage campaigns against other domains, he would create some mischief or another."

"Seems like an excuse to me," I accused.

"I really don't care what you think."

"I don't know" I said anyway. "It sounds like the creators missed their mark with humans. Maybe we weren't ready."

"Maybe they just didn't understand how much we're wired for ambition," Kirsten offered.

Boney studied her a moment, sizing up the worth of his prize. "Now you sound like Steinbeck. I need to find time to deal with that thorn." He glanced quickly at Kirsten's corpus lying on the bed, then at Jones. "Kirsten," he said, "I'd like you to step outside with me."

I felt panic rising up my spine. All this chatter had lulled me from the danger this megalomaniac posed. "You're going to kill her body," I accused.

Boney apparently still wanted Kirsten's cooperation. Her peace of mind was the only card we held.

Boney ignored me. "Come, Kirsten," he coaxed, gesturing for her to follow.

To Jones, I said, "I suppose you lied about your corpus Flock waiting outside."

The traitor didn't reply, but his dark stare gave me his answer.

I was desperate. Boney could just grab Kirsten and leave. "You don't have the balls to admit that you're going to kill her body."

Boney didn't respond, but it seemed that his jaw was slightly clenched. I was running out of stones to throw. I suddenly remembered something I had read a long time ago. I didn't even know if it was true. "Not only are you lacking the balls, I happen to know that your penis is sitting on a urologist's shelf in New Jersey."

Desperation calls for low blows. I'd read that a vengeful autopsy doctor on Saint Helena had removed his member as a spiteful souvenir. It was smuggled to Europe by a crooked priest, and a century later finally made its way to an auction in New York City where the dedicated urologist bought it for $2,900. Desiccated over the years, it has shrunk dramatically, and people who have seen the inch-and-a-half mummified organ compare it to a snippet of buckskin shoelace.

Based on Boney's response, it was either true, or he at least believed it. He strode over, gripped Kirsten by her wrist and pulled her to the door. He placed his palm against it, and a moment later the boy Apostle opened it, looked around, and then left. Boney turned to Jones. "You sure he can't leave?"

He was obviously talking about me.

Jones nodded glumly. "Steinbeck let slip how he can be blocked. I've taken care of it."

It took me a moment to realize that they were talking about my ability to descend back to my corpus, or rather, now the inability.

"Steinbeck is both a dreamer and a fool," Boney remarked snidely. He looked at me and the tiniest smile curled the corners of his mouth. "Goodbye, wonder man." He nodded to Jones, pulled Kirsten outside, and a few seconds later the Apostle closed the door again.

Jones didn't look happy. He sighed. "I don't like this. I don't like it at all."

First Donald, now me. I could barely talk from my terror. "He wants you to . . . dissolve me?"

Jones didn't say anything, which gave me the answer I feared. "You don't have to! I could . . ." But there was nowhere for me to go. The window was closed, and there was no corpus to open it.

Then I remembered. I didn't need the window to be open to escape. "Look, I'll leave through the window. You can tell Boney you did it. He'll never know."

Jones sighed again. "You really think he won't find out? Now you think that I'm the fool."

"Is it worth it? Is it worth a life just to get a piece of heaven?"

But I knew the answer. It was beaming from his eyes. He'd do anything to get back.

I made a dash for the window. Maybe I could get through in time. The tips of my fingers had barely penetrated when Jones grabbed me and pulled me back. I actually saw my fingers stretch as they emerged. The pain was exactly what you would expect from fingers being pulled out of form. I understood what it must have been like for Boney to have his head deformed.

The pain was so consuming, I hardly understood that Jones had wrapped his arm around my neck and was squeezing. The nightmare was becoming beyond comprehension, and my mind sought refuge from the torment. I thought how blessed it would be if I were just back in my body, sitting next to the professor.

Time and distance warped, and I opened my eyes to near darkness. Something tinkled right next to my ear. I didn't understand where I was; not sitting in the professor's SUV, apparently. I was back in my corpus, I could feel my hand lying heavy with mass on my thigh. Actually, I realized that I was assuming that I was back in my own corpus. I had thought it only possible to descend to my own, but I hadn't specifically asked Zorba. What if I had, like, landed in somebody else's? If so, were they still in here somewhere, pushed down out of conscious control? "Hello?" I said, as though that might catch their attention. As I spoke the word, I felt something ruffle my hair, and the tinkling returned. I was beginning to get freaked.

"Hey, man," somebody said. "You awake?"

For one stupefying fraction of a second, I thought that I had commandeered Tod's body, but then it dawned on me that the other voice was next to me, not inside. I reached up to feel my head, and my fingers met something solid, yet light as paper. In fact, from the feel and sound, it seemed to be made of . . . I pulled it off, and daylight flooded my eyes. I held in my hands some sort of homemade helmet constructed from tin-foil held together with cellophane tape. "What the hell's going on?" I asked Tod, who sat in the driver's seat watching me happily.

"I saved your life, man," he replied, beaming.

"What are you talking about?"

"You were, like, in a coma, and demon spirits were waiting to invade your body. They can't, like you know, get through metal."

I was beginning to see the light. "Who told you to do this?"

He lifted his shoulders. "Noshi," he replied.

The professor was outside, pacing back and forth on the sidewalk. I called him over, and his face lit up when he saw that I had returned. "What's this all about?" I asked holding up the tin-foil demon shield.

He chuckled. "Tod here insisted that we needed to do it. I saw no harm."

"You don't know anything about it?"

"No. From your reaction, though, I'd guess that you do."

I shook my head. It didn't make sense. "Steinbeck thought that it would somehow prevent me from descending back to my corpus."

"Why do you say that? Did you see him?" he asked enthusiastically.

"No. No, Jones told Boney that Steinbeck had let it slip."

But that didn't make sense either. Steinbeck was too savvy to let something like that accidentally slip. And in any case, it didn't work. *Ah, ha!* I laughed. "He snookered them!"

"Steinbeck?"

"Yeah! He fooled them into thinking that they could prevent me from descending. They wouldn't have let me get so close to Kirsten's corpus otherwise."

"You found her?"

"Boney let Jones lead us right to it," I replied, my mind racing ahead to the next moves.

"Is she . . . is her body—"

"Yeah, she's alive. Shit!"

"What?"

"Now that I've left, they won't waste time taking care of that problem. I've got to get back in there."

"You're going to ascend?"

I looked at him, then I looked at Tod sitting there not really understanding what we were talking about, but happy to be part of whatever. "No. There's a whole invisible battle taking place out front, and I don't think Boney will let me waltz on up the back way again. It's time to bring in the heavy armament."

"As in molecules," Clintock confirmed.

"Sometimes lumbering muscle and bone comes in useful."

"I'll come with you."

"No, professor. Boney's Disciples may be dangerous."

He reached through the open window and placed his hand on my shoulder. "I'm coming along, Jordan. I've done nothing but sit around while you've been fighting to get Kirsten back. I need to help."

His eyes were full of a yearning to make right a harmful course of events that he'd launched.

I nodded. "Okay," I agreed, opening the door and climbing out, "but you'll have to keep up. Every second counts."

I was getting weary of hearing that.

"Tod!" I yelled as I ran away, "Don't listen to Noshi anymore. He's really Jim Jones—the Jim Jones that murdered a thousand people in Guyana decades ago."

I stopped to let the professor catch up. Tod stood with his hands in his pockets watching us. I couldn't tell if he was sad or angry with me. In any case, he wasn't smiling anymore.

I didn't know the address, but I recognized the front area where the fight between Boney's Soldats and Jones's Flock had been raging. I looked at the quiet plot of grass, the magnolia tree, and the sidewalk and wondered if it was over. It was so strange as I stood there with the professor listening to the soft rush and retreat of the waves beyond the bluff to think that shouts and blows might at that very moment be surging all about me. On the other hand, now that I thought about it, I wasn't even sure it had been a real fight at all, but just staged for our benefit.

"This is the place?" Clintock asked, pulling me from my reverie.

"Yeah," I replied, studying the front entrance, which was nothing but two cement steps leading to a small open landing. A screen door, missing the actual screen, was propped open with a brick. The front door was closed, and I would have bet money, locked. "Give me a minute to get around to the back, then you go to the front door and ring the bell, or knock."

"I'm going to draw their attention while you make the actual penetration?"

"That's right."

"This is the extent of my contribution? A diversion?"

"Sorry, professor. We don't have time to come up with something better."

He nodded. "You're right. Be careful. You never know what these religious fanatics are capable of."

"*You* be careful. Don't provoke them."

"Provocation is in the eye of the receiver, but I'll try."

I ran, crouched, across the short expanse of grass, realizing as I reached the corner of the house that running that way, or at all, screamed suspicious. A cement walk led along the narrow space between the side of the house and the fence that marked the boundary of the lot. Here running bent over made sense, since this kept me below the window sills and out of sight from within. When I rounded the back corner, I was at eye level with the bottom of the windows of the back screened porch. I thought about pushing through one of the screens, but decided that this would make too much racket, and it would be a struggle to climb up, over, and in, giving the Apostles watching TV within plenty of time to come out and cut off my fingers or shoot me in the head. Instead, I continued around to the bluff stairs. Here, though, the vertical railings prevented me from climbing up. I was telling myself that I should go back to the front and force my way inside with the professor, but I knew that this was just me being a scaredy-cat. I could climb onto the stairs; I just had to lean out over the bluff to where the railings were wide enough apart to squeeze through.

I'm not acrophobic, at least not in the technical sense, since I can stand on a stepladder, for example, just fine. Once I'm higher than would be reasonable to survive a fall, however—say fifty feet—I'm terrified if not securely anchored, preferably by a cement wall. Peering out over the edge of the bluff, I felt dizzy and sat back a moment. The trick was to not look down, just concentrate on the stairs three feet away. Sometimes I think there's two of me: there's the amenable team-player me that's willing to try this sort of thing, and there's another me who's the protective, maybe lazy, naysayer. In this case the team-player me reminded the collective that Kirsten's body lay within waiting rescue, and then leaned out to grab the railing before the crotchety me could interfere.

A moment later I was hanging with my legs dangling. I tried to swing them in an arc to catch the stairs beneath the railing with my feet, but in the tenth of a second that they were in contact, all I managed to do was scuff the wood. This was bad. For vengeance, the crotchety me made me look down, and my heart froze. It was a *long* way down. Terror animated me, and frantic squirming and twisting eventually brought my left foot again to the stairs where this time serendipity caused it to get stuck. I couldn't do anything with that foot, but now I was able to pull myself up the railings until I was gripping the top handrail. From there, I brought up the knee of the right leg and placed my unstuck foot solidly on the end of a stair. My groin was stretched beyond its normal range, and it was painful to tug on the stuck foot, but it eventually gave way before my scrotum ripped open, spilling its valued contents. The reason the foot had given way, though, was that it had abandoned the shoe. But I was free, and seconds later, I tumbled through the railings and lay panting from all the exertion. If I ever got out of this mess, I promised myself that I was going to get back to regular gym attendance. Crotchety me scoffed.

I retrieved my stuck shoe and bounded, or at least staggered, up the half dozen steps to the porch. The back door was wide open, and I stepped inside. The TV den was empty, the handful of

Apostles that had been watching the screens were gone. But I heard voices; a heated discussion was taking place off towards the front of the house. I stepped into the hall, and froze when I saw the pressed white shirts of Apostles at the far end. They were listening to the debate just out of view around the corner. Then I recognized the professor's voice. "If God *wanted* you to believe in him, why for heaven's sake wouldn't he make his presence more obvious? Why would he go out of his way to make it so difficult?"

This was met with a chorus of enthusiastic protests. It was as though the teacher had finally asked the class an easy question that they all knew.

"It's like Columbus telling his crew just to trust him that they weren't going to fall off the edge," he continued. "No, that's not a good example. Anyway, to tell you the truth, it seems to me that God just wants the gullible as followers."

The reaction swelled to howls of denial. Good old professor. He probably didn't believe that, but knew it would get a rise out of the Apostles and keep their attention. I was able to walk down the hall to Kirsten's room without them noticing. I opened the door, but just as I was stepping inside, one of the Apostles suddenly spun around, as though tapped on the shoulder. A wraith had obviously been keeping watch.

Inside, the room was the same as it had been when I left so suddenly some minutes before, except that if Boney, Jones, or Kirsten were there, they were, of course, invisible. The young Apostle who had let down the bluff stairs was there, and he was bending over Kirsten's comatose body, but his back was turned, and I couldn't see what mischief he was up to. I slammed the door in the face of the Apostle in the hall, and locked it. The boy Apostle spun around at the sound, and I saw that he was holding a decorative throw pillow. The alarmed look on his face assured that he hadn't been making Kirsten more comfortable.

"Jesus!" I cried, storming over. "Get away from her!"

He didn't resist when I shoved him aside to look at her. "It takes a coward to kill somebody with a pillow!"

That didn't come out right. I meant that if you could use a pillow, then you were killing somebody who couldn't defend themselves, but I didn't really care if he understood. I put my hand against her cheek, and it was warm, but I knew that didn't reveal anything if she had been smothered only seconds before. I watched her chest, and for a few terrible seconds, I didn't see it move. Then I thought I did, but I couldn't be sure. I put my fingers against her wrist, but detected no pulse. "If she's dead, I'm going to kill you," I announced without looking at him. Finally, I did detect a pulse on her neck. "It's okay, honey," I announced in case she was still in the room, "you're still alive." I wondered if I was maybe the first person to utter that particular sentence.

I finally turned to face the boy, and I gasped. He stood five feet away holding a pistol. I had never before looked at a gun so close from this angle. Somehow, foreshortened into a small profile, it didn't seem as threatening.

His face was a different story. It wasn't mean, or angry, or even aggressive; he looked tormented, and this very near caused me to shit my pants. He was agonizing about pulling the trigger, which meant that the possibility fell within the bounds of how his deliberation landed.

I knew what was driving one side of the deliberation. "Boney! Cut it out!"

That was about as effective as telling the rain to stop falling. I knew that as well. "If you shoot me, the police will know it's a murder," I said, reverting to logic. "There'll be blood all over. There's no way you can clean it all up. Modern forensics are like magic."

Of course he would know all about that—the TV arena would have made sure of that—but the weirdness of discussing the details of my own death muddled my thinking.

The boy was sweating; the droplets were rolling down his cheekbones. He looked like he was going to burst into tears. The gun jerked in his hand at intervals. It was as if somebody else was trying to take control, and that was exactly the case.

And then three distinct things happened simultaneously: the boy screamed; an explosion shook the room; and something heavy slammed me in my midsection, causing me to double over. I looked up to see what the boy was up to, and was perplexed for a moment that the young Apostle had dropped the gun. For one blessed second I thought that I was safe, but then I realized that the look on his face had barely changed. If anything, the boy seemed even more tormented than before.

And then it dawned on me that the explosion had been the gun firing. I put my hand on my side where the blow had landed, and it hurt! When I lifted it, the bright glistening blood glared at me, the color of final doom.

He'd shot me.

Chapter 16

I was suddenly weak, so weak that my legs could no longer support my body, and I sat down heavily on the floor. My shirt was wet and sticky in both the front and back. I let myself fall back against the dresser, and the window cleaner spray bottle toppled off, bouncing against my wound so that I howled in pain.

The boy had shot me once. He might pick up the gun and shoot me again. But it still lay there on the floor. I looked up and saw that he was again leaning over Kirsten, suffocating her. "Son-of-a-bitch!" I groaned. The kid was a dedicated psychopath killer. No he wasn't. The truth was more dire. He was controlled by a mind with centuries of megalomanic experience at getting what it wanted.

I tried to stand up, but fell back, helpless. It was as though my legs were no longer connected to my brain. That would happen if he'd severed my spine. The hopeless terror that this thought released made me gasp. I tried moving my foot, and it obeyed perfectly. I might bleed to death, but at least I would die a whole man.

I shouted to the boy to stop, but he ignored me. I pleaded in the name of the god he worshiped, but he might as well have been deaf. I was desperate. How long would Kirsten survive with the pillow smashed against her face? How long before she suffered brain damage? I thought that maybe I could throw something at him, hit him in the head. I looked around, and my eyes fell once more on the gun.

He was stupid for letting it lie there, and I was more stupid for not thinking of it sooner. I reached for it, but it was three feet too far. The effort to just lean out and reach was so painful that I was spent, and I lay down for a moment, letting my blood spill onto the carpet. I was in pain, but Kirsten was dying. I dug my fingers into the carpet and turned myself so that my feet could push against the dresser. Suddenly, the boy's head snapped around. He hadn't seen what I was doing, but Boney had. The Apostle groaned at the complication and ran over and picked up the weapon while I just lay looking up at him. He held the pistol to my head, point-blank. My mind pulled the clutch and slid into neutral. I thought nothing. There was nothing but the gun. There was the time before it fired, and eventually there would be the time after it fired. But for me there was only the former, and I floated suspended in that eternity.

That eternity shook. The gun shook. The boy was struggling like he had the first time. I closed my eyes. I couldn't bear watching him torment over blowing my head open. I heard a whimper, and then the sound of shuffling. I opened my eyes and saw that he'd returned to the pillow. Maybe Boney had gotten impatient with the guilt-conscience reticence. Holding a pillow over somebody who already looked dead had virtually no visible effect, unlike splattering brains across the room.

I was spared, spared to die more slowly. But I was damned if I was going to let him kill Kirsten. And then the obvious answer came to me. It was like I had known it all along, and had been asleep. I wasn't sure if I could pull it off, though. How could I relax when I was bleeding to death? I tried, but it was like taking a nap as terrorists stormed your office building.

But who said that I had to relax? The professor. But he'd never done it. He was just guessing what was necessary, based on the fact that people ended up in a coma afterwards. I tried to recall exactly how I'd done it before. There was the Rohypnol, but that was just at the beginning. No, the only common factor was the professor repeating the palindrome. I didn't believe in magic, but I wouldn't have believed in Halfway either if I hadn't seen it with my own eyes. Maybe magic is just the word we use for something we don't understand. But just hearing the palindrome wasn't enough. The professor didn't ascend. Zorba had said that I was the only person he'd heard of that had ascended without help from the far side, from Halfway.

Whatever it was, however it worked, I didn't care. It just did. I closed my eyes and tried to ignore the pain. "Sator," I said softly. "Arepo, tenet." I heard a sound and looked. The Apostle boy was staring at me. His look turned to alarm. I closed my eyes again and continued, "Opera." I heard his footsteps come towards me. I lifted myself on invisible wings and finished, "Rotas!"

The all-consuming pain was gone. The boy stood over me, but he was no longer looking at me. He was looking at my insensible body lying next to where I sat. Boney was standing behind him, and he jumped at me, but I leapt away. Boney was stronger and probably faster, and he was going to catch me soon. But at least I had pulled the Apostle away from the killing pillow for the time being. There was nowhere to run to. I had closed the door, and had already proved that I couldn't get through the window glass fast enough. Jones had grabbed the Halfway Kirsten, and was holding her off to the side, against the wall. I ran to them. Jones wasn't going to protect me from Boney's wrath, but he was at least an object I could get behind to shield me. Also, it was just natural to try to be near Kirsten.

Boney came towards us, and he gave Jones an annoyed glare. "Let her go," he ordered.

I edged around behind Jones, and he wrapped his arm around her neck. "I don't think so," Jones replied menacingly.

"You're a fool," Boney warned, and reached around to grab me. I was prepared, though, and ran in the opposite direction. The Apostle boy, having been left rudderless, still stood looking down at my dying body. I ran behind him. There was nowhere else to go. Boney seemed in no hurry now. He walked over and calmly placed his hand on the boy's shoulder. The boy immediately lifted his right arm out to the side, and swung it forward. I was trapped, and the arm was a revolving door pushing me inexorably with it. I stumbled on my own body, fell, and was grabbed forcefully by

Boney. A moment later, my neck was being squeezed so that my vision blurred inside my expanding head.

Descending was merely a matter of willing it, and an instant later, I was overwhelmed with the pain and nausea from my wound. The boy seemed surprised. He probably thought that I had died. Marshaling my strength, I lifted my arm and swung it in an arc as hard as I could manage, bringing it to rest forcefully against the dresser behind me. With luck, I had caught Boney in a deadly vice blow. The boy took a cautious step backwards. To him, I probably looked to be flailing randomly in a death spasm.

But the pain and nausea and overall distress of inhabiting a dying body was unbearable, and I decided that there was nothing I could do here. I had left Jones holding Kirsten in a threatening position. I might at least do something about that. I took a breath, closed my eyes, and in one, continuous sequence, uttered the palindrome. The pain and nausea evaporated, and I opened my eyes to the relief of the dulled senses of Halfway.

I was looking across the room at the Apostle and my bloody body. Jones and Kirsten were right next to me. My ascension had placed me fifteen feet away. I remembered that I had twice ascended outside the professor's SUV, and Zorba had been surprised by the feat.

I was disheartened to see that Boney was still there, though, lying crumpled, half jammed under the bed. My swing had at least partially caught its target. I knew that the fact that he was still here at all meant that I hadn't destroyed him, and confirmation of this came when he slowly straightened one leg, then the other.

"Ow!" Kirsten protested. "You're hurting me!"

"Let her go," I said to Jones, but he ignored me. He was watching Boney, waiting for heaven's leader to recover.

"I said, let her go!" I demanded, pulling at the arm he had wrapped around her neck. As a mere Wop, I didn't expect to have any effect on a heaven-initiated rogue, and was surprised that I was able to pull his arm away a few inches. He looked at me, obviously surprised as well, then yanked his arm back into position, overwhelming whatever unusual Wop-strength I had mustered. Then, perhaps to prove the unexpected slip was just a fluke, he grabbed me by the neck with his other hand, and held tight. He couldn't strangle me, as I didn't actually breathe, but he could decapitate me, which I had already witnessed was an effective means of dissolution. I reached up with both hands and grabbed at his fingers, pulling with all my strength. Like bending a barely pliable metal rod, I slowly pulled away two of his fingers. Surprised and angry now, he lifted me off the floor, swung me back, and hurled me through the air. I crashed into something vertical that seemed to break my back in two, then fell senseless to the floor.

The Apostle boy was walking back to the bed where Kirsten's body lay, and it was he that had terminated my flight.

"Let her go," I heard Boney say.

Heaven's leader had recovered, and was getting to his feet.

"Of course," Jones replied, "once you agree that Houston will be autonomous."

"As I said, my Soldats will enter only after prior notice—say, twenty-four hours." Boney placed his hand briefly on the Apostle's shoulder as he walked towards Jones and Kirsten. I could guess the gist of the silent instruction.

"Not good enough, Boney," Jones countered. "That's not autonomous."

"I never agreed to complete autonomy."

As the two continued to argue, I got to my feet. The boy was back at the damned pillow. I wondered how long I could hold off what was beginning to seem like the inevitable fate of Kirsten's mortal body. I walked over and placed my hand on one of his wrists. "Stop this," I said softly. The boy's brow furrowed. "Take the pillow off her face," I instructed.

He lifted his hands and stared at the decorative design on the throw pillow.

"Suffocate her!" Boney called from the other side of the room. "She harbors Satan!"

"No!" I insisted. "That's Satan himself trying to influence you." I thought a moment. This would be blasphemous, but the greater blasphemy would be to just let her die. "I am your God," I growled, "and I command you to remove the pillow!"

The boy jerked as though receiving an electric shock. He grabbed the pillow and pulled it away. I was relieved to see that

Kirsten's face seemed normal, but more importantly, that her chest moved slightly.

Boney cursed, and Kirsten gave a little squeal of pain. I spun to see Kirsten stumbling away as Boney grabbed Jones. The charismatic rogue who had ushered a thousand followers either to Halfway or oblivion grabbed heaven's leader by his throat. Boney stared into his adversary's eyes stonily as he calmly reached out and pinched the edge of the closet door frame, pulling away a taffy extrusion of heaven's thread. Jones had seen this before, and he let go of Boney's throat and lifted his hands in defense. The coils of thread that Boney was deftly wrapping bound Jones's hands tightly against his terrified face, yielding a macabre likeness to Edvard Munch's painting *The Scream.*

I couldn't bear to watch, and covered my face with my own hands. Kirsten screamed, and I looked to find Boney holding coils of limp thread. I knew what would be next on his agenda, and I returned to my ministrations, placing my hands on the boy's shoulders and repeating my message for the few seconds remaining. Boney strode over, and I didn't wait to be tossed aside, but stepped away and let him at the Apostle. There was nothing else I could do.

At least not in Halfway against Boney.

I knew that this was going to be hell. I closed my eyes, mentally contracted myself, and instantly returned to hell. I opened my eyes to a world of doomed torment. Even anticipated, the agony was shocking. The Apostle was leaning on the pillow, grunting and groaning with an effort that was obviously conflicting him, but Boney's invisible commands were impossible to resist within the pliant belief fabric of the young mind. As a flesh and blood Earthly body, I was an impervious force against the imperial monster, but the impervious force was useless lying helpless on the floor. I could throw something, but Boney was invisible to me; I would have to guess where he was standing.

I had to try it. It was my only option. I looked around the floor for something to toss, but religious fanatics apparently valued neatness. But then my eyes fell on the spray bottle that had tormented me when it fell off the dresser. I don't remember what gave me the idea, maybe the fact that the spray handle vaguely looked like a gun. I remembered vividly the effect of the lone sprinkler water droplet back at Roberto's. The tiniest movement brought stabbing pain, so reaching for the bottle was agony. I felt so weak, I wasn't sure I could squeeze the handle. I was too far from the boy. I rolled over on my stomach and willed the strength to push up onto my hands and knees. I cried out involuntarily as I crawled the five feet I guessed that I needed. Then I paused while my vision swam for a few seconds. When I could see clearly again, I lifted the bottle, grunting at the strain, and called to Kirsten to get down. I squeezed and squeezed some more. I swept the bottle back and forth and squeezed. The pungent smell of ammonia and artificial pine scent filled my nose, and the wet spray cooled my face. It seemed ridiculous that something so delicate could be violently harmful to the overlay world of Halfway.

Suddenly my vision fuzzed and I opened my eyes to the view of a sea of carpet fibers receding off into the distance until they merged and butted up against a leg of the bed. I realized that I must have passed out. It hadn't seemed like a long time, but I couldn't tell for sure. I didn't try to lift my head off the floor. I just lay there wondering how long my body would live. It dawned on me that there was a sound that had been there all along, but that hadn't registered. It was the sound of concerted effort. It was a sound of vile intent. With hateful disgust, I realized that it was the grunts of the Apostle boy suffocating Kirsten with a pillow.

I closed my eyes and ran through the entire palindrome as one, continuous stream of syllables, willing myself to appear on the other side of the room. The first evidence that I had ascended was blessed relief from pain and a return to a clarity of mind. The second was Kirsten's hair in my face and her arms wrapped tightly around my chest.

Boney was gone. That, at least, I could be thankful for.

I just wished that I could smell Kirsten's hair.

Chapter 17

"What happened to Boney?" I asked Kirsten.

"It was terrible . . . I mean, it was great—terrible for him, though. If he didn't hate you before, he does now."

"So he didn't dissolve?"

"I couldn't tell. He just disappeared and then the screaming stopped."

"There was screaming, huh?"

"Lots."

"Good. Oh, shit," I exclaimed, letting go of Kirsten to sprint across the room. I'd forgotten for a moment about the Apostle.

With Boney gone, he readily lifted the pillow off her face. I wondered what kind of reasoning facility the kid had that he was so compliant to waffling, sometimes conflicting, suggestions.

"Are you . . . dead?" Kirsten asked.

She was standing over my bleeding body.

I knelt next to me. "I'm still breathing."

I felt sorry for me, not for myself, but for my body. I liked my body. It was *me*.

"Well, thank God you're here," she said.

I looked at her.

"Safe," she explained. "Your body can die now. You're safe."

She was right. I hadn't thought about that in all the turmoil. "I'm not ready to let it go," I decided.

She shrugged. "Looks like you don't have much choice."

I thought about it, and shook my head. "No! I've worked too hard to save your body. I'm not going to be stuck here alone."

She smiled at me and took my hand. "I'm not leaving you. Let them both go. We'll be together here. Maybe someday we'll get to heaven."

Halfway would indeed be unbearable without her. But it wasn't a real existence. Her hand was soft in mine, but there was something missing: the warmth, but something more, some subtle tactile sense below the level of the consciousness. In Halfway practically all we had was consciousness. We would be two ghosts wandering the world, invisible and unnoticed, watching life bloom and struggle and procreate and perish, but not be part of it.

"I'm not done making love to you," I declared.

Her grin was self-conscious. If she had blood, she would have been blushing. "Is that so important?" she asked.

"Yes. *Yes!*" I exclaimed. "It *is* important!"

She leaned in and wrapped her arms around me. "I guess I shouldn't have made you wait so long."

"It wouldn't have mattered. It's not like one day I would just decide that I've had enough. There's no 'enough.' "

A loud quarrel outside interrupted our debate. The professor had abandoned his logical arguments, and was berating the Apostles for being criminally stupid. Our young assassin was at the door, shouting through it, trying to understand what was going on. I tried to draw him away to call an ambulance for me, but the tumultuous activity with his colleagues was disrupting. I couldn't keep his attention long enough to convince him that God wanted him to seek help for me, particularly since just minutes ago God was telling him to kill everybody in the room.

"I have to go back," I finally concluded.

"To there?" Kirsten protested, pointing at the bloody mess that was me.

"I have to call for an ambulance, maybe slow the bleeding somehow."

Her eyes suddenly went wide. "You—your body—could die any second! If you're there when it does, you'll die with it!"

I looked at me. I really was a mess. It wasn't obvious that this blood-drained shell could be saved.

"I have to try. I can't give up on life, on a life with you."

Her face was exactly like when she cried, but of course there were no tears in Halfway. "Jordan, you can't leave me here alone!"

I took her in my arms. "I'll be back for you. I promise."

"How can you promise when you don't know what's going to happen?"

I squeezed her, wanting only to hold on forever. "You're right, but I promise to try my best."

I let go and turned away from her. A moment later, I was in hell gazing across an expanse of carpet.

I had seen a phone on the nightstand next to the bed. My body had had a few minutes of rest; maybe I could manage now. I pulled my hands in under my chest and pushed up. I managed to crawl to the nightstand on hands and knees, but then collapsed. After a few seconds, I corralled the strength to lift myself up again, but fell back against the bed. I knew that there was a real danger that this brain would fall into unconsciousness, and then I would be trapped until it died, and me with it.

I saw the coiled handset cord hanging in front of me. I grabbed it and pulled, but it was made to flex and stretch. With a gasp, I gave it a good tug, and the handset came tumbling down, knocking me on the forehead, then rolled under the bed. But I had a glimpse of good news: the handset *was* the phone, including the dial buttons. Laboriously, inch by inch, I pulled the coiled cord again and again until the phone slid out from under the bed. I didn't even have the strength to lift it to my ear, so I let myself fall, taking my head to the phone. I heard nothing. I moved my head to make sure I was listening to the earpiece. The phone was dead. When everybody has a cell phone, why pay for a landline?

I was screwed, but I felt too weary and sick to even be disappointed. The only thing left to do was try to slow the bleeding. The hole, or rather, the two holes were in my side between my ribs and pelvis. I knew that if a tourniquet couldn't be applied, the next best thing was to bind the wound, applying pressure. Maybe I could take off my shirt and tie it around my middle. This seemed a monumental task; just taking off my shirt was surely far beyond my capabilities.

I was screwed.

Suddenly a boom filled the room. It sounded like the door. The yelling in the hall rose to a higher pitch, and then the door burst open, and Tod stepped inside. The professor was right behind, standing backwards, holding his hands out to ward off the Apostle mob trying to follow.

The assassin boy had jumped back and was fumbling with his hands behind his back. From where I lay, I could see that he was reaching for the pistol that he had tucked into his pants.

"Gun!" I yelled in warning, but it came out as a whisper, no louder than the hiss of a soda can opening.

I was dying, and my priorities were drawn inward to the next breath and a few more heartbeats, but I liked Tod, and once the Apostle boy shot him, the professor would be next. I gathered my strength and bellowed, *"Gun!"*

This weak warning might have been heard by an attentive person, but it went completely unnoticed in the excitement. I watched, helpless, as the boy pulled the gun from his pants and brought it around at Tod. The aging hippie blinked at the sight, and then in one smooth maneuver, spun around in a circle with his foot extended. The gun bounced off the wall and fell behind a small table in the corner.

I couldn't see the boy's face, but Tod looked at him with disapproval, like a parent facing a child about to be punished. Our bus driver screwed his mouth at the unpleasant task at hand and with the same fluid dance, grabbed the boy's wrist and spun him around. In one flick of an eyelash, the boy was his prisoner, his arm twisted behind his back. Tod turned him around to face the crowd of Apostle colleagues, as sort of a warning, or demonstration of the mistake they'd be making by trying to come in.

I think I blacked out then, for the next thing I remember was that the professor was using one hand to hold something soft against the hole in me, and with the other was pressing a cell phone to his face. He was obviously calling for an ambulance because Tod had to hurt the Apostle boy a little to tell them the address. "We have some social aberrants here who might interfere," the professor said, "so you should also bring along the police."

He closed the phone and let it drop, then he noticed that I was awake. "How are you doing, son?" he asked with a serious concern that he didn't even try to hide.

"Okay" I mouthed.

There was nothing more that I could do here. "I'm leaving," I whispered.

I felt his hand on my side jerk a little in alarm, and he leaned in closer. "Hang in there, Jordan. Help's on the way."

It took me a few seconds to understand the confusion. "No," I said hoarsely, "ascend."

After a few moments, that sunk in and he nodded vigorously. "Sator," he started, but I ran quickly through the rest in my mind, *arepo, tenet, opera, rotas,* while imagining myself across the room where I had left Kirsten. The relief was beyond description as I opened my eyes with a clear, pain-free mind to see the professor hovering over my blood-drenched wreck of a body. He was still finishing the palindrome.

"Too bad."

It was Boney. He stood on the bed, and he was holding Kirsten. A Soldat stood by his side, and two more stood on the floor in front. "I was hoping we were about to be rid of you," he said. Nodding down at the professor he added, "At least we'll soon be done with half the problem."

I was holding out hope that my body would make it, but the consensus was stacking up against that.

"Let her go," I said.

He laughed.

It sounded retarded even to me. "I'll make a deal," I tried, putting my mind to better use.

"A deal implies something of value proffered by both parties," he replied. "Besides, I still have a bad taste in my mouth over the supposed deal with Jones."

"Maybe I have something of value. If you let Kirsten go, if you promise not to hurt her, I'll return and take my chances with . . . that," I offered, gesturing towards the failing mass of flesh and bones. "I won't bother you again."

"Jordan! Shut up!" Kirsten yelled, but Boney gave her a little shake to quiet her.

"You're being presumptuous. There's an assumption that you have the power to bother me."

"I squashed your head like a dropped pumpkin, and chased you back to heaven with window cleaner."

He glowered at me, whether from remembering a deformed head or my insistence on calling his home heaven, I wasn't sure. "Perhaps you're right," he agreed, sneering. "Maybe it is time to put an end to this troublesome bother."

"Jordan! Look out!" Kirsten suddenly yelled.

I started to turn, but two arms clasped me from behind like a vice-grip. Boney nodded to the Soldat that must have come in from the hall, and the vice-grip began to close, squeezing my torso like a tube of toothpaste.

I had only one option, and a moment later, hell engulfed me. The pressure that the professor was applying might have been slowing the bleeding but it was also radiating pain like a fusion agony source. I gasped, and the professor peered into my eyes. "You're back?" he asked.

I didn't answer. I didn't have the strength. I saw one of the Apostles in the hall suddenly start forward, but Tod, still holding the boy in an arm lock, twisted and kicked, and the man fell back groaning. Boney was determined to get me, whether here or in Halfway.

I tried to guess where the attacking Soldat had been, and then zipped through the palindrome, concatenating the five words into one.

Tormented hell was replaced with clarity, and I was standing behind and to the left of the Soldat. He must have caught my arrival out of the corner of his eye, for he spun to face me.

Switching back and forth like this was going to make me dizzy. I was about to return to hell, when somebody said, "You've met your match, Boney."

The voice was familiar, and I turned to look. It was Steinbeck, standing with his arms crossed over his chest! He had wormed his way through the Apostle crowd. Behind him, still half hidden in the bodies, I saw Zorba.

"Then why did you run away like a scared rabbit?" Boney asked.

The author studied heaven's leader through his blue and gold eyes. "Insisting on feigned ignorance is dishonorable in its dishonesty."

"Ha!" his adversary exclaimed, but the humor seemed feigned. "Surely you're not referring to this," he spat, pointing at me, as though I were a little steaming pile of dog shit.

I looked at Steinbeck and he returned my gaze steadily. "Please, Boney," he replied, looking back towards the bed, "you're embarrassing us all. You know I am referring to him."

"A freakish ability by some . . . mutant to return from Halfway hardly constitutes a threat."

"Boney, you've never underestimated an enemy before. I don't believe that you are now. This is your chance to retire with grace."

I was expecting Boney to howl with derisive laughter or perhaps pretend mock fright as an insult, but the French general stared at Steinbeck a moment, and then looked towards me. He nodded to the Soldat, but before the soldier could react, Steinbeck caught his wrist. "Careful, my friend" he said quietly. Then to me, he said even lower, "Let me show you," as he reached with his other hand to pinch the edge of a bookshelf and pull away a strand of taffy— heaven's thread. The Soldat tried to grab the thread, but Steinbeck deftly wrapped it around the soldier's wrists, drawing his hands together and binding them. "Now you," he urged, nodding at the bookshelf.

I had no clue what to do, other than pinch at the edge of the shelf. There was no reason to expect that it would be any different than all the other times I'd bumped up painfully against the impervious objects of the real world.

"It's not the shelf you grasp," he explained, "but heaven's twin inside."

I shook my head. "I don't know how."

"Yes you do. It's the same as when you ascend."

"But that's the palindrome."

"No, it's you. The palindrome is just a verbal touchstone. Now try it."

One moment Steinbeck was standing there, and then there was a flick of motion and he was gone. Another Soldat had come through the door and grabbed him. He'd have to fend for himself for a moment. I pinched the edge of the shelf, and my thumb and forefinger slid right off. It was obviously more than just pinching. I placed my thumb and finger back in position and this time held them there with a slight force. *Now*, I told myself, *do what you do when you ascend*. But that was just the palindrome. There was no time to study this; I just ran through the words in my head. Still nothing but solid shelf. I had obviously done more than just listen to the Latin words. I closed my eyes and ran through them again, but this time I ignored the chaos swirling around me and imagined that I was ascending from Earth to Halfway. The solid shelf remained a solid shelf, but at the same time, there was another shelf that was pliable. It was extremely strange, and difficult to explain, because my thumb and finger were grasping two different objects that occupied the same space. Imagine that you have two hands doing the same motions, but applied to different things. Or maybe imagine that you first pinch a hard shelf, and then later pinch one made of stiff clay, but then superimpose the two sensations on top of each other.

In any case, when I pulled my hand away, my fingers slid off the hard shelf, but also pulled away part of the soft one, the one from heaven. I was holding a strand of heaven's thread.

I heard a grunt behind me, the involuntary kind that could be a groan. Two Soldats were holding Steinbeck, who struggled forcefully. If he hadn't kept them occupied, they would have already grabbed me. One of them froze when he saw me, and Steinbeck managed to pull away from him. The heavenly wraith was staring at my hand, the one that held the thread from heaven. The other one noticed, and paused enough for Steinbeck to yank his other arm free. "Behold your doom," Steinbeck declared, and two men looked at each other uncertainly.

"Grab him, you fools!" Boney bellowed.

This jarred his soldiers from their trance. One tackled Steinbeck, while the other came for me. I had seen how effective the thread had been for both Steinbeck and Boney, and I tried to wrap it around the Soldat, but in attempting to swing it around the man's head, I managed to get my neck caught as well, so that we ended up with our heads bound together, lovers, posing for a picture.

If this was their doom, then the world vastly misunderstood the power of the *Three Stooges'* Curly.

My co-bundled Soldat, on the other hand, had a trapped victim to molest, and he didn't wait to partake. Despite the entanglement of the resisting thread, he was able to wrap his arm around my neck, and he gave a mighty squeeze. I had the second or two that I needed to prepare, so when he jammed the vise closed, I popped like a pinched lemon seed back to hell.

I was expecting an explosion of pain, and so was surprised to find . . . nothing. I rose from the depths to consciousness, and the pain and nausea and devastating complete malaise was almost welcomed. I wasn't dead quite yet.

The professor must have seen my eyes open. "Hang in there, Jordan. They're on the way."

I had thought that someone was crying, but I realized that it was the wail of a siren. The room was so still after the raucous mayhem of Halfway. The gang of Apostles stood quietly in the hallway, as though waiting for permission from Tod to proceed. Despite my unbearable distress, I marveled at how two worlds could coexist, one on top the other, and yet be seemingly light years apart. As far as I knew, maybe they were.

Wherever Halfway was in space and time, I had to get back. I tried to remember the layout. Boney and Kirsten and his three personal Soldat guards were still at the bed, and Steinbeck was wrestling near the door, while my abandoned bundling partner was there near the bookshelf. I had started thinking of this purposeful ascension to a specific location as targeting, and I decided to target myself near Steinbeck's struggle.

My targeting was a little too precise. I appeared right between a surprised Steinbeck and his assailant. My appearance had pushed them apart, and Steinbeck used the distraction to break free from the Soldats grasp. I jumped away to let them go at it again, and leaped towards the Soldat I had just left. He was pushing the thread off his head, but it was stiff and unyielding, and it was more the case that he was ducking below it to get free. I wasn't sure whether I could repeat my trick, but it was far easier this time. I had the feel. I pulled away a thick strand of heaven's thread from an overhead lamp, and when he lifted his hand to intervene, I shoved it under his armpit and then around his neck, and finally back over the hanging lamp. I gave a hard tug, pulling the harness tight, and then took a couple of wraps around the lamp's hanging cord. Although the thread was like soft taffy to me, for the Soldat, it was stiff plastic.

Heaven's thread deteriorated after a few minutes, but that might be long enough.

"Help!"

It was Zorba. One of Boney's guards was trying to grab him as he danced around the oblivious Tod and his captive Apostle assassin. I ran over, and the Soldat immediately gave up on my friend and grabbed me by my arm, and then my throat. The only object within reach was Tod. It seemed disrespectful somehow to pull away a piece of him, but I pinched off a thread from his belt. The thickness of heaven's thread was evidently related to the size of the source, and this thread was a mere string, but I managed to entangle us both before retreating back to hell.

Hell was hell, and I didn't stay long. I targeted Steinbeck again, and when he let himself be taken by his Soldat, I pulled a thread from the door jam and bound his adversary.

"You make good bait," I remarked.

"Happy to oblige," he replied, turning to Boney and his two remaining guards. "Have you seen enough?" he asked Boney, while I reinforced the thin thread bindings of the Soldat that I had tethered to Tod.

"Enough to know that the simple tricks you've taught your Wonder Boy are tiresome; they compliment the mundane air of Halfway. I need a breath of fresh air."

I saw that he had wrapped his arms around an uncooperative Kirsten. She squirmed rebelliously, but his heavenly strength was overpowering. I started forward, but Steinbeck pulled me back. "No," he warned. "Not now."

"Why not?" I demanded, trying to pull away, but he held fast.

"The transition can be dangerous. You could kill her if you interfere."

"What transition?"   A wonderful, miraculous thought illuminated my mind. "He's taking her back? To her body?"

Steinbeck just stared at me solemnly.   He nodded in their direction.

They were disappearing, both of them.   I could see the wall behind. Then they were gone, leaving the two guards who watched a moment, then clasped their hands together in front of their faces, closed their eyes, and disappeared as well.

"He's taken her to . . ." I couldn't finish it.

Steinbeck sighed. "Heaven."

Chapter 18

"I'm sorry," Steinbeck said, leaning over with his hands on his knees. The old guy was pooped. "I didn't expect it so soon. It all happened so fast."

"You mean, Boney taking her off to heaven?"

He nodded.

"You didn't expect it so *soon*? Meaning, you *were* expecting it?"

He shrugged and nodded again.

"When were you planning on telling me, for God's sake?"

"I'm telling you now," he offered, standing up straight again.

"After she's gone? Was that the plan? You were going to tell me *after* she was gone?"

He looked at me carefully and said, "Yes."

"So, what, you actually planned to have Boney carry her off?"

I said this sarcastically, hoping to poke at him and force a reaction.

But his response was, "Yes."

I just looked at him. I felt what would have been goose bumps on my real body. "Oh—my—God! You're working *with* Boney!"

He smiled, laughed, and shook his head. "Oh, no. Quite the opposite, my young friend. I've been waiting for you for a long time."

"For *me*?"

"Well, not you specifically. Somebody with point-one percentile innate potential."

"Which happened to be me."

"Which happened to be you. Ninety-six percent of people fall within ten percent of the mean capability spectrum. One percent are above the eighty-five percent capability level, and only point-one percent—one out of a thousand—have innate potential above ninety-seven."

I was getting lost amid all the numbers. "I'm one in a thousand," I summarized.

"That's right."

"But there's, like, three-hundred million people in the U.S., that's a lot of one-in-a-thousands."

"Yes, ascension potential is required, but by itself is not sufficient. Without all the other qualities normally associated with a hero, the ninety-seven level capability is just parlor tricks."

It was my turn to laugh. "Are you kidding? Me a *hero*? Mr. Steinbeck, I'm afraid you've wasted a lot of your time." I became sober. "And endangered my fiancée."

He shook his head and placed his large hand on my shoulder. "This is something which you can't see. You wouldn't be a hero if you did. You have sent Boney running off to his heaven. Trust me, you're the one."

My head was spinning. "It wasn't a coincidence that Kirsten ascended just as you were connecting with the professor, was it?"

He watched me carefully, sympathetically. "No."

I felt anger simmering. "You and the professor purposefully convinced her to ascend!"

"You would never have embraced such an outlandish idea as Halfway otherwise."

I swung my fist at him, but he easily dodged. "You bastard!" I cried. "You're no better than Jones or Boney!"

"That may be," he agreed. "But I hope that at least my motives are less shameful. Jordan, you don't understand what's at stake. The creators never intended for heaven to be limited by tyrant gatekeepers like Boney. They certainly never intended the various heavens of Earth to wage war against each other. The endless succession of heaven's dictators must be broken."

I wasn't swinging at him anymore, but my fists were still balled tight.

"Jordan, can you guess why Boney abhors the term 'heaven'?"

I shook my head in quick little jerks. I didn't want to give him the satisfaction of replying with words.

"It's because of Josephine."

I looked at him. Despite myself, I was interested.

"You see," he explained, "before he embarked on the Italian Campaign, Boney—Napoleon Bonaparte—promised Josephine heaven. It became their little joke. He would end his letters from the battlefields with that reminder."

I lifted my palms. "So?"

Steinbeck looked at me a moment. "The dictator of heaven at the time prevented her from ascending to Halfway. He let her perish."

"Oliver Cromwell," I added.

"Yes. Perhaps the most despised man ever to inhabit heaven."

Pieces of the puzzle were coming together. "You didn't want me talking to Kirsten at the Rancho Santa Fe mansion because you had to keep the carrot just out of reach. You couldn't let me take the bait that easily."

"That perspective is a bit harsh. I didn't want you to convince her to return. You still had a lot to learn."

My mind raced forward in time. "You purposefully misled Jones into thinking that I couldn't descend if I had tinfoil on my head, to let me get close to Kirsten."

Steinbeck laughed heartily. "Jones had the gift of charisma and persuasion, but he suffered from his own gullibility."

"Why did you keep company with the dick?"

"He was effective camouflage. I was able to stay under Boney's radar, at least for a while. But time is wasting."

"What do you mean?"

"I mean that we have to rescue your lovely fiancée."

"You have some plan to trick Boney into bringing her back?"

Boney's nemesis, the man who had been scheming to bring the tyrant down just looked at me, his student who was missing the obvious answer.

"You're going to heaven?" I asked.

"Not just me."

"I think he means you." It was Zorba, who had come over and stood next to us. He was nervous, glancing at the trapped Soldats who glowered at us menacingly.

"Me!" I exclaimed looking at Steinbeck, who just nodded. "I don't know *how!*" To Zorba, I said, "You told me it took months to prepare."

"Yeah, but Wops can't pull heaven's thread and stick their heads through glass," he reminded.

"He's right," Steinbeck concurred. "Jordan, you'll just have to accept that you are special. But every minute counts. We really must be going."

"I've been racing against time ever since I ascended from the professor's car, like, days ago."

"It was five hours, and every minute we wait here will make it that much harder to find Boney."

"I know, I know, every second counts. Show me what to do."

"First, Zorba, I suggest you take off," Steinbeck said. "You don't want to be here when these threads dissolve and Boney's henchmen are free to wreak havoc."

My first friend in Halfway looked at me. "It's really cool that you're going to heaven." He paused, searching for words. He shrugged, giving up on the effort. "Good luck with Kirsten," he said, and turned to go.

"Wait!" I called.

He turned back.

"Listen," I told him, "you'll get there, I know it. Things are changing."

"That, they are."

Steinbeck gave him a little shove. "Now g'it!"

Steinbeck waited until Zorba had weaved his way through the Apostles, then told me to help him secure the three Soldats with fresh thread. "Why did you hustle Zorba away if we were going to re-secure them anyway?" I asked.

"I'll explain later," was all Steinbeck would say.

When we were done, he led us out of the room. As I passed Tod, I put my hand on his shoulder and said, "Good job." He smiled.

Once in the hall, it was an obstacle course getting through the Apostles and back to the central news monitoring room. "Why did we come here?" I asked.

"To get away from the Soldats."

"Does it take that long to ascend?"

"No. I just didn't want them to watch us."

"Ah, I get it . . . that's why you sent Zorba off?"

He nodded, glancing around, studying the layout. He looked down the hall and out the windows and then sighed, not satisfied. He put his mouth to my ear and said in a whisper, "Follow me—do exactly as I do," then he strode over to the lone Apostle guarding the back door. The man stood peering up the hall, trying to catch all the commotion, but when Steinbeck put his hand on the side of his head, the Apostle furrowed his brow, opened the door and walked out onto the back porch. "Come on!" Steinbeck called as he led the man along to the outer porch door.

I ran to catch up. The man opened the screened porch door and stopped, holding it wide. Steinbeck slowly pulled his hand away, making sure the corpus was going to succumb to his inexplicable urge to stand holding an open door.

"Ready?" Steinbeck asked, but didn't wait for a reply. "Exactly as I do," he reminded, and then he sprinted off across the landing . . . and leaped into thin air.

I stood looking at the vista of the Pacific Ocean beyond the wooden railing where the rogue author from heaven had disappeared. He had said exactly. Besides, although it would hurt like hell, I doubted the fall would deform me to the point of dissolution. I took a breath and tried to pretend that I was running off the high dive at the college swimming pool. I tore off across the wooden planks and screamed as I launched into nothingness. A few seconds later, the scream became embarrassing and I shut up and enjoyed the ride. My weight in Halfway had always seemed normal, but the air rushing past me now was more like water, or maybe what it would feel like to jump into a huge vat of styrofoam balls.

Nevertheless, the rubble of sandstone lying at the base of the bluff was approaching at a disconcerting rate. I saw that Steinbeck was picking himself up ten feet beyond the rocks, and I positioned my arms and legs to catch the wind and glide away from the cliff face. I was so intent on my acrobatic maneuver, I forgot that I might want to turn myself to land feet-first. I missed the rocks, but landed on my chest, executing a belly-flop on sand that was hard as cement.

I don't think it's possible for an ethereal Halfway mind to temporarily lose consciousness, but I wished that I had. The scream that I'd stifled at the beginning of the leap returned.

"That's enough," Steinbeck reprimanded as he helped me up. "Now hurry."

I followed him as we ran to the stairs. "Ascension to heaven is the same as to Halfway," he explained, edging in behind the vertical wooden structure, "but more difficult. The Soldats that you saw follow Boney were actually drawn up by him after he arrived. As far as I know, nobody's discovered this but me. Once you wrap yourself, pull it tight—as tight as you can bear."

Before I could ask what the heck he was talking about, he reached out and pulled a strand of heaven's thread from the back of the stairs. Starting at his ankles, he wrapped his legs, taking the thread behind him, and then transferring it to the other hand to bring around the front. Alternating like this, he wrapped his way snugly to his waist, and then tucked the extruded, thin tip under his belt. He then did the same from the top, starting with his head and working down until he tied the tips together. Only his arms were free, and with some effort, he slid his hands under a couple of wraps so that he now looked like an inadequately prepared mummy.

"The trick," he instructed, "is to lean into the thread as you ascend. Let it merge with you."

His mouth was partially immobilized so that his words sounded strained, almost painful.

"What if I don't make it, like, all the way? What if I get stuck with the thread half merged into me?"

"Don't," was his only answer. "I'll do what I can from the other side to help you up. Hang on to a piece of thread as you ascend if you can. You might find it useful; it might help when you return. Now I have to go."

He closed his eyes and concentrated. Then he leaned sideways, letting himself fall over. The threads pulled tight, then stretched, and I could see them pressing against his clothes and skin. And then they seemed to melt, but I knew that they were simply sinking into his body. His face was pulled tight, and his mouth froze in a grimace. If I didn't trust my new friend, I would have thought that he was drawing me into some kind of horrendous torture.

But I trusted him.

He disappeared. One moment I could see the waves breaking on the beach through him, and the next there was just the waves. The threads fell limply to the ground.

It was my turn. I mimicked the thread wraps, but decided that the loops around my chest were too loose, and started over from my head. I pulled each wrap tight as I worked downward, and felt a little panicky as I slowly and methodically bound myself into complete immobility. If the Soldats or Boney caught me here now, I would be served up like the catch of the day caught in a net.

Finally, only my arms were free. Like my teacher, I worked my hands under some wraps. I remembered what he'd said about hanging on to a piece of thread, and I grasped one of the wraps with each hand.

Now to ascend. But how? Steinbeck had said that it was just like ascending into Halfway. First, I had to lean so that the threads pressed against me. They hurt! It wasn't exactly pain, but that didn't make it any less tolerable. Walking on a foot that had fallen asleep wasn't exactly pain either, but just as excruciating. I was scared, terrified, actually. I hadn't known—or believed—enough to be frightened the first time I'd ascended to Halfway. Now I had at least a vague idea of the dangers involved.

But I trusted Steinbeck. How could a man who had written *Of Mice and Men* let me down? I trusted him.

I did what I had done each time before, I ran the palindrome through my head as I imagined myself lifting upwards. My self-induced trance was almost broken when I felt the threads merging into my body. Imagine that you keep your eyes closed and continue to breathe deeply as a knife is slowly inserted into your belly.

I fell, but somebody was holding me up. "Well done," Steinbeck said as he steadied me to stand on my own.

I looked around, then at him, alarmed. "Why didn't we ascend?"

He shook his head. "What do you mean?"

We were still huddled under the bluff stairs, and the ocean still lunged and retreated up the sand. Most tellingly, I kicked at the sand, and it was soft. It was sand, not cement.

"You think we've returned to corpus Earth?" he asked.

I nodded, but already I was doubting the idea. The ocean sparkled with sprays of light that seemed to dance in coordinated joy, as though the sparkles were alive and desiring nothing more than to weave subtle, hypnotic patterns together. The sky was an impossible blue, a blue that I had never seen before, and the scattered puffy clouds were not so much condensed droplets of water, as perfectly formed decorations whose sole purpose was to complement and give depth to the dome of the sky. Where senses were dulled in Halfway, they were amplified in heaven. The gentle breeze that wafted in from the water was achingly rich with salt and oxygen and just pure cleanness. It was a smell that I remembered vividly when I was five and gazed out on the Pacific for the first time after our family moved to San Diego from Missouri.

"The corpus Earth is a foundation upon which the world of Heaven resides," Steinbeck explained softly, obviously aware of my fascination at the truth. "Or maybe, think of Earth as a model—heaven is the bright apparel on the mannequin corpus world."

My attention was drawn upwards. I gazed directly at the sun, and it seemed appropriate that I should be able to do so. I wasn't surprised that the light didn't burn my eyes. But, oh the light; if the sparkles on the sea were dancing Tinker-bells of joy, the sun, their source, was a concentrated fusion of purified beauty. Gazing at the golden glowing ball, I was convinced, with no evidence other than the effect it had on me, that this represented the completion of everything I had ever desired.

"That's the portal," Steinbeck explained.

I looked at him. "To where?"

He gave a little shrug. "The creators. This is what everybody assumes. No one knows for sure, of course. I don't necessarily trust those who have come closest to it, but their stories at least agree."

"You can get close?" I asked, mesmerized by the prospect.

"Not me," he said. "I wasn't here nearly long enough to gain more than a middling altitude. No, I'm afraid that honor is reserved for heaven's leaders, not because they necessarily deserve it, but simply because they've usually been here the longest and they decree it, like kings of old carried in a litter on the shoulders of their subjects."

I was still gazing around, fascinated by every little detail. "People here can fly?" I asked. I was ready to believe anything.

"I am usually disappointed when people answer a question with something like 'yes and no,' but yes and no. They don't have wings, and you don't see them swooping around in the air like birds. In fact, you don't see them at all from the ground, at least not the dimensional aspects."

I turned my gaze from the wonders of heaven to look at him. "Do you expect me to understand that?"

He sighed. "I'm not sure anybody really understands it. Heaven is multi-dimensional. The world you see around you, the clothes on Earth's mannequin model, is just the most easily comprehended by our Earth-born minds. Another dimension extends upwards. It's not really upwards—'outwards' would be more accurate—but that's how we perceive it, at least at first. You don't jump back and forth between the dimensions, you exist in them all at the same time. It can be disconcerting at first. There's other dimensions as well, but they're more subtle, too ethereal to perceive as distinct alternate existences."

I wanted to fly. I wanted to soar up into this impossibly pure air and feel the glorious heat of that joyful sun on my face. "How do I do it? How do I go up in that other dimension?"

He sighed again, this time with a hint of frustration at an anticipated difficulty. "I'm afraid it's beyond instruction. It's something you learn to feel, like riding a bicycle. But I fear that it's also something that you're going to need to get a handle on very quickly."

"Why?"

"Navigation into the dimension we perceive as altitude—what they call 'the balcony' here—is the most important skill you'll learn, at least with regards to your struggle with Boney."

"*My* struggle? Isn't it 'our' struggle?"

He laid his hand on my shoulder, and it was warm and organic; alive, where in Halfway it was hardly more than a coagulated ghost. "I've taken you about as far as I can."

"You're *leaving*?" I asked in a panic.

"No. No, I'll be with you as long as I can keep up. But you're going to have to learn to go where I can't if you have a hope of saving Kirsten, and . . ."

"And what?"

He just looked at me.

"Ha! You still think I can somehow beat Boney?"

He didn't answer me. Instead, he pointed. "You'll want to hang on to that."

It was the piece of heaven's thread that I had been gripping between my two hands when I ascended. Here in heaven it was translucent, like elastic plastic piping. I coiled up the two-foot piece and shoved it in my pocket.

"We should leave before Boney finds us," Steinbeck said, glancing up the stairs. "You have a lot to learn before we tackle the next hurdle."

I heard voices, excited, insistent chatter. I looked, up, but the stairs blocked my view. There was no way to leave without being seen anyway, so I stepped out and saw a line of men standing at the railing far above. They were looking off to each side, up and down the beach, but one of them glanced down and shouted, and the chatter rose a few Decibels as they all saw me.

"Lousy traitors," Steinbeck growled, disgusted as he joined me.

"Who are they?"

"Boney's lackeys. They like to call themselves generals, but they're nothing but yes-men. Every megalomaniac needs constant praise and fawning, even if it's insincere."

Boney's lackey generals' attention was again directed up and down the beach, and I now saw why: a squad of soldiers was approaching from each direction, pounding along the firm sand just above the waves' reach.

"He was a step ahead of me," Steinbeck said, defeated. "He anticipated that we would ascend. I'm sorry. We tried."

I watched the Soldats as they grew larger and larger, descending on us with grim determination. "Is that it?" I asked. "Is the trying over?"

Steinbeck didn't answer. We both just waited for Boney's troops to arrive.

Chapter 19

As Boney's soldiers approached, I saw that they were distinctly individuals. This was worth noting, since in Halfway it was difficult telling them apart; they were more like caricatures, their faces smooth, with few defining features to differentiate. I had felt bad after dissolving the two in the mansion, but I would have felt far worse had they appeared like they did now. It had felt more like I'd scored a few points in a video game. I realized that even Steinbeck was now more "real." The wrinkles on his brow and neck were sharply defined. He looked his 66 years.

My own body apparently comprised a substance closer to that of Earth, for I had scraped my arm on the stairs when I ascended, and it still hurt. There was a red rash, red from blood spilled from tiny capillaries. I didn't have time to ask Steinbeck about this, as the Soldats had now arrived, and they grabbed us roughly. There was no use in struggling, so we didn't.

The ones not holding us suddenly moved to the side and stood at attention. The clomp, clomp coming down the stairs explained why. Boney didn't say anything as he stepped onto the sand and looked us over grimly. I had grossly deformed his head and sent him scurrying back to heaven under a rain of painful window-cleaner bullets. I didn't imagine that he was one to shrug those off lightly.

I looked up at the sound of more activity on the stairs, the syncopated scuffling of someone being led uncooperatively. It was Kirsten, pulled along by two Soldats. When she saw me, her eyes opened wide with joy, and she stopped struggling. Seconds later, she stood behind Boney, held fast by her Soldat escorts. Boney's generals followed in single file, and fell in along a line behind them.

The little general had lost his characteristic condescending sarcasm. Now when he spoke, it was all serious intent. "Welcome to my home," he said loudly for all to hear. He didn't sound welcoming at all. "It's too bad your visit will be so short."

I had experienced a great deal of pain since my first ascension seemingly so long ago from the professor's car, and I had watched as Soldats and Jim Jones had perished. Maybe it was because it was all so fantastic, and had unfolded so quickly. I don't remember, but whatever the reason, I felt no sense of mortal danger, like a dream where you are aware that the crouching tiger is just a dream.

"The creators didn't construct this world for you to use as your exclusive home," I countered with my hallucinated sense of impunity.

I wouldn't have thought that his face could get any darker. Steinbeck looked at me with surprise, and what I took to be admiration.

"What could you possibly know of the creators?" Boney accused. He had lowered his voice, as though not wanting the spectators to hear my answer.

"I know that they never intended it to be restricted by a tyrant."

His eyes narrowed into perilous slits of hatred.

"I know that Halfway was never intended to be used and abused as a purgatory," I declared. I hadn't formed these thoughts prior to this, but after seeing just a few minutes of heaven, they seemed blindingly obvious. "Halfway is supposed to be just that; a temporary staging point on the way here. A way station. A platform to make an otherwise impossibly long ascension possible. It's not half of anything when it leads nowhere else." I now raised my voice to a roar. "It was never meant to be a prison to serve as a tyrant's gate!"

"*Enough!*" Boney screamed.

Silence imploded on the beach, leaving only the swish and gurgle of the waves to whisper to the impossibly blue sky.

The ruler of heaven regained his composure. He carried a leather strap here—what I took to be a riding crop—which he waved as if shooing away my accusations as though bothersome flies. "Nobody cares about your imbecilic ramblings. We must proceed with the sentences."

That stopped me cold. There weren't many ways to interpret that.

"And what are the charges?" Steinbeck demanded, looking Boney straight in the eye.

"What do you think, John?"

"I think that you dole out sentences to suit your whim."

"*Treason!*" Boney yelled, then quickly caught himself. "Treason," he repeated more calmly.

"Treason against whom?" Steinbeck asked, the voice of patient reason.

Boney turned to his generals. "McKnight?"

The man on the left replied, "Treason against mankind, sire."

Boney looked to Steinbeck. He'd been given his answer.

"How have I betrayed all mankind?" he asked, still with measured calm.

"By defying the code! By sneaking in this mutant cancer," he exclaimed, shaking the crop at me.

"But this is *your* code," Steinbeck continued doggedly. "It wasn't treason against all men, but just treason against you."

"And that is the same!" Boney cried. He wasn't trying to maintain his composure any longer. "Treason against me is treason against all mankind!"

Boney turned and stomped off to his line of generals. I had the strange sense that I was watching the debate unfold from the observation deck of a courtroom.

"Jordan," Steinbeck said softly.

I looked at him.

"Listen, son. There's something I need to explain. Here, you must go up to go down."

The look he gave me indicated that this was the preamble to something important he wanted to communicate. He never got the chance to finish the enigmatic message, however, for Boney stomped back. He still held the riding crop in his left hand, but now he had something else in the other. Steinbeck suddenly began struggling with his captors, but they were prepared, and held their ground against his twists and squirms.

At the last minute, I realized that it was a small hunting knife that Boney gripped in his fist. "John Steinbeck," heaven's tyrant declared with ferocious intent as he advanced upon the struggling author, "you are sentenced to death!" Without a moment's hesitation, Boney cocked his arm and drove the four-inch blade into my mentor's stomach. The knife penetrated to the hilt, and Steinbeck instantly froze, his face cast in a grimace of horrible shock. Boney gazed determinedly into his eyes a moment, then yanked out the knife and jammed it in again, this time just below his ribs. Steinbeck jerked once, but the three additional thrusts that followed were superfluous, my friend was beyond shock or caring.

Boney stepped back, surveyed the lifeless man, and then waved his red-smeared blade to the Soldats to let him fall to the sand.

Silence once again fell upon the beach for the barest second. Whatever sense of false impunity that remained evaporated as I watched John Steinbeck's blood flow.

Then, a bloody scream rang out like a siren. It was Kirsten, but her cry was not an involuntary wail of terror, but rather overwhelming anguish and anger. She blasted Boney with a barrage of verbal projectiles, slamming him with words I didn't even know she knew.

As Boney turned and advanced on me, the sense of observing from on high was even stronger. In fact, I realized that I was actually watching myself and the approaching tyrant from above. I had taken it for an inner visualization, my mind running its own mental simulation, but I understood now that it was truly an alternate view. This must be the other dimension, the balcony, that Steinbeck had talked about. I couldn't imagine what else.

Boney stopped in front of me, the bloody knife held at his side. My Soldat captors tightened their grip in preparation. My heart, a real heart, beat a pounding thump in my chest. I sensed that my usual method of escape by descending wasn't an option, at least not in the short time before the knife pierced me. In any case, I couldn't leave Kirsten here alone, not knowing if I could ever return without Steinbeck to help me.

Suddenly Kirsten bellowed with rage and stomped on the toes of one of her Soldat guards, then spun and drove her knee into the crotch of the other, leaving them both doubled over in pain. My beating heart told me that I had a functioning anatomy, and I was glad that the guard's testicles were functional as well.

Kirsten raced the short distance across the sand and leaped onto Boney's back, wrapping her legs around his waist, and tearing at his face from behind, searching for his eyes to gouge with her fingers.

My captors tried to hang on to me while using one hand to reach out and help their leader. Their distraction was my open door, and I took a lesson from Kirsten and kicked one in the shin, and turned to knee the other, but missed. But somehow, my twist jerked my arm from his grasp, and I jumped at Boney, knocking the three of us to the ground. I punched and kicked and even bit, hoping it was Boney's flesh and not Kirsten's. Amidst the fog of rage, I realized that Boney had no advantage of strength now; we were on equal footing in heaven.

As I scrabbled murderously to do whatever damage I could, I sensed that Boney had somehow regained his feet, pulling Kirsten and me along. But that couldn't be, because I could still feel the sand digging at my elbows and spraying my face. It was the other dimension, the balcony. It was just as Steinbeck had said. I was in two places at once: I was rolling and kicking in the sand, and I was also rising into the air, wrestling with the man the professor had warned about, the devil.

As we rose, I could tell that I was gaining strength in both dimensions. Soldat guards were trying to pull me away on the beach, and I kicked them aside like so many barking toy poodles. I understood what Boney was trying to do; if he could gain altitude in this other dimension, he could best me with superior strength. Steinbeck had said that nobody rose higher than heaven's leaders.

But I could flit back and forth between Earth and Halfway; I could pull heaven's thread; and I had ascended to Boney's home less than a day after entering Halfway.

I was special. Steinbeck had said so.

I followed Boney up into the expanding heights of the balcony dimension, hanging on, but also pulling myself along to keep up, to keep him from gaining an advantage.

"You—can't—do—this!" he growled.

The shouts and commands on the beach were still close by and audible, but they occupied an increasingly smaller portion of my consciousness as we rose higher and higher. The world spread and opened below us. I could see all of southern California, from Mexico to the San Gabriel mountains of Hollywood. I had an expanding view of breadth, but also of depth. From an altitude, I could clearly see that heaven was indeed a fabric, an overlay, lying on top of the Earth I knew so well. We were perhaps eight miles high and rising, but I could see both people of heaven and Earth, and because I was seeing with my mind and not my eyes, I could discern details of people as though standing in front of them. It was overwhelming, and I had to look away, focus on my struggle with Boney or he would get the upper hand.

Up and up he rose, and up and up I followed, being careful not to let him get too far ahead. The sky was growing darker. We were leaving the atmosphere, but the body in this dimension didn't breathe. Far, far above, the glorious light of the creator's portal still blazed, but as the air thinned, I could see that the source was not in fact the sun, but something closer. Still very far away, though.

Way off on the horizon to the north above the Sierra Nevada Mountains, another source of light shone, with a fraction of the intensity, but comprised of the same animated quality of beneficent energy. As we rose even higher still, I could tell that this source hovered high in the sky, and I wondered if perhaps this was a portal to one of the other heavens, perhaps Asia's, or Africa's.

"Enough—is—enough," Boney gasped, and surged ahead.

I guessed that he was perhaps reaching his limit, and I strained to keep up.

"Who for the love of God *are* you!" he cried.

"The man John Steinbeck found to depose you," I replied, "but I doubt you have God's love."

I thought of my mentor and the life he gave as I called on the last ounces of strength to advance up and ahead of him.

"But you forget something," he groaned, straining with effort.

We were rising like speeding rockets into space, but far below we were also still wrestling on the beach. He raised the bloody knife high, poised to drive it home into my back, but I had outdistanced him now above the atmosphere, and I caught his wrist in my hand and held it. I was now the stronger.

I had forgotten Kirsten, however. She was still there with us in the sand. Her balcony dimension floated far below, trying to follow us, but having climbed only perhaps a mile. Boney reached with his free arm and wrapped it around her neck, yanking her to his chest. At our extraordinary dimensional height, I knew that he could snap her neck bone like a toothpick. I punched him in the face. It was all I could do to distract him, but this was exactly what he wanted. He was able to wrench his wrist free from my grasp, and an instant later, my back exploded with pain as he plunged the knife down.

I found out then just how similar my heavenly body was to that of my Earthly one. The knife in my back couldn't possibly have inflicted more pain if I had been skewered before ascending. My mind was pure agony, and I saw that I was losing altitude. This was the end if I let Boney go now. I tried to grab him, to hold on from falling, but he knocked away my hand and laughed.

I was desperate. Altitude was all I had, my only hope. I needed to hang on somehow and not fall away, leaving him victorious holding the high ground. I needed a tether, a line.

And then I remembered. John Steinbeck had advised that I hang on to the scrap of heaven's thread. It might be useful.

I pulled it from my pocket. Here in space, filled with the direct light from the creator's source, it seemed to glow with life. I had fallen significantly below Boney, and I clenched my teeth and cried out with pain and effort as I harnessed tattered remnants of will to rise back up. Slowly, slowly he drew nearer, a look of puzzlement on his face as he peered down. When my head drew near, he cocked his foot to kick me, but I caught it in a loop of the thread and took two turns around his ankle.

And then, taking a few wraps around my own hand, I gave up.

I fell, and Boney fell with me. He tried to free himself, but it was impossible to loosen the fantastic little scrap of heaven's fabric. He kicked at my hand, and cursed, but I ignored everything and hung on against it all. We were falling fast, but the lower we fell, the more control Boney had, the more he could resist the plunge. Soon, he would be able to counter the freefall, and stop.

Something flashed by, and soon after, Boney finally halted the mad nosedive. Grunting with effort he slowly began the long climb again, back to where he would have the strength to deal with me.

"You're hurt!"

I opened my eyes. Kirsten was on her hands and knees on the beach, peering down at my face, but she was also floating next to me in the air as Boney pulled us ever higher. It was her that had flashed past us, and she now hugged my waist, pulled along, all three of us by Boney striving for altitude.

"Let go," I said weakly.

"No! Why?"

"I have to leave. I'm going . . . home."

"Jordan! No! You can't leave me here, not without you!"

"I don't even know if I can . . . return. I don't know what will happen. We might just . . . perish."

"I'll take my chances, but by damn, Jordan, you are not leaving here without me! Do you understand?"

The only way I knew to leave was to try to descend like I had from Halfway. And the very thought of attempting it without knowing the consequences, without knowing if it could even be done at all, instilled intense anxiety.

And so, I had come full circle, back to my first return from Halfway seemingly so long ago. I had used my anxiety then, perhaps it would serve me now.

"We could die," I said.

"We could," she agreed.

"Okay," I concluded.

I lifted her higher and wrapped my free arm around her waist and held tight. "It might help," I said, "if you close your eyes and just imagine yourself returning."

"Like Dorothy," she said.

I smiled. "Exactly like Dorothy. Here goes."

I fabricated the worst possible outcomes I could think of in my mind: that we would evaporate into nothingness; that Boney would win, and would display our heads on stakes on the beach as a warning; and worst of all, that I might return safely, but never see Kirsten again.

That last was our ticket. As I felt myself drowning in my fabricated sense of hopeless doom, I marshaled my well-traveled coping tools and focused on simply being back in my own Earth-born body.

I felt everything fall away beneath me, and I fell like a stone. Kirsten gave a little squeal, but we clung to each other for our lives, for our love. My other hand was still wrapped in the thread, and I realized with an abstract curiosity that Boney was screaming, he was coming along. The little scrap of heaven, glowing with creator's light, was dragging him along on the long irresistible descent.

Suddenly the gray, static world of Halfway surrounded us, but just for an instant. The next instant, lasting perhaps a millisecond, my body, and my head, and Kirsten, and the whole rest of the universe exploded, and for that infinitesimal millisecond my last glaring thought was that I had made a terrible, terrible mistake.

ж ж ж

I was in hell. Boney was still screaming, though. I had forgotten how horrible the pain and nausea had been. A very tiny part of my brain reminded me that I was lucky to be alive. The vast majority of the rest of my brain begged to disagree that this was luck.

The screaming wasn't Boney, though, but a siren. A very loud and very close siren. Something pressed against my nose and mouth, something that delivered a rush of very needed oxygen.

I opened my eyes. It was a struggle. A young man was holding the oxygen cup in place over my nose and mouth, and he saw me and said, "It's going be okay. We're almost there."

His face said something different. His face said that I probably wasn't going to make it there at all.

My only chance was to ascend, to abandon this dying body and spend the rest of eternity in the purgatory of Halfway.

I couldn't, though. There was nothing left, not even the strength or will to let my soul fly free.

Besides, Kirsten wouldn't be there.

I closed my eyes and let myself die.

Chapter 20

I opened my eyes to heaven, to a different heaven. This heaven was a white painted wall with neat trim and a TV mounted in the corner. This heaven was a place where there was no pain. I was lying in a bed. I moved and discovered that heaven was not completely pain-free.

"Well, hello there."

It was Kirsten. She was sitting in a chair reading, and she placed the book carefully aside and spun around to take my hand.

I recalibrated. This was indeed heaven with or without pain. "You made it back," I said. The joy at seeing Kirsten again in the flesh and blood was overpowering. She blurred as my eyes watered up.

"I didn't do anything except hang on. How do you feel?"

"Alive. Fine, other than a hole in me."

"Oh, they patched that up with no problem. The bullet didn't do much damage. It was the loss of blood that almost did you in."

"How long have I been here?" I asked.

Through the window I could see cars racing past on the freeway. I guessed that I was in Scripps Memorial. I started panicking about how much my insurance was going to cover, but forced that aside. We were both back; everything else would take care of itself.

"Two days. They kept you sedated, but the doctor came by about an hour ago and said that he was going to let you come out of it for a while. The police want to talk to you. I think he was supposed to call them *before* he woke you up, but I've been driving him crazy with questions, and maybe he thinks this will shut me up."

I had vague half-conscious memories—being rushed down a hall on a gurney with people on both sides hurrying along and looking concerned, being lifted onto a bed and someone calling out in warning that I was awake, a male nurse leaning over me and telling me that I was going to be all right, but that I had to sleep some more. "How's the professor?"

"He's fine. He's been in and out for the last two days. Tod's here as well. He went down to get some food. The professor had to leave an hour ago for a class."

"Well, he'll be sorry when he gets back."

"Why?"

"We have a lot to talk about. For one, he's going to pay for whatever my insurance doesn't cover—"

"Jordan! What the heck are you talking about?"

"I'm talking about how he scammed you into ascending, when he knew damn well that—"

"Honey."

"What?"

"Shut up. Professor Clintock feels bad enough already."

"You, uh, talked to him about it?"

"Of course. What do you think we did the last two days waiting for you? He feels like he was manipulated by Steinbeck—"

"Which I had to drag out of him!"

"Thank you, dear. Now please shut up. Professor Clintock didn't even believe it all himself at first. He spent his whole life in worlds that existed only in books. His job was to teach college students about those imaginary worlds. He wasn't connecting his fascination—and later mine as well—about Exiguus's writings with anything real. It wasn't until he began getting subliminal communications from John Steinbeck that he began to take it seriously."

"Uh, huh. So you're saying that the professor got snookered by Steinbeck as well."

"Maybe the professor would prefer to think of it as becoming engaged, but I guess, yeah, he got snookered. In any case, after I ascended, he began to get the idea that Steinbeck had tricked him, or at least had led him along, and he was ashamed about that, so he didn't mention it at first. But he did believe Steinbeck when he communicated that I was in danger, and that you were the only one who could save me. And, of course, he was right."

"I see. But Steinbeck did knowingly put your life in danger?"

She shrugged. "He must have had faith in you."

To tell the truth, I was satisfyingly complimented by that. But at the same time, I shuddered to think how many times our butts had been pulled from the fire by pure chance. Maybe I would have pulled it off anyway in the end. But maybe not.

"Zorba thinks that he was looking for somebody like you for a long time," she went on. "There were rumors over the centuries about occasional special talents. Normally the leader in heaven finds out about them before they even hardly know it themselves, and gets rid of them."

"Er, how do you know what Zorba thinks?"

She smiled slyly. "Oh, we've been talking."

At this, I tried to sit up, and fell back groaning.

"Oh, take it easy. I don't mean actually talking; we've been in contact."

"Oh yeah? I didn't think his Wop influence was precise enough to discuss details like that."

"We use my laptop."

I looked at her, trying to decide if she was joking. "Okay . . . so, he commandeers your computer like the cyber geniuses in the movies?"

"Not quite. Zorba commandeers my fingers. I just look off into the distance and type random stuff, and I sort of let him do his thing. I think of it as a high-tech Ouija board. What I type still looks like a bunch of gibberish, but if I look at it carefully, I can see that he was getting words through. It's kind of tedious, but it works." She glanced around, as though she could actually see if he was listening, and then leaned close and whispered, "I think that he really enjoys it—Halfway can get pretty boring."

I grinned and nodded. Unless somebody happened to be watching a TV show you liked, you were pretty much stuck watching the world literally pass you by.

"Well, does he have an idea how I managed to get us back to our bodies?"

"Yep. It was apparently that piece of heaven's thread you had, the one you used to lasso Boney."

"Yeah," I agreed. "Steinbeck mentioned that it might be useful."

"Zorba says that ever since we returned, rumors have been flying around Halfway about it. Word came down from heaven that Isaac Newton hypotheses that this was the only way you could have dragged Boney out of heaven."

"I did?"

"Apparently. He's gone. You dragged him through Halfway and all the way back to normal Earth. He didn't have a body waiting so he . . ." She made a fluttering motion with her hands.

"Huh," I said, pleased, but at the same time a bit uneasy at extinguishing a soul, even one so bastardly as Boney.

"Yeah, 'Huh.' Both heaven and Halfway are in quite a turmoil—ding-dong the witch is dead."

Just then Tod strode through the door, not noticing right away that I was awake. "You shouldn't be eating this factory food from the cafeteria. I got you a chicken salad; it was the closest thing to real food I could find—whoa!" he exclaimed, stopping short when he noticed me. "You're back!"

"From the dead; at least that's the way it felt. Thanks for coming, Tod. Hey! I probably owe my life to you back there at the loony house. That was amazing the way you handled them."

"Nah," he said, handing Kirsten the plastic salad container and then taking a seat in the other chair in the far corner. "They were a bunch of weenies. The more they lean on some imaginary connection with God, the easier it is to push them over."

"Unless they have a gun. But where in the world did you learn moves like that?"

"You mean that kickboxing? Mostly in the Army, but I kept it up over the years in clubs."

"The Army teaches kickboxing?"

"Green Beret training, at least in the seventies."

"You were a Green Beret?"

"Nope. Almost, though. I was about ready to head off to kill a bunch of gooks in Vietnam when I discovered pot. The Army discovered my discovery and canned my ass. Probably saved my ass. Green Berets' life expectancy was pitiful in the jungle. The Vietcong were fighting on home territory."

I just looked at him. I couldn't imagine this stringy old guy with a long, gray ponytail sneaking through the brush with a blackened face. On the other hand, I wouldn't have imagined him manhandling those Apostles the way he did, either.

He just sat watching me, happy and content. I hated what I was about to do. "I'm really sorry, Tod, but I'm afraid that Noshi is dead."

His smile was patronizing. He shook his head. "No. He's alive and well."

This news created a little knot in my stomach right next to the patched-up hole. "Why do you think this?"

If Jones wasn't gone, then maybe Boney wasn't either.

He shrugged. "I just know. He's talked to me."

I stared at him. "When?"

He thought a moment. "Well, just before he transitioned into phase three, I was in the van listening to Pat Metheny. You were sitting next to me passed out."

"Phase three?"

"Yeah. He gets more gentle with each transition. The last thing that phase two Noshi told me was to save you with the deflection hat."

"The tin-foil thing."

"Yeah. It worked."

I looked at him. "Because I'm still here?"

"Of course." He chuckled. "Then you told me that Noshi was Jim Jones. You remember?"

I nodded.

"Here's the sad part: I believed you at first."

"What convinced you otherwise?"

He smiled at the memory. "After we got the loony boys under control, he told me I'd done a good job. I could tell that he meant it."

I blinked. "Oh, Tod, that was *me*!"

He looked at me sideways, gauging whether I was fooling with him. "As I recall, you were lying on the floor bleeding to death."

"No, I mean . . . my, er, my spirit. I was in the same place that Noshi had been—that Jim Jones had been."

He nodded slowly, patronizing me. He looked at Kirsten. "Can you get me some of those drugs he's on?"

I sighed. It wasn't important that he understand.

But that let another thought bubble up. "What happened to the Apostles?"

"The police arrested the boy with the gun," Kirsten replied, "the one that shot you. They searched the house and found a large stash of weapons."

"So, the whole gang was locked up?"

"Nope."

"Why not, for God's sake?"

She shrugged. "All the guns were properly registered and legal."

"Wait, you're telling me that they're still on the loose?"

"Of course. There was nothing to charge them with."

"But . . . but, what about you! What about kidnapping *you*?"

She lifted her palms. "They all stuck to the same story, that it was just the boy who did it all. He's taking the fall. They claimed that they were trying to get into the room to stop him."

"But that's ridiculous, how can they get away with it?"

"The detective told me that the Apostles had apparently been flying under the radar, but now either the FBI or ATF, or both, will be keeping an eye on them. That's all they can do for now. The professor didn't help the cause."

"Why? Because the nurse at the hospital saw us taking you away?"

"No, she never actually saw my body—but speaking of which, Jordan, a laundry cart? But that's a whole other topic. No, it was because Professor Clintock insisted on trying to tell the truth. It's in his genes. They initially arrested him, you know."

"What for? We were trying to *save* you!"

"The police didn't know that until I woke up. Between fanatic religious Apostles and an old man who insisted that your soul was only temporarily absent, they didn't know what to make of it all, so they arrested the whole bunch."

"Including me," Tod chimed in. "They took my pot."

"I guess we're all glad we got you back in your body," I said to Kirsten. "Hey, is Zorba still here?"

She joggled her shoulders. "I guess so. We talked not too long before you woke up."

To the air, I said, "Hey, Doctor Zorba! I think I maybe know how to get you into heaven. It just takes a little thread." I remembered my speech just before Boney murdered Steinbeck. "In fact, there's a lot of people I'll have to show—all of Halfway, I guess."

At least, I hoped I could show them how. It was daunting to think that I might have to personally escort all those thousands of souls. Maybe I could get some folks from heaven to come down and help. Not Soldats, of course. But then I thought about it; they were just soldiers following orders. Who was I to say they were all as evil as Boney?

Kirsten interrupted my musings. "Everybody?"

"Eh?"

"Do you want to help even the rogues?"

"Well, no. Not if they're like Jim Jones. Stuck in Halfway forever is what they deserve."

Kirsten just looked at me expectantly.

"What?" I said. "You think I should just let everybody up?"

She lifted her shoulders, then let them drop.

I got it. "You're right. I'd be no better than Boney if I began assuming that kind of authority." I sighed. "What a mess; I'm damned if I do, and damned if I don't. At least there's one decision I won't have to think about; Zorba will be my first and most honorable ascension."

Kirsten was wrinkling her nose.

"What? Did I say something wrong?"

"No, not at all. Zorba and I talked about this, actually. He's going to hang around in Halfway for a while. He thinks you're going to need a lot of help at first."

I nodded knowingly. "I see. You two have worked out my whole future, saved me the mental strain."

"Just the next year or so," she replied. "Zorba can manage things in Halfway while you're keeping heaven from exploding out of control."

I thought she was kidding, but she watched me levelly, waiting for my response.

I gave it to her. "No way."

"You mean to say that now that you've deposed the leader, you're just going to walk away and leave everybody there to their own devices?"

"Sounds about right."

But she had me feeling uneasy.

"You're going to help all the rogues back into heaven, and then let them run amuck," she pressed.

"Hey! You trapped me! First you convince me that I have to let everybody in, and then you point out what a big problem that is."

"It wasn't a trap, just facing reality. Zorba and I have had a lot of time to think about this while you dozed peacefully there in bed."

"So, you think I should be, like, the sheriff of heaven."

"To quote you, 'Sounds about right.'"

"No way."

She just glared at me.

"Okay, okay, I'll think about it. Man, what the hell has the professor gotten me into?"

I saw her grinning, looking from me to the door.

The professor was standing there. He must have just arrived back from class. He blushed and said, "Um, maybe I should come back a bit later," then turned to leave.

"Professor!" I called.

He turned back, looking sheepish.

I let him stew a minute. "You convinced Kirsten to ascend, knowing it was dangerous."

I thought he was going to collapse in on himself. "You are absolutely correct, and I can offer no excuse, other than that I believed—"

"Professor!" I exclaimed, cutting him off. "I don't really care about that; there's just one thing I want to know."

He sighed. "And that is?"

I couldn't maintain the act, and I grinned despite myself. "That magical palindrome—was it really necessary?"

He slowly smiled, then grinned ear-to-ear. "That's a question I've been mulling for a good while, and in fact, I do believe—"

"Uh, oh," Kirsten said. For the last minute, she had been tapping away madly at her laptop. She looked up from the screen. "Zorba says that—" She peered at it again. "David . . . er, Kiresh is here."

"Who's David Kiresh?" I asked.

"She might mean David Koresh," Tod offered. "But he's dead."

"That sounds familiar," I replied. "Was he a minister or something?"

"I'd pick the 'something' choice on that one," Tod said. "Koresh was the leader of the Branch Davidians."

"Ah, yeah!" I exclaimed. "The militia Waco whackos that all burned up when the ATF tossed teargas canisters inside."

"Er," the professor quickly reminded, "he's listening to you."

"Oh, yeah. Sorry! I mean, that's just what I heard."

Kirsten was studying her screen again. "He wants to talk to you."

I took a deep breath, and winced. "Now? I'm, like, wounded."

"Uh, oh," Kirsten reported, looking up. "It looks like T.E. Lawrence just showed up."

"What? Lawrence of *Arabia*?"

Her fingers tapped away madly, and then she studied the screen again. "They're arguing. Zorba thinks you'd better get up there fast."

"I'm *wounded*!" I protested.

I looked around, but everybody—Kirsten, Tod, the professor, and probably Zorba—were watching me. "The police are going to be here any minute," I objected, but the silent eyes stared at me. "Oh, dammit to hell, anyway—Professor, do the honors, will you?"

I sat back, closed my eyes, and listened to the ancient words unfold.

"Sator, arepo, tenet . . ."

Blaine C. Readler

About the Author

Blaine C. Readler is an electronics engineer, inventor of the FakeTV, a Beverly Hills Book Award-winner, three-time San Diego Book Awards-winner, and an IPPY Bronze Medalist. His novels have been described as quirky, captivating, creepy, eccentrically wild and irreverent, wonderfully succeeding, top quality, a surprise winner, intense and chilling, hilarious, deft, weird, whimsical, witty, entertaining, and intelligent.

He offers no comment.

He encourages you to visit him:
http://www.readler.com/

www.ingramcontent.com/pod-product-compliance
Lightning Source LLC
Chambersburg PA
CBHW050510260626
47157CB00004B/1261